The Outlaw Melodiac

A. R. Maxwell

ISBN-13: 9798367439397

Cover design by: Hannah Linder Designs
Library of Congress Control Number: 2018675309
Printed in the United States of America

To the state of Maine, where I learned everything I know about winter.
May you ever enjoy white Christmases and cold Moxie.
And to my husband, who has Maine in his veins.
207 forever, my love.

He gives snow like wool;
he scatters frost like ashes.
He hurls down his crystals of ice like crumbs;
who can stand before his cold?
Psalm 147:16-17

WRAP UP WARM. IT HAS
BEGUN TO SNOW.

JAEL'S NARRATIVE

Four hundred years ago, the lights went out. The snow buried the nuclear desert. All the flowers died.

One day, winter began...and it simply never ended.

They called it "The New Ice Age". Winter crowded into the spring and summer months. Glaciers grew over cities until they looked like glass paperweights. Snow covered the ground for ten months of the year. All the flowers died.

As the snow mounded up to their window frames, the scientists in their warm laboratories and the politicians in their padded chairs argued about what started it – whose fault it was – until the grid collapsed, and they were left shouting accusations into the dark. As it grew colder, Rattlelung came, then the famine; war dealt the death blow. Nuclear bombs hurled back and forth across oceans devastated half the world's population. Soon, it became too cold, even for war.

Technology became too expensive to produce. There was no more oil and nothing to run with it anyway. Electrical transfer stations turned into children's playgrounds. With their numbers cut down by two-thirds, a shivering, impoverished humanity slipped slowly back in time until modern life looked like frontier life. Humankind traded the farmer for the hunter-gatherer, the pharmacist for the herbalist, and the mail service for a boy on horseback with a saddlebag and a sharp knife. Most people no longer lived in cities. Instead, they clustered in outposts of two or three hundred near forests and mountains.

Just when the world began to settle into its new arctic way of life, the Gravarians arrived.

They landed in a copper shuttle no bigger than an outhouse: two humanoid creatures with pale translucent blue skin and visible black veins. They stood seven feet tall, had smooth bald heads, wore no shoes even in the snow, and carried heavy metal cleavers on their backs.

Humans greeted the strangers with typical human hospitality and tried to kill them.

The Gravarians used their cleavers to sweep heads from shoulders and cut off human limbs, but they were outnumbered. The humans left their dead bodies in the snow for the birds.

Two days later, a second, larger shuttle arrived. This time a dozen Gravarians stepped, blinking, into the sun-blinding snow. They took even more heads and limbs with them to an icy grave.

Two days after that, the shuttle returned with fifteen Gravarians. It returned with more that evening. They poured in like ants until there were almost as many Gravarians as humans.

At first, humanity thought this was an invasion. But the Gravarians mostly avoided the humans the way you avoid a nest of skunks. They set up settlements, and the humans set up outposts, and the two groups gave each other a wide berth. If a human came near a Gravarian settlement, he would likely get a crossbow shaft through his throat. If a Gravarian came near a human outpost, he would likely get a knife in the back. There were routs, an occasional dispute over land, and then that horrible night at Eveness.

Eveness is why music was outlawed.

In the midst of all this, the Klifrari emerged. They were a rough clan of mountain men and women who knew the secrets to life in the endless winters. If you hurt yourself, you went to a Klifrari Lithna, and he stitched you up or gave you Klifrari blood taken from Klifrari veins and carried over the mountain by a Klifrari Berablotha. If you needed medicine, you found the Klifrari Yushta and she gave you a concoction of herbs to cure you. You went to the trading post for game killed by a Klifrari Vayda or furs from a Klifrari Gildru. And all these services cost you something. A dozen bundles of firewood for a few stitches. A mare for a buckskin. A woolen blanket for two jars of beans.

The Blockade Runners were one of the only essential services not run by the Klifrari. They carried the mail through

Gravarian-dominated land to the outposts on the other side. If you lived in Rustypike outpost at the foot of Ram's Head Mountain, and you needed to send a letter to your aunt who lived in Hellspite outpost on the other side of the valley and across a gauntlet of Gravarian settlements, you sent your letter with a Blockade Runner. They were mostly young boys, some of them barely teenagers. Sometimes they went on horseback, and sometimes they went on foot. They were frequently killed or wounded and made a thriving business for Klifrari Lithna. As a matter of fact, most outposts with Blockade Runner barracks had a resident Lithna who worked with the Blockade Runners exclusively.

There were four modes of travel left on Earth. Horses, dogsleds, trains, and your own two feet. Old iron steam trains crisscrossed the continent and made up for most long-distance travel. Horses and dogsleds were common for the everyday man and, of course, Blockade Runners. Your own two feet was the Klifraris' preferred method and the only way to get over the mountains.

The Gravarians, or Gravs as humans began to call them, had a shuttle that went from Earth into the sky somewhere – presumably to their home planet Gravarus. It arrived at a specific Gravarian settlement, dropped off more Gravs, and then left again. No one knew how and no one cared. They came, and they were here, and they were annoying, and there was no way to get rid of them.

I was born four hundred years after the New Ice Age began. I have one memory of my mother, or, rather, of her shins as I was too small to remember any more of her. I remember her shins standing on the other side of the kitchen, and her voice, far above me, saying to my father, "The child's a little creepy, don't you think?".

I think I was holding an injured squirrel, but it may have been a possum.

"The other children won't play with her, you know. They think she'll give them a disease."

She said this because I was born with a skin condition that causes white patches to grow all over my black skin, especially around my eyes and mouth.

I don't recall if my father agreed with her, but not long after that, he woke me before sunrise and told me to dress warmly. He took me to the nearest station, put me on a train, and told me to find his second cousin Birch at Rustypike outpost and tell him that he must train me to be a Klifrari. When I told my father that I didn't want to be a Klifrari, he responded briskly, “Yes, you do,” and left.

I found Birch chopping wood outside his cabin. When he saw me, he looked like he'd seen an apparition. My unusual appearance often startled or frightened people.

“My name is Jael,” I said. “My father is your cousin. I want to be a Klifrari.”

Birch put his axe down and looked at me for a long minute, deciding, I think, if I was real or the result of too much ale in his water that morning. Finally, he said, “But I don't want you to be a Klifrari.”

“Yes, you do,” I replied.

“Well, what kind then?” Birch asked with the air of someone who has just posed an unanswerable question.

“The type that climbs over the mountains,” I replied with the air of someone who's just been asked a very stupid question.

“Klifrari don't just climb over mountains for fun,” Birch said. “There are the Laidish, who are guides, the Vayda who hunt, the Berablotha who carry blood from outpost to outpost, Lithna who treat wounds, and the Gildru who trap furs, and the Yushta who gather herbs for medicine. Which would you be?”

“Lithna,” I replied without a second thought. “I want to heal people.”

“Then you have to be a Berablotha first.”

I don't know why he agreed to take me in. Perhaps it was because he'd never seen anyone like me before. Perhaps he felt sorry for me. Perhaps he was growing old and needed someone to cook for him.

The other Klifrari children Birch trained came from generations of their own kind and were all born like hinds on the mountain, but I was a stranger, a usurper, and because I wanted increasingly with every snub and side-eye to be one of them, I tried very hard and accidentally surpassed them all, which made me more of an outcast than before.

We discovered pretty early on that I had an almost perfect sense of direction. So Birch decided to put me to the test in a way only Birch would.

I was five years old. Birch took me to the mountain, turned me around five times, and left.

I was home by dinner.

The next day, he took me to the peak of Ram's Head, turned me around five times, and left.

I was home by breakfast.

The following day, he took me across the pass to a mountain I did not know and left.

This time, I was afraid. All the trees looked the same. The clouds obscured the stars. I cried for three hours, then I got up, wiped my face, and put on my snowshoes.

I was home for breakfast on the third day.

Whatever I was asked to do, I did. I excelled in every Klifrari skill. I was set to be as good as Birch, perhaps better. But when I turned sixteen, and the other children took their Klifrari trials and proudly returned with new totas – a carved animal worn on a chain to symbolize that you are a true, initiated Klifrari – the council never seemed to get around to me. I wrote letters. Even Birch went to the council and pleaded for me. They made excuses, but Birch and I knew the truth; I was an outsider and the Klifrari simply didn't want me. It took two years before my persistent complaining became annoying enough that the council relented.

One blood bag, to be brought over Ram's Head before it had time to spoil. If I did this, I would be a Berablotha and, someday, a Lithna – a healer. The animal Birch picked as my tota was a bear —a symbol of strength and wisdom.

THE LOVE LETTERS OF CAPTAIN HARRISON CRADDOCK

Dearest Helena,

Please don't name the mushrooms in the kitchen; they're not alive. I can hear your voice right now explaining that they are, in fact, alive, but they're not. And they're probably poisonous, so don't chuck them in one of your stews. And definitely, don't give them to the pigs.

I've been fighting with the boys to keep their barracks clean, but it's a losing battle. I tried to get the oldest boy, Luca Paxton (we call him Pax), to help because the other boys look up to him, but it's no good. He's always either on a run (I sometimes think I give him too many runs, but he's the oldest and the fastest, and he's just very, very good at it), sleeping off a run, or playing his fiddle. And about the fiddle, he plays it no matter what I say. It's not safe, but the boys don't care. I should be firmer and make him stop or snap the instrument over my knee, but I can't. Pax made it by hand, and it's a work of art. Anyway, if you teach a boy to ignore all his fear receptors before he's got hair on his chin, you have to make allowances. But the barracks are a little like a squirrel cage. I've heard other Captains say their Blockade Runners are the same, but I'd hoped I'd be different. Seems I'm not.

Did I mention that I'm hoping Pax will stay with us at Christmas? I should have told you earlier, but I know you won't mind. And maybe Henry too. Pax is training Henry now, and he's doing a terrible job. Frankly, Pax is a good Blockade Runner, a skilled musician, and a great artist, and he can cut a Grav's jugular before it has time to blink, but he's too gentle. Henry needs a firm hand.

I'm a little concerned about our Sawbones, Ed (The boys call the Lithna "sawbones," and I've been picking up their jargon, unfortunately). He's gotten so old and blind that I think he might fall over dead any day now. Ed says he knows Klifrari medicine "like the back of his hand", but he doesn't appear to have been able to find a toothbrush or a full sentence in his life, so I'm incredulous. The boys do still go to him before and after their runs, which is regulation because they think he's funny.

In fact, it's the only thing they do that's regulation. I always imagined I'd run a tight ship, but that was before I met Pax and Co. I'm thwarted at every turn.

I miss our little farm (even if the pigs do burrow out too often) and your stews (even if they do give me food poisoning because you're always tossing mystery ingredients in), and your lovely face (nothing but praise on that account). Send up a few prayers for me as I try to keep this cage of squirrels in line.

See you soon,

Crad

THE PERSONAL LOG OF OBSIDIAN, ONCE CROWN PRINCE OF GRAVARUS

I am, of course, elated to report that the assassination attempt on my mother was a failure. The queen lives, and my brother Aresis, the failed assassin, her favorite child, and the (former) heir to the throne has been banished to Earth -- my mother's prison planet. I'm heartbroken to hear that my only brother, my younger brother, who so gallantly won the right to rule when I was disinherited over an indiscretion so minor it hardly bears mentioning, is now also disinherited, and I will never see him again. It's tragic. I'm sure he would have made an excellent ruler; he's got such a genius for strategy. It's hard, you know, to kill a seven hundred-year-old woman who is sleeping, alone, in her bed.

My most excellent mother, who suffers no fools in her court other than her most esteemed self, will name the new heir to the throne when she has chosen who is best fit for it. There's a plethora of options, of course.

- General Oberisk, the brave individual who lost his last campaign to a band of farmers armed with kitchen utensils.

- My uncle Anekzandar, who is only nine-hundred-and-sixty-three and sometimes forgets to put on his pants in the morning, but we all have our absent-minded moments, don't we?

- My cousin Petra, who is seventeen months pregnant with quadruplets.

- My cousin Gregorikus...oh, never mind, he was involved in the conspiracy against my mother and is also banished.

- And me, Obsidian, the oldest son, the original heir to the throne, disinherited over a slight indiscretion but the victor of twenty military campaigns against actual soldiers armed with real weapons.

I'll give her all the space and time she needs. I'm sure this will be a mind-numbing decision.

THE LOVE LETTERS OF CAPTAIN HARRISON CRADDOCK

Dearest Helena,

I am not sorry that I missed your pig fiasco. I've told you to keep the fences mended, and I know you ignore me. You have to bury the wire at least six inches into the ice and freeze it down with water, or they burrow out. You never listen to me, which is why you spend so many afternoons chasing the pigs.

Ed the Sawbones died. There wasn't anything wrong with him; he was just a million years old. Now I've got no Sawbones, and it's hockey season. The Klifrari will send another Sawbones whenever they feel like it, which is based on nothing and no one and timed to cause me maximum inconvenience.

You asked about the Klifrari, so I shall tell you that all stories you've heard about them are heavily romanticized. I've met more than my share now, and they're not clever, mysterious mountain people; they're toothless, crass, smelly mountain people. They have a superior attitude even though most of them can't spell their names. They're all pretty sullen, and they keep to themselves. Oh, and if you do need them to help you, they charge you an arm and a leg. One of my boys broke his leg, and he and Paxton had to chop wood for weeks to pay the debt. Sometimes they take people's cabins, their horses, the snowshoes off their feet.

It's not as though I think it ought to be free. Nothing is free, but I know they're taking advantage of us.

But here is the real news.

Yesterday, a Blockade Runner came from an outpost on the other side of the Shadbone River with a package for us to take through the Gravarian blockades to Hellspite. He must have carried that thing for days. And he'd been shot to pieces. Whatever he had, the Gravs wanted it. Since we have no Sawbones and no blood bank in Powderkeg, he died.

I sent the package with Pax yesterday, and he hasn't returned yet. He should be back by now.

I keep thinking about the Blockade Runner who brought it here bleeding out at the clinic and asking myself what possessed me to send it with Pax. Why not Henry? Why not Ben? Here I have a barracks of thirty boys, and I send it with my best one. Whatever that package is, the Gravs are desperate for it. I wish I hadn't sent it at all. I wish I'd burned it and buried the ashes.

I will send you news when I hear it.

Your own love,

Crad

JAEL'S NARRATIVE

As I hiked between Ram's Head's icy shoulder blades, I watched the clouds riling over the summit. It was the afternoon of my second day on the mountain, and I was so far ahead of schedule I could have taken the afternoon off for some skiing if I'd wanted to. But my goal was to get home early so I could stride into Becky's yaupon shack, blood bag in hand, to the gasps of a room filled with astonished Klifrari. The council would scramble to give me my tota.

As I climbed up the mountain, I felt the warmth of confidence. Bring a blizzard; I've got time.

When I breathed, I felt the blood bag, tucked close against my skin to keep it from freezing, squish between my shirt and my stomach.

The snow pummeled on as night wrapped its arms around the mountain. I decided to head for a small cave I knew to rest and warm my fingers. I had turned my back to the wind and started downhill when something bright red caught my eye. Kneeling, I found fresh drops of blood, already frozen, leading down the mountain. In case it was another Klifrari in trouble, I followed the trail for a hundred feet before I found the source.

I groaned. It wasn't the first time I'd found some poor idiot who was too cheap to hire a Laidish, gotten lost, and ended up frozen like a popsicle in the snow. I shrugged off my pack and pulled a red flag from it, which I meant to wrap around the corpse's wrist so someone could find it and bring it down the mountain after the storm, but when I grabbed the arm, the corpse sprang up and had a knife at my throat before I had time to gasp.

"Hey, hey," I shouted, "I'm Klifrari!"

He pulled his knife away and knelt in the snow, slapping

his arms with his ungloved hands. He wasn't wearing furs like a sensible person, but the lighter, bleached buckskins and a loud red, green, and black plaid wool shirt like a Blockade Runner. No mittens. No coat. No hat.

"What are you doing up here?" I shouted. In the wind, my words blew away like bubbles. I grabbed his arm and pulled him up. "The way you're dressed, you're fingers'll drop off like..."

He held up his hand. "I know, I know!"

"We're not far from a cave!"

He pointed to a red stain on his pant leg above his knee. I nodded and took his arm around my shoulder.

It was only a quarter mile to the cave, but it took us an eon to get there. The sun was down when we walked out of the wind into the dry, dark entrance.

As was the custom, the Klifrari before us had left a small pile of kindling. I knelt and had the fire started in a minute. The living corpse knelt next to it and held out purple hands.

There were blankets and some medical supplies stashed at the back of the cave – Klifrari look out for each other's emergencies. I gathered bandages, iodine, alcohol, a bone suturing needle, and some thread and returned to the fire.

The corpse, looking less corpseish and more personish by the second, had dark hair, a compact, athletic body, and black, almond-shaped eyes lined with thick lashes. I guessed he was around my age, perhaps a year older. He wasn't tall or imposing, but he prickled with nervous energy, like a flannel blanket snapping off static sparks. Just standing across from him made me feel tired.

"Hope my fingers don't drop off," he said with a chuckle, which felt misplaced, given the very good chance that they would. Like all Blockade Runners, he had a small tattoo above his left thumb of a buck deer. Every year Blockade Runners survived, they added a point on the buck's antlers. I had heard that if they earned six, they fulfilled their conscription and could retire. This boy's buck had five points.

He stared at me over the fire with a slightly startled

expression. I waited for him to say something about my skin.

"The white patch over your left eye looks like a raven," he said.

"Yes, I know," I mumbled. My voice came out croaky, and I had to clear my throat.

He smiled. "I'm Luca Paxton. I'm a Blockade Runner."

"Jael Jannigan," I replied. "Klifrari-in-training."

His resting face was a half smile, a little higher on the right side, which gave him a perpetually wry expression like he was always laughing about some amusing secret.

"Sit and let me look at your leg," I ordered.

It occurred to me suddenly that, after three days of preparation and two days on the mountain, he was the first person I'd spoken to in almost a week. I wondered if I looked as awkward as I felt.

As I bent over him, he crinkled his nose a little, and I remembered that I'd rubbed my face over with boar fat that morning to keep the cold off, and I must have smelled rank.

The gash above his knee was deep but clean, and the cold had already helped stem the blood flow.

"I got caught trying to get a package through to Hellspite, and the Gravs cornered me," he volunteered. "They shot my horse right out from under me, closed me in on three sides, and I had to come up the mountain. I jumped from Chimney Rock."

I smiled incredulously. "You can't jump from Chimney Rock. It's too high."

He gestured at his leg. "Well, you can, but I don't recommend it."

I dug around in my rucksack until I found a little jar of tea tree oil salve, which I'd made myself.

I dabbed the wound, and he sucked in his breath.

"It'll sting," I said.

He sat up, reached into his pack, and pulled out a little fiddle.

"What's that?" I asked.

"What does it look like?" He set it on his thigh and touched the bow to the strings. It 'plinked' like a wind chime.

"A little risky, don't you think?"

He laughed. "There's no Gravarians up here."

"If music carries down the mountain, there will be. Besides, it's illegal," I said.

He shrugged me off.

"I guess you've never heard of the Eveness Massacre," I mumbled.

He tuned the instrument and ignored me, leaning his ear close to the strings and listening to each tone, then twisting a little nob at the top of the fiddle's neck until the sound satisfied him.

As I cleaned his wound, he played a nervous dance. When I pulled out a needle and thread, he played faster. When I punctured the skin with the needle, the fiddle screeched and bounded into a frantic jig. The music made my heart race.

"Would you please stop!" I cried. "This is delicate."

He dropped the bow abruptly and drummed a tattoo on the back of the fiddle.

"Can you just sit still?"

"Would you rather I scream?"

"I'd rather you sat still!"

He lay down again, set his fiddle on his stomach, and plucked the strings.

"What kind of Klifrari are you?" He asked.

"I'm not one yet. I'm doing my trial now, and you're slowing me down," I squinted at the needle passing through the skin, "but when I pass, hopefully, I'll be a Berablotha and then, someday, a Lithna."

He let out a tiny, almost inaudible "humph".

"What?" I demanded.

"Nothing."

"What?"

"It's just...I have this buddy, and a few months ago, he fell and broke his leg so the bone broke through the skin. You people charged him half a cord of firewood for the blood they gave him, another half for the setting, and then a pelt for every stitch."

"We've got to make a living," I said.

"Yes, but how was he supposed to get a cord of firewood with a broken leg?"

"Maybe you could've helped him."

"I did."

I finished the stitching and set to bandaging. "What's in the package?" I asked.

"A book, I think."

My curiosity sparked, and I held out my hand. "Can I see it?"

He shook his head. "Mail's private. Can't let anyone open it."

"What'll you do with it now?"

"Take it back to my commanding officer and let him deal with it. With everything going on with the Gravs..." his voice trailed off.

"Yeah," I said, without knowing what he was talking about.

He looked up at me with surprise. "You know how this one Grav and his followers are suddenly burning down villages?"

"Um, I think I may be spotty on the details," I said.

"Do you live under a rock?"

I gestured around us. "Kind of."

"Well, ever since Aresis came to Earth..."

He read my blank expression. "You don't know who Aresis is, do you?"

"I'm a little spotty on the details."

"Have you ever even seen a Gravarian?"

"I live on the mountain," I said defensively.

"Ok, well, that's...not healthy."

His leg freshly bandaged, I put some chicory and yau on the fire. Klifari mixed yaupon holly leaves into chicory to make coffee, and the resulting drink was called yau. Everyone loved yau, and yau sales were probably the Klifraris' most profitable business. As I waited for it to boil, I took out my tota – a little bear carved in ivory. It was smooth as butter under my fingers. I imagined putting it on and walking into Becky's with it glinting, white and new, around my neck.

"Your tota?" Luca asked.

"If I make it back in time."

"May I see it?"

I held it out for him to see, but when he went to take it, I pulled back.

"Sorry. I won't touch." He inspected it quietly. "Incredible workmanship. Did you make it?"

"No, my teacher did. That's how it works for Klifrari. The teacher carves the tota for the student."

"It's beautiful."

"Did you make your fiddle?" I asked.

He nodded, looking it over with the critical eye of an artist.

On the lower bout, he'd etched a wolverine into the wood – snarling, its paws up, claws swiping. He'd carved the teeth jagged and the eyes glinting. He'd carved every last hair. The tongue had texture. The little nose somehow looked wet. It was so intricate I thought I glimpsed the creature breathing.

"You don't meet many musicians anymore," I said. "Not since Eveness."

He shrugged. "Life is for living."

As I sipped my yau, he played a cheerful composition, which I suspected he was making up on the fly. I'd rarely heard music in my life. It somehow made the firelight brighter and the wind less mournful, and something in my chest rose to it, like smoke spiraling toward the sun.

THE PERSONAL LOG OF OBSIDIAN, ONCE CROWN PRINCE OF GRAVARUS

My most esteemed mother has made her decision, and I'm sure it is very wise despite all appearances to the contrary. All appearances. There is no scenario in which this decision doesn't appear to be the product of a rambling, senile mind.

Also, I'm completely positive that my mother didn't devise this plan just to spite me. My mother is never spiteful. The fact that my father was murdered by mysterious assassins only hours after he denied my mother's request to exterminate all life on Earth and turn the planet into a giant solar farm is, I'm sure, pure coincidence.

She decrees that whichever of her two sons can go to Earth and bring back a dirty little human music book will inherit the throne when she dies. Apparently, she has forgotten that my crime pales in comparison to Aresis' crime. He did try to assassinate her. But perhaps she doesn't see assassinating a member of the royal family as wrong.

I leave for Earth immediately. Earth is just...so lovely. All the snow and...ice and things. There's nothing I relish more than spending months wandering aimlessly over a frozen, desolate planet looking for a human artifact that was probably burned centuries ago to keep some peasant's backside warm.

And if the murderers, thieves, and artists weren't enough, the place is teeming with human beings. Human beings always bring down the value of real estate.

But I suppose it's not humanity's fault that, after four hundred years as my mother's prison planet, they've let Earth get a little slummy. It's not as though it's a royal prison planet for traitors or conspirators, except for my brother Aresis and one or two others, but mostly it's just an ordinary prison for ordinary prisoners.

Humans are pretty disappointing. They batter on about love and friendship and honor, but they're backstabbing little reprobates, every one.

I will get to Earth, get the book, and get back as soon as possible.

JAEL'S NARRATIVE

When the snow slowed, I stood and doused the fire.

"We should get going."

He shouldered his rucksack. "Thanks for the help."

"I'll be heading to Rustypike outpost to the east. What outpost are you from?"

"Powderkeg."

"You'll need to go west – Powderkeg is on the other side of the pass from Rustypike. The pass will close soon, but you might make it home if you hurry. Good luck with the rest of your trip."

I started for the entrance, but he hung back.

"Which way..." he hesitated.

"What?"

"Which way is east?"

I stared at him. "You don't know?"

His face reddened.

"You're a Blockade Runner!" I cried. "How do you not know how to get back to your own outpost?"

"I have a terrible sense of direction."

"But you're a Blockade Runner!"

"I memorize the maps and all my routes. There aren't any maps of the mountains except what the Klifrari have, and even if there were, I wouldn't know them."

"Klifrari don't use maps," I said proudly. "We know the way by instinct."

"Could I come with you? I can contact my outpost from Rustypike, and they can come pick me up."

"I'm already behind schedule, and with your leg the way it is, it'll take us an extra day to get down the mountain."

His face fell.

"Besides," I added, "you're not in good condition to hike that far."

"I'm fine," he said quickly. "I've hiked further in worse condition."

"I'm on my trial. If I don't get to Rustypike by sunrise, I'll fail, and they won't let me wear my tota or become a blood initiate, and I'll never be a real Klifrari, and my entire life will be ruined."

"Is being a blood initiate a good thing? It doesn't sound like a good thing."

"In order to be a real Klifrari, you have to give blood for the blood bank."

He grinned. "Blockade Runners call Klifrari toothless vampires".

This annoyed me, and I bristled. "I bet your friend with the compound fracture wasn't calling anyone a toothless vampire when he got our blood in him."

"He was when he was stacking wood in a hip splint."

I cleared my throat. "Anyway, I need to get going."

With a slightly forced shrug, he sat beside the fire and poked at it with a stick. "Could you send someone back for me?"

"I'll come back for you myself," I said. It slightly softened the battering on my conscience. "It won't be more than two days. Keep the fire going in case of wolves."

He swallowed.

"Do you have food?" I asked.

"We don't carry much with us on our runs. I'll be fine. Do you have spare bandages?"

I grimaced. "I used them all. Sorry."

He pulled his fiddle out, leaned against his pack, and began to play.

The music followed me for a mile.

THE PERSONAL LOG OF OBSIDIAN, ONCE CROWN PRINCE OF GRAVARUS

Today was my first day on Earth. The sun is rather too bright, and everything is covered in cold white crystallized water. It's very drab.

There are two ways to travel: riding on the back of a bony, hairy, smelly, four-legged mammal called a 'horse' (What kind of word is 'horse'? Sounds like a fungal infection you would get on your feet.) and an iron machine called a 'train'. Trains are very, very heavy, and behind them, they pull boxes on wheels. Humans have used them to transport goods and even to transport themselves for centuries now, and I've decided to travel by train. I can pass through human settlements without being noticed.

I found an old train built centuries ago but still well-maintained. All in all, it looks very much the way it looked when it was manufactured, except I've retrofitted it with an auto-pilot control. I just tell it where I want to go in the morning, and it goes there—no need for a human conductor. I wasn't able to bring much with me from home, but the autopilot control was a good use of baggage space.

I think I will need to hire a human or two to help me get food and supplies from the towns I pass through since I can't be seen. This should be easy. Humans will do anything if you pay them enough.

I've easily located Aresis. You know the saying, 'where there's smoke, there's your homicidal psychopathic brother'? He's using the scorched earth method to find the book. He goes to a human settlement, kills everyone, turns the place inside out, and then burns it to the ground. So elegant. So subtle. He'll be an original kind of king.

JAEL'S NARRATIVE

He'll be fine, I told myself. *I'll come back for him. The wolves probably won't find him all the way up there in a storm.*

Maybe, replied a voice in my head, *if he stays still, but if he tries to find his own way, he'll fall into a crevasse. Break a leg. Die of cold and starvation. His wound will get infected.*

I need my tota, I argued. *Imagine all the people I could help if I had a tota. Imagine how crushed Birch will be if I fail! It's unfair to Birch. I owe it to him for everything he's done for me.*

The snow came thick as a white scrim.

I stopped, the freezing wind clawing my face.

The Klifrari code dictated that Klifrari help one another, but there is no obligation to strangers. And strangers must always pay for help. But I felt guilty. Anyone would get lost in this storm, and a fresh wound should be changed every morning.

Maybe we could move quickly. If I was only a few hours late and had such a good reason...

I turned around and followed the music back to the cave.

Luca smiled at me when I walked out of the snow, like he'd known all along I'd return. Without a word, I pulled his arm around my shoulders. He leaned on me, heavier than I'd imagined, and we limped out into the storm.

It wasn't as slow going as I thought it would be, but the hours piled up like sticks on a dam. Luca used my shoulder as a crutch, and we pressed through the white-out.

"How on earth do you know we're not going in circles?" He panted.

"I just know," I replied.

Six hours later, we reached the glacier near the base of the mountain. The snow stopped abruptly, and we could see the smooth, sloping ice and the lights of Rustypike outpost below.

"Do we have to go down here?" Luca asked.

"We could go around, but if we go this way, I'll buy back the time I've lost."

I braced myself for an argument, but he shrugged. "Ok, looks interesting."

They say you have to be a little mad to be a Blockade Runner.

I took my knife and cut an anchor for the rope in the snow, then tied it around myself. "We'll tie together and then climb down the front of the glacier."

I fastened the rope around his waist. "Can you repel?"

"Of course."

"Well, don't. Try to climb down."

He looked at his nearly treadless boots and nodded. "Great."

He didn't look confident, but he didn't look frightened either, and both of those things made me second-guess my decision to climb down instead of going the long way around the glacier. If this worked, though, I'd still get to live my fantasy of striding into Becky's with my tota around my neck – not hours early, as I'd envisioned, but at least on time and with a great story to brag about while surrounded by my new compatriots.

Finally welcome.

Finally, one of the pack.

I kicked my spiked boots into the ice and started down. Luca followed me slowly. I could tell from the little red smear he left behind that his leg was bleeding again. I told myself I'd redo his stitches when we made it to the outpost. I told myself that getting him there sooner was better and this wasn't a selfish, stupid thing to do.

I told myself a lot of things.

Everything went well for twenty feet. The glacier sloped downward until it was sheer and smooth as glass, and here, not surprisingly, Luca's foot slipped. He slid a few feet but caught himself with his fingertips, showering snow down on me. I lost my balance, and my boot clicked out of the ice. I swung out on the rope, away from the glacier, and then slapped back into it. The impact jarred me, and a jag in the ice tore my coat. Red splattered on the blue wall.

I hung there for a moment, stunned.

Luca called from above me, “Is that blood?”

I slowly bounced against the ice, hanging limp as a marionette on a peg.

“The blood bag burst,” I said.

THE LOVE LETTERS OF CAPTAIN HARRISON CRADDOCK

Darling Helena,

Are there Gravs at the farmhouse? I wasn't sure if I should believe him or not. He said they were. I don't know how he knows where you live. I don't know how he knew I existed. I'm so confused.

Aresis came to me last night. I don't know how he knew about the package I sent with Paxton, but he did. He told me that if I didn't tell him where the package was and who had it, he would...well, that doesn't matter now. Maybe he's bluffing and doesn't know about you and the farm, but he seemed like he did, so what was I supposed to do?

He's burning villages. Just burning them to the ground. Maybe, if he gets the package, he'll stop. Maybe it'll save lives, him knowing. Maybe Paxton will give it to him, and he'll let him live.

But Paxton hasn't returned yet.

My love, I'm sick over it all.

But it doesn't matter. All that matters is that you are safe now. Tell me in your next letter if there really are Gravs there, and what they are doing.

I've always believed that there was a clear line between the right thing to do and the wrong thing to do, but yesterday, I couldn't see it.

Stay in the house and don't trust anyone. Don't speak to anyone. You must butcher the pigs. I know you've probably named them, and I'm sure you want to keep them forever, but don't. You need bacon this winter. I know you love the pigs, dearest, but I told you not to get attached to them. Sometimes survival means sacrificing something you love.

I love you, and don't be afraid. I'll keep you safe, somehow, and I'll come to you soon,

Crad

JAEL'S NARRATIVE

I left Luca shivering on the porch of the Klifrari clinic in Rustypike and slumped inside, an hour late, stiff with frozen blood.

Inside, ten or fifteen Klifrari milled around rows of beds, binding sprains, stitching wounds, pouring medicine into spoons. Birch stood behind a desk with four older Lithna, arguing over how much to charge a woman to treat her broken collarbone.

With an audible whoosh, they all turned. Everyone stared at me. Birch hurried over.

"Please tell me that's your blood," he said.

I took his arm and pulled him away from the others. "I have a reason."

"What?" he said too loudly. I shushed him.

"There was this Blockade Runner I ran into in the storm. He hurt his leg, and I had to help him down the mountain."

"Jael, if you're going to lie to me, make it believable. Otherwise, it's insulting."

"No! I'm serious! His name is Luca Paxton. He's sitting on the porch; you can talk to him."

Birch looked behind him at the little knot of waiting Klifrari. "It's only an hour. They shouldn't care."

Speed isn't important to Klifrari. Dependability, instinct, planning. Those were the pillars of their world.

"I'll try to explain this to them. Wait for me outside."

"Birch," I caught his arm. "The blood bag burst."

This was a cardinal sin. Losing a shipment meant no dependability. No instinct. No planning.

"That was your task, Jael! You cannot break a blood bag!"

"I know, but I was making up for lost time. Time I lost

because I was helping someone!"

"Helping someone was not your task! And making up for lost time is not the Klifrari way. Better to be late and still have your blood bag! You know this!"

He looked over his shoulder at the others and groaned, "Wait for me outside."

I stepped onto the porch and joined Luca, who lay on his back, plucking at his fiddle strings. A few other Klifrari came and went, ignoring me. No tota, no greeting. Behind us, a man begged a Lithna for a bag of blood for his wife, who had just finished hard labor. The Klifrari bartered for firewood. The man insisted that, without his firewood, the new baby would freeze.

The man left distraught. Luca watched him, muttering something about vampires.

The snow began to fall again. A little band of skinny, grubby boys came down the street from the train station and ran toward us, shouting.

Luca grinned.

"What are you doing here?" He cried. "How did you get here?"

They mobbed him, laughing and talking at the same time.

I edged away, feeling like I'd stumbled into a stranger's Sunday dinner.

A tall man with red hair and a gray-streaked red beard strode up. "I told you he'd show up somewhere," he said, smiling. Luca reached his hand out to the older man, who pulled him to his feet. They embraced in the violent, back-thumping way men do. From my perspective, standing behind Luca, I saw the man look up to the sky for half a second, his eyes brimming, but he pulled himself together quickly before any of the boys noticed.

Balancing on his good leg, Luca gestured for me to come closer. "This is Jael Jannigan," he said. "She found me on Ram's Head, patched me up, and rolled me back down the mountain again."

The older man shook my hand. "Captain Craddock. Pax here," he slapped Luca's shoulder, "well, we have to keep him around because none of us knows how to play the fiddle."

A freckled boy raised his hand, "I do!"

"No, you don't," everyone shouted together.

"I'm learning."

Luca threw his arm around the boy's shoulders, "Henry, I'll teach you more when we get home. Bye, Jael! If you ever need anything from the Blockade Runners, let me know!"

Supported by his friends and their captain, Luca was borne across the street back toward the train station. This time of year, trains ran to Powderkeg by way of the pass. It would close soon as the weather got colder, and then there would be no way back and forth except by foot over the mountain. I watched them with a thrill of longing.

The door behind me opened, and I turned. Birch came out onto the porch, followed by the council leader, a big man with a beer keg belly and a beard to his knees.

"Birch spoke to me," he said.

"I know, but I can explain."

"You lost your blood bag."

"Yes," I said quickly, "but I met this Blockade Runner..."

"Why was a Blockade Runner on the mountain?"

"He was lost. A band of Gravarians forced him..."

"None of this matters..."

"No!" I cried, "Listen! I can explain everything! I found him in the storm, and I stitched his wound, and I even helped him down the glacier!"

"Why come down the glacier instead of going around it?"

I swallowed. "I thought...I thought I could make up for lost time."

"And you broke the blood bag on the glacier?"

"Yes."

"Because you were rushing?"

I hesitated and commanded myself not to cry. "Yes."

"Better to arrive late with the blood bag than on time without it. And even better, leave the Blockade Runner on the mountain and bring your blood bag."

"But I did what we're supposed to do! I guided a lost person off the mountain!"

"NO!" The old man shouted. "Klifrari are not just guides! We are the lifeblood! We carry supplies. We carry mail. We carry medicine and food. Without us, the world shrivels, and the world dies. Klifrari do not stop to help people – we press on, no matter what. And we never help anyone without payment."

"But it was just one blood bag. I couldn't let him freeze for one blood bag!"

"Every blood bag is a life. You simply traded one for another."

I focused hard on my bootlaces and held my breath against my temper and shame.

"There will always be reasons to stop, but you can never stop. This is why you aren't ready to be a Klifrari. You are not granted permission to a tota."

My lungs folded up like a book. Birch sought my eyes, but I looked away. If I looked at him, I'd fall apart and do something unthinkable – like cry.

There was nothing to say. It was definitive. Done. I turned and walked away, back toward the mountain. I spent the rest of the afternoon punishing a pile of firewood behind Birch's cabin.

Birch came to me at blue hour, riding his sled behind his team of happy, panting dogs.

"Come with me to Becky's," he said.

"I'll never show my face in Becky's again."

"I'm too old to ride around in the snow alone."

"I'm not a Klifrari, so they won't let me in."

"I own Becky's. They'll let you in."

I put the axe down with a sigh and climbed into the sled.

Becky's Yau Shack, a crooked, two-story building snuggled close to the mountainside, could only be accessed by dog sled or snowshoe and the bouncer only let Kifrari past the front door. Becky's boasted a little porch complete with two rocking chairs for the two or three weeks of warmish weather we sometimes enjoyed in the summer. The snug dining room included a dozen raw-edged wooden tables, a bar made from a white pine log, and a fireplace big enough for a grown man to stand in. Upstairs were two narrow rooms with beds, wash stands, and nothing else. The basement held the blood bank and a hefty stockpile of supplies. Every day, a Klifrari child took a dog team four miles down the mountain to the Lithna clinic with blood from the blood bank.

On the front porch, we had to avoid three men struggling to fit a sheet of glass into the window. Glass was rarer than gold and twice as expensive. The Klifrari had to sell five hundred blood bags to afford this luxury, and it had been a topic of much excitement and pride for weeks.

When we stepped out of the snow into the warm wood smoke scented dining room, everyone acted as though they didn't notice us, but I saw the whites of their eyes flashing in the dim room as they darted looks in our direction. I noticed Menda Wright pull her tota from inside her jacket and let it hang where the light shone off the carved ivory. Menda was only fifteen – three years younger than me, and already she had a tota of an eider in flight.

Behind the counter, a stout woman named Mag poured yak milk into yau and stirred it with a small wooden spoon.

"Yau?" She asked.

I nodded.

As she poured, she leaned toward Birch. "Rent is late again this month, but times are hard. You don't suppose you could..."

Birch held up his hand. "Don't worry about it."

"The old Yushta woman up the mountain is stealing our customers with her cheap salves and medicines."

Mag and Birch looked at me, and my cheeks burned.

"I'll let you pay me back later," Birch said.

"The little thing about her trial won't...change anything, will it?"

Birch's eyes flashed. "Should it?"

"It's not my fault she didn't make it back in time."

"Not mine either," I said.

A woman with gray braids and a walrus carved from a narwhal horn hanging around her neck sipped her yau and mumbled to her male companion, "Just because you've got boar fat on your elbow doesn't make you a Klifrari. Until you've got a tota..."

"Bold talk for a woman who lost her teeth but none of her fingers or toes," Birch murmured, just loud enough for the woman to hear him.

She slammed her mug on the counter and swung her stool toward him. "Birch, if you weren't a hundred years old, I'd knock your teeth out."

"Maeve Mulligan, if you had teeth to knock, I'd do the same."

Maeve leaped off her stool, but I grabbed Birch's arm. "Let's just go."

"Don't take this opportunity away from me, Jael!" he shouted as I pulled him out the door. "I've dreamt of this moment since I was ten!"

I pulled him onto the porch and shut the door against the commotion.

"Let them fester," Birch sighed.

"They'll never accept me," I said. "It doesn't matter what I do. They'll never get over this mistake, and they'll never get over my birth. If it were Menda, or Isla, or even Jecka, they'd let them have a second chance. You know they would."

"I'm tired of your griping," Birch said.

"I have done more hiking and healing and hunting," I continued, my voice trembling and my face and neck suddenly hot, "then half the people in there. I am better at this than them. It's not fair. It's not fair."

"When I die, you inherit everything I have. The cabin, the dogs, and," he waved his hand at the yau hut, "Becky's. They'll let you in when you own it."

I sat down on a log and put my face in my mittens. "What was I supposed to do? Leave that boy to freeze to death on the mountain?"

Birch shrugged. "Don't ask questions you don't want

answered."

"If I ever see him again, I'll throttle him."

THE LOVE LETTERS OF CAPTAIN HARRISON CRADDOCK

Helena, my dove,

I'm glad there are no Gravs near the farmhouse. They could arrive any day. Aresis knows where you live, so keep the doors locked and don't let anyone inside.

I told Aresis where to find the package, but he didn't get it. Paxton escaped. That boy is made of tougher stuff than he looks. He's all smiles and big, dark eyes, but he's cunning.

But I'm afraid. I don't know if my deal with Aresis still stands since he didn't get what he wanted. Maybe he doesn't know. Maybe he thinks the package was lost with Pax on the mountain. I think I should meet with him again. I can just hand him the package and reinstate our deal. No more fuss or danger. He can go back where he came from and leave us alone.

Keep the doors locked, and please, please butcher the freaking pigs. What did we get them for if not to eat them? They were born to feed you this winter so let them fulfill the purpose they were born for. Think of it as noble if it helps. It's not complicated. Draw the knife across the jugular and then hoist them up in a tree so the blood drains. It's messy, so don't wear anything you like. It may take a few days to get the blood out from under your fingernails.

I'll write you again soon,

Yours forever,

Crad

JAEL'S NARRATIVE

I sat in Ama the Yushta's cluttered kitchen, my feet hooked around the legs of a tall stool, as I peeled pine needles off a bough and dropped them into a mortar. In the heavy air, their cool citrus smell felt like a current of cold water in a hot spring.

Ama sniffed a bubbling brown concoction over the stove and made a low 'Mmmmm 'through her nose.

I spent most afternoons with Ama, perhaps because in a world fenced in by Klifrari rules and traditions, the chaos of herbs and old books in her little cabin felt like a reprieve. She was an independent entity, not a Klifrari but still vital to the ecosystem of the outpost. People needed her, and after half a century of experience, the Klifrari both resented and relied on her.

When I was still very small, I'd appeared on Ama's doorstep like a wandering wood sprite. I hadn't slept in two weeks because of the itching white patches all over my body, and I was desperate for a salve. While she mixed her 'magic potion, 'she sent me to the greenhouse for some herbs, and I got lost among the shelves and pots of sweet-smelling plants. For the first time in weeks, I forgot I was miserable. When I came back flushed and happy with an armful of leaves – half of which were the wrong kind – she smiled at me, and it was the first time anyone had smiled at me in days. She put the salve on my skin and let me lie down on her little squirrel hide mattress. I slept for nine hours. After that, I stuck to her like a burr on a boot.

I wasn't supposed to see Ama, but I couldn't help it. Ama taught me things the Klifrari wouldn't teach. She taught me out of an old, old book about a man named Joshua who healed people just because he loved them. How he touched the untouchable, and the rank, and the festering, and their pain melted away. She said that we should try to be like that.

Now, I could mix my own salves. Ama joked that I'd surpass her soon, and I knew she wanted me to take over when she died, but I didn't want to spend my life in a dark kitchen, smoke in my face, endlessly stirring a bubbling gunk on the fire. I wanted to be out on the mountain or racing around a Lithna clinic, stitching wounds, binding breaks, delivering babies. Helping real people right in front of me instead of handing a jar to a Lithna to take to some faceless villager or lying awake at night trying to imagine the cause of some child's rash.

I wondered if there was some way to be every type of Klifrari in a lifetime...

Ama looked out the window with milky, sightless eyes and fingered a marigold leaf. She knew every herb by touch and smell. People came from miles around to purchase her woefully underpriced medicines and balms and, with a sad enough story, usually walked away with whatever they wanted for pittance

When I was there, I would meet them at the window, do some figuring in my head, and then charge them the Klifrari way. The upshot was that nobody came around when I was there anymore.

"Forget being a Berablotha or a Lithna," Ama said as she dropped a handful of dried bael leaves into the pot, "and be a Yushta instead. The Lithna are nothing without the Yushta."

"It's too lonely," I said.

Ama laughed. "And carrying bags of blood over the mountain isn't lonely? I see more people in a day than you will in a month."

"Being a Berablotha is just a stepping stone."

Ama's cloud of bushy gray hair blew a little in the steam as she leaned over her pot. "Berablotha smell bad," she said.

I chuckled to myself. Ama was one to talk when she smelled perpetually of garlic, and boar fat.

"They're going to send me away," I said quietly. It was cracking thin ice over a frozen pond.

Ama swung her ample body around in a swish of skirts and

looked over my head with one hand on her hip. "Child, don't you let them do that to you."

"I spoke to Birch. He said if I go to Powderkeg and work there in the clinic and teach for a few years..." I rushed so she wouldn't interrupt me. She did anyway.

"TEACH?" She bellowed. "They won't let you be one of them, but they'll let you teach their children?"

The hypocrisy was not lost on me. I counted four pine needles and dropped them into the bowl.

"Don't count them out, child," Ama waved my hands away, "weigh them out in your mind. You're too precise."

She pinched the bough between her fingers and ran them down the length of the branch. The needles fell away.

"They'll let me retake my trial after two years," I said.

"Bearhie, you'll be a grown woman by then."

"Better than nothing."

"Forget the Klifrari. I'll let you have all my recipes when I die, and you can take over."

"Birch says the same. He'll leave me Becky's."

"HA!" Ama turned back to her boiling pot. "Well, then they'll have to let you in."

She dried her hands on her apron and pushed a plate of gash cakes across the counter to me. She always baked with a pinch of cardamom; everything she made tasted a little like grief.

"If you'd had the chance to earn your tota, wouldn't you have taken it?" I asked.

She laughed. "Oh, they gave me a chance."

I stared at her. "And you didn't take it?"

She shook her head. "I didn't like the task. I'm not a Vayda."

I finished my gash cake and licked the maple syrup off my fingers. I spent the rest of the afternoon stacking wood behind the cabin.

Two days later, I left for Powderkeg.

I hated Powderkeg outpost. I'd always hated it. My home, Rustypike, was cleaner, and there were Klifrari everywhere.

Here, Klifrari came and went every day, bringing shipments and mail over the mountains from Leatherstrap and Brokentooth for the Blockade Runners to take through the Gravarian settlements to the villages to the north, but they never stayed. They would stomp into the clinic, covered in snow and looking like pastries dropping powdered sugar on the floor, leave their blood bags, glare at my spotted face and lack of tota, and then leave.

The Blockade Runner barracks was large in Powderkeg, and the unnervingly young Blockade Runners made up most of my patients. I often treated boys with round faces and no whiskers, armed with a machete in one hand and playing with a yoyo with the other. Some of them were adept with hatchets, some used pitchforks. I saw a bigger boy with a splitting mall strapped to his back. I once saw a boy with a hacksaw filed down to a point at the end. They wore ragged bleached buckskin pants, fraying at the hems and split at the knees, and plaid woolen shirts under shearling lined buckskin jackets. The plaids ranged from green and black to reds, blues, and yellows; the brighter, the better. Dyed cloth was expensive, and plaids even more so, but the blockade runners took great pride in their colors, and each barracks had its own distinct tartan. They always looked cold.

A man named Pat ran the clinic with his wife and grown daughter. They were Klifrari living on the wrong side of the mountain. Pat had a cough and sore throat most of the time, which left all the teaching to me. His wife, Gib, said she was blind in one eye, though she clearly wasn't, so I had to do all the stitching, and their daughter said she had to care for her aging parents, though they seemed able to take care of themselves. They all had totas, which miffed me considerably.

I closed the clinic in the evenings, cleaned everything, and went to my room. I was bored out of my mind, so I got creative, and my mind turned to my clothes.

I wore what most Klifrari women wore: a buckskin tunic to my mid-thigh, buckskin breaches, a pair of fur-lined boots with laces up the front, and a huge, rabbit-lined coat with a hood. So, every evening, after I closed the clinic and sat listening to the silence humming in my ears, I took up a needle and thread and embroidered my tunic.

Soon, pine trees sprouted up from the hem, with caribou peering out behind the branches. Then I added a flurry of snowflakes. When I finished the hem, I sewed ivy twisting up the sleeves; then I set to work on the collar. I embroidered my favorite constellations all around it and at the front, over my collar bone, bigger than everything else, a bear—my tota.

When I finished with my tunic, I set to work on the coat. I started with snowflakes down the sleeves; then, around the hem, I embroidered an exact picture of the mountain range where I grew up, with Ram's Head at the center. When I was done with that, I stitched a raven over my shoulder blades, the same shape as the white patch over my eye. It was good stitching practice, and it filled my empty evenings.

Most of my job consisted of checking the Blockade Runners before and after their runs. Mostly, I bound sprains, stitched gashes, and made them drink bone broth. They were tough miniature men who wouldn't come to me unless Craddock forced them to.

Three weeks after my arrival, I was binding the twisted ankle of the little, freckle-faced boy named Henry when Craddock came to see me. Henry had just returned from a run and was asleep on the table. I knew Gib would chase him out with her belt when I was done, but I wanted him to get his sleep, so I was taking my time. Craddock tapped me on the shoulder and startled me.

"What?" I snapped.

"I need you to come out to the barracks and look at one of my boys."

"Tell him to come here," I said. I applied a special salve I'd invented for sprains to Henry's ankle. It should have cost him extra, but I mixed all my Yushta recipes in the evenings. Gib caught me once and threatened to report it to the council, but I bought her silence by giving her free lavender balm for her hair.

"He won't come here," Craddock said. "Says the Klifrari

charge too much."

"Well, it'll cost you extra for me to go there."

"I'll pay it."

"Who do you want me to see?" I asked. I checked to see that Gib wasn't watching and slipped a jar of the sprain balm into Henry's pocket.

"My lead runner," he said, "Luca Paxton."

THE LOVE LETTERS OF CAPTAIN HARRISON CRADDOCK

My beloved,

I miss you beyond my vocabulary. I miss your voice, and your tender hands, and the way you smell. I like to bury my face in your scarf and take a long breath. Even after all these months, it still smells of you. But mostly, I miss your eyes. I miss the light in them. I miss the hope in them. I miss their gentleness. I want to see your eyes again, and touch your little nose, and feel your hands on my cheeks. I can't put it any other way. I miss you to the point of physical pain. I miss you to hell and back.

I've contacted Aresis, and he has assured me that our deal will remain if I give him the package and...I have to get rid of Paxton. I've told him I agree, but I'm not going to do it.

I'm going to give Aresis the package. I don't care about that, but I'm not going to hurt Pax. It's going too far, and I simply draw the line at murder. I mean to take the package and the boys and flee Powderkeg. I'll get the package and get out – take a train and go straight to the meeting place. Aresis means to burn Powderkeg anyway, something to do with covering his tracks and throwing his brother off the trail. But when I go, I'm going to leave Paxton behind. Then I'll tell Aresis that I did what I was asked, and I'll save you, the other boys, and Paxton all at once.

Paxton will make it. Paxton is clever. He's a survivor. I'm certain. More than certain. Absolutely positive.

This seems right. A small lie. A small risk. A little gamble is part of war.

My beloved, I will see you soon.

Wait for me.

Yours forever and to eternity,

Crad

THE PERSONAL LOG OF OBSIDIAN, ONCE CROWN PRINCE OF GRAVARUS

Curse Earth, curse trains, double curse humankind.

It is snowing and slowing me down, and my brother hasn't burned anything recently, so I've lost him. On top of that, I got my map from, of all people, my Uncle Anekzander, and it's so outdated I'm hopelessly lost. I should have known better than to trust Anekzander. In addition to his senility, he killed his own brother over a puvvle orchard last century, and then he was too stupid to properly harvest the puvvles, and they all rotted on the branches.

But I can't judge him too harshly. I'd kill my brother over a puvvle. Half a puvvle. One bite of a puvvle. Not because they're particularly good, but because my brother is particularly awful.

Aresis could be on the shuttle headed back to Gravarus by now, and I could be stuck on Earth...alone...forever. It's not as though I can ever return home with Aresis on the throne. He'd have me beheaded in an instant. I'll be stranded here, forever, in the snow.

I'll never see...

Well, I'll never get to see...

Now that I think of it, there's not much to see on Gravarus. But there's not much to see on Earth unless you like gigantic rock piles touching the clouds. Humans love them, but I don't understand it.

"Yay, if you climb to the top of this thing, you can't breathe, and your face is freezing off, but you can see really, really far! Might die on the way down, but who cares because I got to see farther than anybody else!"

So you saw a lot of things far away, but you also now have

no nose or fingers.
Humans are so stupid.
I want to go home.

JAEL'S NARRATIVE

I went to the barracks at blue hour. The Blockade Runners lived in eight log A-frames arranged in a circle, facing each other across a small courtyard. The sky, the snow on the roofs, the drifts taller than my head, everything swam in deep river blue. It looked like a town underwater.

In the center, I saw Luca. He was standing over a slapdash grill, a leather apron tied around his waist, flipping venison steaks with a pair of hand-carved wooden tongs. When he saw me, he shouted, "Hey, hey!" and waved the tongs in the air.

Seeing him again brought the last month tumbling back, and I had a sudden urge to snatch a nearby snow shovel and bean him with it.

"You ruined my life!" I shouted when I was still across the courtyard.

His face fell. "What? They didn't give you your tota?"

"No!"

"Dang."

"My words exactly."

I approached and held my hands out over the grill. "Apparently, Klifrari aren't supposed to get distracted by stupid, lost Blockade Runners."

He laughed, which annoyed me, and I eyed the snow shovel again.

Sitting down on a nearby log bench, I gestured for him to join me. He sat on the opposite end of the bench and extended his leg between us. He was wearing the same leather pants, still torn and stained. I wrinkled my nose.

"I only own two pairs," he said defensively, "and the other is drying by the fire."

I took my scissors from my rucksack, tore the rip in his

pants wider, and went to work on his stitches which, I noticed with irritation, had pulled and healed ugly and ragged.

"I did such a good job on these, and look what you did to them."

I cut the thread sadly. A work of art, ruined.

"What happened to the package the Gravs were so eager to get?" I asked.

"Gave it to Craddock," he replied, leaning away from me and trying to flip his steaks. I accidentally poked him with the scissors.

"Sit still!"

"Steaks gonna burn."

"What was in the package?"

"I'm not really allowed to..."

"You ruined my entire life."

He groaned. "It's a book of..."

He hesitated.

"A book of what?"

"Can I wait until you're done with the scissors?"

"No."

"Crad said it's a Klifrari manuscript or something."

"Klifrari?" I looked up at him. "How do you know?"

"I'm just telling you what Crad told me."

"Where is it?"

"Still sitting in his office for all I know."

I looked around at the barracks surrounding us. "Which one is his office?"

Luca laughed. "I'm not telling you that."

"You ruined my life."

He gave me an indecisive look and then said, "You can have a steak."

A little bundle of Blockade Runners blew in from behind the barracks and surrounded us. They fell into cheerful conversation, and I finished with Luca's leg and left.

I glanced over my shoulder at them as I walked back toward the clinic – a knot of rowdy boys, laughing and shoving, with

Luca in the center, like the warm heart. Something inside me reached out for that.

Captain Craddock stepped out of a building at the far end of the barracks and watched them solemnly with his hands in his pockets.

There was no wind that night. As I lay on my cot in the storeroom behind the clinic, stitching a moose onto the collar of my coat and feeling the purring cat gently vibrating at my feet, I heard a fiddle playing brightly from the direction of the barracks. A shout shot through the cold every now and then, followed by clapping as the boys danced and sang and burned off their bad memories like paraffin in flame.

Soon the rumors wafted in with the snow. A Gravarian the size of Goliath, with a furious horde. They showed no mercy. They left no survivors. Some people were frightened. Some claimed it was all just empty talk. Some said it was a lie from the Klifrari.

Then, on clear days, we started to see smoke in the distance.

The first refugee came on a sunny day. I saw her arguing with Gib on the clinic's doorstep. My eyes stung because the wind brought an acrid smoke down the river and the woman seemed to have blown in on the smoke itself. She was barefoot, frostbitten, and carrying a toddler who was crying to keep himself warm. Gib shouted at her and pointed down the street. The woman turned away, weeping.

The baby buried its face in her shoulder and wailed. The skin on his tiny knuckles was raw and bleeding. My heart broke. I was supposed to teach a little group of Klifrari children how to treat frostbite. What better way?

I chased after her and grabbed her arm. "I can help you."

"I don't need your help," she snapped. "They'll come for you too, you know, and then you'll know how it feels."

"I'm not technically Klifrari, and I can help you for free if you don't mind a few observers."

She looked me up and down and shrugged.

Once she and the baby were thoroughly bandaged and my students thoroughly taught, I helped her to the train station and bought her a ticket.

She turned to me before she got on the train. I expected a 'thank you 'but I didn't get it. "The Gravs who burned our outpost," she said, "were looking for something."

"What?" I asked.

She shrugged. "I don't know. A book or a letter or something."

The train began to puff and strain against the weight of its cars.

"They'll be here soon," she said.

I stood on the platform as the train groaned and dragged toward the glassy tundra, and a sinking dread swamped me. I turned back toward the outpost and noticed Craddock at the postman's window, paying to mail a letter.

An idea seized me, and I tramped toward the Blockade Runners' barracks. As I entered the split rail fence that encircled the barracks, I was nearly trampled by Luca Paxton swinging by at breakneck speed on a little brown mare. He didn't notice me. This wheedled me, and I couldn't understand why.

Craddock's office door was unlocked. I rifled around in his desk until I found the brown package. It still had Luca's bloody fingerprints on it. I picked it up and turned it over in my hands. Then I gently untied the string and unfolded the wrapping.

Inside was a small, leather-bound book. It felt like a fragile, dying bird. Like a set of broken wings, the hardcovers barely held together and left a fine brown dust on my fingers. The pages crackled when I opened them, like breaking bones.

On the first page was a poem written in Klifrari shorthand. I couldn't immediately comprehend it. On each following page was a melody neatly handwritten in black ink. An animal was sketched above each song at the top of the page. A bear, a beaver, a stork, a buffalo…

My breath caught in my chest. This was an ancient Klifrari Melodiac. Probably a hundred years old. They were banned after the Eveness Massacre.

Craddock shouldn't have this, I thought. I should have this. This belonged with my people, not some Blockade Runner Captain at a desolate outpost.

Maybe if I brought them a real, handwritten Melodiac, the council would let me take my trial sooner, and I could get out of this flat wasteland and go home.

I pulled a Klifrari guide to bone setting from my jacket, wrapped it in the brown paper, and then laid it where the Melodiac had been. I slipped the Melodiac into an interior pocket of my coat.

Footsteps crunched in the snow outside, and I hurried for the door but bumped into Craddock in the doorway.

"What are you doing in here?" He asked. I saw his eyes travel to the desk.

"You never paid me for the other night when I came out here to take out what's-his-name's stitches."

I knew his name, but I didn't want to look like I was secretly harboring a crush or a grudge against Luca. Which I was. Which one, I couldn't quite decide.

"Put it on my bill," he said.

"That's not really how it works..."

He glared at me, and there was something dangerous in his look. He blocked the doorway, and I felt a little frightened.

"Now get out," he snarled.

"I can't. You're blocking the..."

"GET OUT!"

I ducked under his arm and ran all the way back home. I escaped to my little cot in the storage room and, when I felt safe, opened the book again. Very carefully, I began to translate the verse on the inside of the cover.

By midnight, I'd managed one verse:

Water silent, southward flowing;
Glacier sliding – ice toboggan.
Rest my Darling, feel the snowflake

Stardust falling on your lashes.

And I was starting on the second when I heard the first far-away rumble. The ground thrummed slightly. I sat up and glanced around the room. A hanging lantern swayed with a tiny creak. Another boom made the yau pot on my stove clatter. I walked to the window. Outside, beyond the outpost, a red glow like hot metal pulsated in the night sky.

I pulled my coat over my shoulders and fell asleep wondering when Craddock would notice the Melodiac was missing.

Pat's daughter woke me in the middle of the night. She burst into the room, breathless, pitchfork in hand. "I said this would happen. I told everyone that this was going to happen."

"What's happening? Is it the Gravs?"

"They're just a few miles down the road. They've already burned Leatherstrap. He'll burn everything to the ground..."

Something shrieked overhead.

"That's it!" she screamed. Something struck the clinic, there was a flash of fire and a rending sound, and the world flipped upside down.

THE LOVE LETTERS OF CAPTAIN HARRISON CRADDOCK

I have the book and the boys, and we are safely on a train headed to our meeting place. Everything is going according to plan, and I feel I can breathe again. Paxton was supposed to be on a run when we left, but he returned early because the Gravs blocked his route. I had hoped we could escape while he was gone. As we got on the train, Henry was injured by an explosion. Pax turned back for him, and I ordered the engineer to go. As we left the station, he looked up, and our eyes met, and Helena, the look on his face. It was pure betrayal. I see it every time I close my eyes. But I did it for his own good. He thinks I abandoned him and that pain is a knife to the stomach. It is bleeding out.

I'm glad you're safe, and I'm glad you butchered the pigs like I asked. Don't cry over it. There's no point crying over a thing once it's done. Close your eyes and collect your courage and push through the terrible act. Because sometimes it takes a little courage to sin.

I will end this war, and save you, save my unit, even save Paxton in the end. I had a moment of weakness at the beginning, but once the book is in Aresis' hands then, it'll all be over. Oh, how I want it to be over.

I want to wake up with you beside me and the curtains are open and the snow is falling outside, and I want us to be at peace. I want to feel the deep pillow under my head and the drowsiness after a long sleep, and I don't want to be afraid anymore. I want to have no worries again, and I want to be in love again. Don't you feel like this is becoming a heavy love? Don't you feel this is a heavy love? Don't you miss a light love? One with no dread in it? One that doesn't fear loss?

All love is made terrible by loss. Because losing you would be death.

It would be burning alive.

It would be hell.

But I will see you again. We will be together, and the snow will be falling outside the window, and you will bring me peace.

I love you more than life.

Yours,

Crad

JAEL'S NARRATIVE

I awoke with dirt in my mouth. I lay face down on the floor, sheltered by a shattered wall fragment. Spitting, I pushed the debris aside and got unsteadily to my feet. I still had the Melodiac clutched in my hands. I rummaged around a moment until I found my rucksack and I stuffed the Melodiac inside. A slow snow of gray ash blew in little flurries and stuck in my hair and eyelashes as I struggled over the piles of broken paneling and collapsed ceiling toward where the door used to be.

It was early morning – the sky a baby-powder blue. I limped down the empty street, looking for other survivors, but all I could hear was the light breath of the wind, the crackling fires, the loose sole of my boot snapping against my foot. Nothing stirred, and the street was littered with relics. The twisted skeleton of a child's tricycle. A pie plate with half a pie smeared beneath it on the ground. A wooden box, cracked and hanging open, papers wafting out of its open mouth and drifting away like dandelion seeds.

Insanely, I ran toward the train station. There must be a train. There's always a train.

I heard hoof beats and sprang aside as a horse with no rider streaked past me, running toward the Blockade Runner's barracks and dodging madly from side to side with its nostrils flaring and foam spattering its flanks.

The platform was deserted. A squirrel ran down the tracks, holding half a heel of bread in its mouth. The glass at the ticket booth was shattered, and the ticket agent lay slumped on the desk in a puddle of blood.

Could I be the last living person in this entire outpost? The last living person on this side of the mountain?

I ran to the back of the train station, which faced north.

In the distance, smoke billowed into the sky, and a wall of fire crept slowly toward me. The Gravs were returning, purging the region, making sure there were no survivors. A silent destruction. No sounds of panic. No screams.

I really am the only survivor.

I couldn't stay here. I couldn't run. I stepped back onto the little platform and sat down on a bench. Except for the ticket booth's broken window, the train station was oddly untouched. I half expected the bag boy to come around the corner and ask me if I needed a tag for my luggage.

Then I heard a sound.

"Who's there?" I called.

"Help me!"

I stood up and ran to the end of the platform. Luca Paxton staggered down the street toward me, supporting a bleeding young Blockade Runner.

"Oh, it's you," he panted.

He dropped to his knees and eased his friend onto the ground.

"Hang in there, Henry. You'll be ok," he said.

"Get me something to use as a bandage," I ordered.

Luca jumped up and ran into the train station.

Henry groaned. His side was open, the skin blown away, and the muscles and ribs shattered. He took a shuttering breath and just...died.

Luca returned with an armful of curtains.

"I'm sorry," I said quietly.

He let out a long breath and walked away down the platform. I covered Henry's body with the curtains and followed him. He sat on a bench with his rucksack at his feet and leaned his head against the wall behind him.

"That's everyone."

"Did you have family here?"

He shook his head.

"And the other Blockade Runners?"

He gazed blankly into the middle distance. "They left."

"Without you?"

"They got on the last train. When Henry fell, I went back for him. They didn't wait for us."

A breeze picked up and swirled the smoke around us. Luca leaned forward and ruffled his hair spasmodically with his fingers. We sat silent for a while, watching the smoke curling into the brightening morning sky as Luca made a rhythmic ticking noise with his mouth.

"Odd how the smoke does that," he said at last.

I didn't know what he was talking about, but I said "yeah" anyway.

"There's always a way out," he murmured.

"Not necessarily," the smoke stung my eyes to tears, "sometimes you run out of options."

"There's always a way out. Come on."

Wearily, Luca stood up, brushed the ash off his pants, swung is rucksack onto his back, and then began walking down the platform and back into the outpost. I followed him. For a few minutes, no one disturbed us.

In my mind, anyone who could get lost on Ram's Head had no right to lead, so I shouldered in front of him. He sped up and got in front of me. I double-stepped until I was in the lead again. I instantly regretted it.

A huge, blueish creature burst out of a half-collapsed log house.

I'd never seen a Gravarian before, and the shock struck me dumb. The size. The black veins webbed under the milky blue skin. The impassive look on its heavy face. Luca shoved me back, knocked me down, whipped a knife from his belt, cut the Gravarian's forearm and bicep, pushed him forward, and cut his leg. It happened so quickly that the Gravarian was howling on the ground before I hit the dirt.

Luca grabbed the back of my coat and hauled me up.

"HEY!" I shouted, angry, as I scrambled to my feet, but my complaint was cut off by a metal shaft striking the brick where my head had been a second before.

Another Gravarian appeared at the end of the street. Luca ducked through a broken window, and I followed him, tumbling gracelessly onto a smoldering couch. Metal arrows struck the opposite wall. We crouched and ran into the kitchen with our hands over our heads. I was so distracted I tripped over a woman's body next to the oven. She lay on her back, her eyes open, her hair in braids. She wore a flowered apron and clutched a cast iron dutch oven between her hands. Something red leaked out of it and pooled around her body.

"Don't look at it," Luca said, taking me by the arm and pulling me up. We heard footsteps at the front of the house, and Luca led the way out the back door into a dim backyard, but the second I stepped over the threshold, a Gravarian appeared from nowhere and swiped at me with a weapon like a cleaver. He'd have cut me in half from head to toe if Luca hadn't snatched me out of the way, stepped in front of me, and cut the Gravarian's hand off.

I turned and ran back into the house – I don't know why.

"Don't!" Luca shouted, running after me. There was a boom, the house trembled, and everything went black.

I awoke in a bed.

Of all the places I'd imagined waking up (both Heaven and Hell had flashed across my mind as I lost consciousness), a bed had not been one of them. But here I was, warm and comfortable, tucked under a clean white sheet and a red chenille blanket.

I sat up and looked around. I lay on the top rack of a narrow bunk. I assumed, from the way the room rocked steadily back and forth to a rhythmic tick-tick-clank, that I had somehow found my way into the passenger compartment of a steam train. The room was about six feet square, with green carpet, a bunk bed, and a bench nailed into the wall and upholstered in frayed green brocade. Beside the bench, which served as a couch, stood a small porcelain sink. At the end of the compartment was a sliding door with a frosted glass window, and opposite that, on the exterior wall, a small window looking out on the white countryside flashing by. The walls were covered in fading green fabric wallpaper.

I slid off the bed and looked out the window, wondering who'd rescued me. At that moment, the door opened, and Luca walked in, looking rumpled.

"We need to get off this train," he said.

"Why?" I demanded. "We've been rescued."

"We were not rescued," he said. "We've been captured by Gravarians."

"Ridiculous!" I cried. "Gravs don't take prisoners."

He held up his hands, and I saw that his wrists were tightly bound.

"Untie me and we can jump."

"I'm not jumping off this train!" I cried. "I'll break my neck."

"Not your neck," Luca scoffed as if it was the silliest thing he'd ever heard, "just your legs. Possibly a wrist."

I backed away from him. "You jump. I'm taking my chances here."

"I'm kidding! You'll be fine."

"No."

"Just duck and roll when you hit the ground."

"No!"

He came toward me, "I'll hold your hand."

"NO!"

"When you hit the ground, just crumple. There's snow, so it'll cushion your fall."

"GET BACK!"

I reached into my jacket and felt a little burst of panic in my chest.

"The Melodiac is gone!" I shouted.

Luca stopped and looked back at me. "The what?"

"They took the Melodiac!"

"You have a Melodiac?" I'd piqued his interest.

"I did, but they took it!"

"They didn't take anything."

"How do you know that?"

"Some of us have stronger constitutions."

"Your constitution didn't keep you from nearly turning into a popsicle on the mountain."

He ignored me. "The Grav pinned me down, tied me up, and threw me in the compartment. I've had a good look at the train, though. There's about five of these passenger compartments on each side of a narrow corridor. There are three other cars; I think they're mostly supply cars. I think the Grav is in the next one over."

"None of that matters. I won't leave this train without the Melodiac," I cried. "It's an ancient Klifrari artifact. It's priceless. And I need it to take back home to Rustypike."

In a panic, I tore open my rucksack and dug around inside. My fingers brushed against the feathery pages, I let out a long sigh and pulled out the Melodiac. "It's here. I found it."

"Is that..." Luca came back across the train car toward me, "is that from the package I gave to Craddock?"

I found my knife and cut his bonds.

"Did you steal that?" Luca asked, rubbing his wrists.

"That's none of your business!"

"You stole it! Give it to me!"

"NO!"

"It was my packet that I was entrusted with. If Craddock doesn't have it, it's mine."

"No," I said, hugging the Melodiac against my chest, "it's a Klifrari artifact, which means it's mine."

"You're not even a Klifrari!"

"And whose fault is that?"

He raised his hand, and I flinched. Luca looked shocked and offended.

"I'm scratching the back of my head!" he said. "I'm not going to hit you! What type of animal do you think I am?"

I stared at him, confused. Birch had hit me a dozen times in my life, and it never occurred to me that it was strange or excessive or even shameful, but clearly Luca thought so.

"Now," he said, softer than before, "we need to get off this train before the Grav comes back and finds us with that."

But it was too late. The compartment door opened, and a huge Grav stepped in. Luca took the knife from my hand and pushed me behind him.

"Go out the window!" He ordered. "Hurry!"

THE PERSONAL LOG OF OBSIDIAN, ONCE CROWN PRINCE OF GRAVARUS

Aresis burned another village. When I arrived, the smoke still stood in the air. He shelled the place with some kind of old human artillery he was carrying around on his train. The carnage he left behind was lamentable, even if humans are a lower species. It sits badly with me.

I rescued two humans who somehow survived: a male and a female. I decided to bring both because I've heard conflicting reports on which sex is more intelligent, and this seemed my safest option.

I will admit that these two little things did fight off Aresis' scouts fiercely. I was impressed. Of course, their building was shelled, and some ceiling caved in. The female one instantly went unconscious. Apparently, this is something humans do when life gets a little too uncomfortable for them. Just sort of drop dead for a few hours and then come back around.

The male one nearly slit my throat, and I almost crushed him while trying to get him tied up and on the train. Feisty creature. Lots of teeth.

But this is the beautiful part: the female human has the Melodiac. Yes, the book that will restore my ancestral right to the throne. I have it. It's on my train. Aresis thought he could get it by killing humans and burning their villages. Well, I got it because I had mercy on two helpless creatures. To use a rather crass human idiom, I don't quite understand but find very fun to say, "Put that in your smike and poke it."

We are headed to the next village, Eveness, which is where the Melodiac is said to be from. There we will gather supplies, turn around, and head back to the Gravarian settlement I started from, where I will climb on the shuttle and take off back home, and all my problems will melt away like ice. I would feel rather cheerful if trains weren't so agonizingly slow! There has got to be a faster way to travel. But the route is impassible by any means other than train or dog sled, and I'm not about to be whipped around the countryside by a bunch of slobbering, yapping rodents.

When I went to greet my human companions, I found them together in the female's compartment, trying to leap out an open window. Just hop right out. As if we weren't traveling at a breakneck speed through mountainous terrain.

I had to hit the male one quite hard to prevent him from gutting me, and he just dropped like a dead pomrat. So I assumed I'd killed him, which quite shocked me. I let out a little shriek, and the female, who was halfway out the window, came back into the room shouting, and for a moment everything was rather chaotic, and the female kicked me so hard in the shins I'm surprised she didn't break her foot.

I didn't know what to do, so I just retreated out of the compartment and shut the door behind me.

It seems if you hit humans even a tiny bit hard, they take one of those little death naps I mentioned before.

I stood awkwardly out in the corridor for quite some time until I heard voices. I put my head in to see if they were both alright, and the female human screamed and threw a knife at me. It stuck in the door as I shut it again. It took the rest of the day to coax them out of the compartment, and I had to offer them food. Humans will risk anything for food.

Now, both humans are sitting on the floor of the rations car, and the female one is holding a chunk of ice against the male one's face and looking at me with great ire. The male one's eye has turned purple. It's unnerving.

Their names are Jay-el and Luke-ah, and they're...the worst. I hate them. And the rumors are true. Gravarians can smell human emotions, and it's disgusting.

Right now, they're both very angry and scared, and so they

smell like a very spicy curry, and it's making my eyes water.

I've decided not to tell them I want the Melodiac. If they know I want it, they'll run off somewhere.

Our first peaceful interaction was awkward. I didn't know how to make them understand that I mean them no harm, so I just kept giving them food. The entire time we talked, whenever the spicy curry smell grew potent, I thrust bread and cheese at them. They'd take it, nibble on it, then eat it in big bites, all the time growing calmer. When they'd swallowed the last bite, they'd get stinky again; I'd stick more food under their nose, they'd take it and calm down. Miraculous discovery.

Luke-ah is not feeling cheerful because, apparently, his human friends left him for dead, which made him quite nervy. When I asked him about it, he suddenly smelled like grief, which is bitter smelling, like camphor, and I ordered him to go back to his compartment before he asphyxiated us all. He left very willingly, and I haven't seen him since.

The female isn't comfortable with me but isn't overtly hostile. She's not very emotive (thanks be). Odd looking for a human. I've seen varying degrees of pigment in human skin before. It's quite beautiful that they are made that way. But this one has dark skin covered over with white patches. It's stunning. It's utterly gorgeous. All other humans must be so envious of her.

She says she will stay on the train as far as Fool's Bridge. I let her keep the Melodiac in her compartment. I know it's a gamble, but it's keeping her feet on the floor instead of vaulting out windows.

As we spoke, she began to tremble all over and said she wasn't feeling well, so I left her alone on the condition that she wouldn't try to leap out the window again. She agreed.

JAEL'S NARRATIVE

My body was gripped with violent shaking, cold chills skittered up and down my spine, and my head weighed a thousand pounds. Then my throat ached, and my stomach turned, sending me rushing to the sink.

I dug around in my rucksack until I found a little bottle of charcoal, which I poured into my water skin and drank before, I crawled into my little bunk and pulled my blankets over my head. I was freezing cold and nauseous, and I wished I were dead. I was a few minutes into a heavy, lethargic sleep when Luca burst into my compartment.

"What did he say to you after I left?"

"Nothing. Now go away. I'm sick."

"Look, I know this Grav says he's helping us out," Luca said, dropping onto the couch.

"Go away," I moaned, "I'm sick."

Luca ignored me and rambled on, "I've dealt with Gravs for the better part of the last five years, and they don't help humans. Not even grudgingly. They kill humans. I don't think we should trust this one."

"I'm too sick to care," I grumbled.

"I thought he seemed cagey. Did he tell you why he's here? Where he's going?"

"He's trying to catch Aresis," I mumbled.

"Why?"

"I don't know. War crimes or something."

"That's it? Aresis isn't the first Grav to commit war crimes on Earth. There's something else going on. He wants something, and he's not just keeping us on board to guide him across the country. Did he say anything else?"

The words went into my mind, but they got scrambled up

before I could comprehend them. I pulled the blanket down under my chin.

"Earth is a Gravarian prison planet," I said. "The only Gravs you've dealt with in your life were criminals. This one isn't a prisoner, he's from Gravarus itself, and he seems decent. Plus, he's letting me sleep in this warm compartment on this nice bed, and I'm sick, and I want to be left alone."

"Oh, are you sick? I'm sorry about that."

"Yes. Now go away."

"We need to decide if we're going to stay on this train or get off at the next stop and make a run for it."

"We're not prisoners," I said. "We can leave whenever we want."

"So?"

"SO, we might as well stay where there's food and shelter for free until Fool's Bridge."

"I need to find my unit," Luca said, touching his black eye and wincing.

"Great. We both have achievable goals. First step to success. Now go away."

Luca was about to respond when his face went green. He doubled over and looked desperately around the room.

"SINK!" I shouted, pointing to the little porcelain basin between the couch and the window. Luca ran to it and vomited violently.

"Bearhie, I think I might be sick," he panted when he was done.

I pulled the blanket over my head again. "Skin you, I can't believe you gave me the flu."

"I gave you the flu? I think you gave me the flu."

"I felt fine yesterday."

"So did I."

He rolled over to face the wall. "Do you think the Gravarian can catch a human virus?"

"Probably not. Go away," I moaned. "Let me die in peace."

After a minute or two of silence, Luca said in a small voice,

"Do you really want me to leave?"

"I guess no one should die alone. Just be quiet."

He rolled off the couch and crawled out of the compartment on his hands and knees.

"I said you could stay!" I called after him.

A minute later, he returned with his fiddle and a little, hand-carved wooden flute.

"You know," I said, "every time I interact with you, my life takes a dramatic turn southward."

"Can I see the Melodiac?"

"No."

He took it from under the bottom bunk sheets, lay back on the couch, and began playing one of the songs. "What are you doing?" I shouted, leaning out of the bunk and plugging the end of the flute with my finger. Luca coughed.

"I'm trying these songs."

"Have you forgotten that we are on a train with a Gravarian? It's illegal, and it's dangerous!"

He rolled his eyes. "Have you ever seen a Grav kill somebody because they were playing music?"

"No, because I've never seen anyone stupid enough to play music around the Gravs. Have you never heard of the Eveness Massacre?"

"Legends and fairytales," he said, putting the flute to his lips again and starting to play. I hopped off the bunk, pulled it out of his hands, yanked the window open, and threw the flute out.

"Hey! That was a custom piece!"

"Get out of here!" I cried, pointing at the door. "Go get murdered in your own compartment!"

He shrugged, got up, and took the Melodiac with him. I grabbed his arm.

"Leave that here."

"No. You don't even know how to read it."

"But it's Klifrari, so it belongs to me."

"No."

"Give it to me."

"Take it then."

I tried to snatch it, but Luca had lightning reflexes, and he evaded. He made a run for the door, but before he made it out, he doubled over, hand over his mouth, and ran back to the sink, dropping the Melodiac on the way. I picked it up and shoved it up my shirt. It was a stupid, childish thing to do, and if I'd been on that train with a lesser man, I might have learned a hard lesson that day, but Luca was kind to his core.

He glared at me. "That's cheating."

I waved at him, and he left.

I crawled back into my bed, tossed the book on the couch, pulled the blankets up to my ears again, and let out a long sigh.

There was a knock at my compartment door.

"What?" I snapped.

The door slid open. Luca walked in. He saw the book lying on the couch, grabbed it, and walked out.

"You're a dirty thief!" I shouted after him.

A moment later, thin fiddle music drifted from Luca's compartment.

THE PERSONAL LOG OF OBSIDIAN, ONCE CROWN PRINCE OF GRAVARUS

Something in the air makes my heart heavy. I remember things I'd meant to forget. I feel restless.

I am unwell. My body aches and my throat feels as though I'm swallowing uncut diamonds, and my joints burn. I believe I am dying. I have caught some vile human plague and will soon be dead.

Gravarians should not be able to catch human plagues. It's absurd. It's unscientific. My physician assured me that I would not need any kind of special precautions as humans are an alien race, and their bacteria would not affect me.

I feel very affected at this moment.

I am regurgitating my stomach contents.

My skin is warm and moist, but I feel cold.

This is the end.

Curse these disgusting, unsanitary humans. I should have left them behind. The male bit me. Perhaps I have rabies.

But, if this is my appointed time, I have no regrets.

Well, one regret.

Two.

No, maybe three.

Very well, I have several regrets.

I wish I hadn't listened to my mother. Ever. I wish I had never listened to my mother.

I wish I could have saved my father.

I wish I'd strangled Aresis in his sleep when I had the chance.

I wish I'd never come to Earth in the first place.

I wish I'd never met the humans.

I wish Earth were gone like it deserved to be hundreds of years ago.

I wish I were home in my own bed.

I hate everyone and everything, and the world is a very bad place. I want to be alone in my room, and I want it to be dark and cold, and I want a servant to bring me some tea. I want to sleep for days and days. I want my physician to come and heal me.

But instead, I'm stranded here. I will be buried under ten feet of snow, and no one will ever know what became of me. Not that anyone cares.

JAEL'S NARRATIVE

Too thirsty and miserable to sleep, I dragged myself out of my bunk and staggered down the corridor and across the coupling to the next car. The next car was identical to ours with the faded carpet and dark wood ceiling, except the Grav had removed the walls that separated the compartments to make two large, long rooms on either side of the corridor. On the right was the supply room, stocked with water barrels, a rust-pocked potbellied stove, a table and some chairs, and a dozen boxes of dried fish, which is apparently one of the only things Gravs can eat on Earth. On the left were Obsidian's quarters.

As I refilled my water skin, I could still hear Luca's fiddle playing a sad tune, but even louder I heard Obsidian weeping in his compartment. This surprised me as I'd always heard that Gravs were supposed to be emotionless.

When I returned to my compartment with some water, I curled up in my bed and tried to sleep, but I couldn't shut out the angry jig Luca was playing on his fiddle now.

Footsteps out in the corridor made the floor of the car shiver. I crawled down from my bunk and peered out.

Obsidian stood outside Luca's door, breathing heavily, his face contorted, and he held a knife in his hand.

I felt like I should shout, but my voice died in my throat.

Obsidian's hand found the latch.

The fiddle music stopped abruptly and was replaced by loud retching.

Obsidian shook himself. His face relaxed, and his muscles softened. He looked down at the knife like he didn't know where he got it, then looked around like he didn't know where he was. His eyes brushed past me, and he froze.

"I'm sorry," he said. "I'm in the wrong compartment. I'm not feeling well."

He put the knife in his belt and walked calmly back down the corridor and out of the car. I watched him until he was out of sight.

Next door, Luca vomited on. With a sigh, I went to his compartment and knocked softly.

"What?" said a gravelly voice.

"I have something to make you stop puking so I can get some sleep."

"The door's open."

I slid the door open. Luca lay in the fetal position on the floor.

"I wish I were dead," he said.

"Drink this, and it'll help."

I took his water skin and poured some charcoal inside.

He looked at it skeptically.

"What is it?"

"Charcoal. It helps nausea and vomiting."

"Where did you get it?"

"I made it."

"Where did you learn how to make it?"

"I trained with a Yushta."

"I thought you were a Berablotha. Actually, I thought you weren't a Klifrari at all."

"I'm not because I felt sorry for this pitiful Blockade Runner who got lost on a perfectly chartable mountain, and I failed my trial."

His face went pale, and he gagged.

"Just drink it!" I said, retreating quickly from the room.

THE PERSONAL LOG OF OBSIDIAN, ONCE CROWN PRINCE OF GRAVARUS

I have rabies.

I looked it up in the Guide to Human Maladies that the female human leant me, and I have all the symptoms. And my emotions are bouncing about like a trapped babbit.

One moment my heart is heavy as a locomotive; the next, I want to throw a chair through the window, and the next, I feel like dancing. And I'm in a haze. Like I don't quite know where I am. At one point, I awoke outside the human's compartment with a knife in my hand.

What was I thinking of doing?

Increased aggression is a symptom of rabies.

Oh, mercy, I have rabies. Soon I'll be slobbering and spitting, and I'll die in dreadful spasms.

Curse Earth!

Curse humans!

The human came by a moment ago and offered me some concoction that she said would help my stomach. I drank it, and it does seem to help a little. I'm so sick I'm drinking mysterious human medicine now. This is the end.

I hope Aresis gets what's coming to him because this is all his fault. If only he'd managed to assassinate my mother properly.

JAEL'S NARRATIVE

Finally, I went back to my compartment and crawled into my bed. A tattered, light sleep was creeping over me when I heard a shout from the next room. I groaned and covered my head with the blanket.

My door flew open, and Luca staggered into the compartment. "What did you give me?" He gasped.

"Charcoal, I told you..."

"My puke is black!"

"Yes, but..."

"IT'S BLACK!"

"I know, it's because..."

"WHY IS IT BLACK???"

"LUCA!" I shouted.

"WHAT?"

I pushed the blanket down just below my eyes and looked at him. "What color is charcoal?"

"What?"

"What. Color. Is. Char.coal?"

He thought for a minute and then threw himself on the couch with a groan.

"I threw up on my bunk," he said.

"You can stay there as long as you're quiet."

"Thanks."

There were footsteps outside, and Obsidian burst in.

"HAS ANYONE ON THIS CIRCUS TRAIN HEARD OF PRIVACY?" I shouted.

"WHAT DID YOU GIVE ME?" Obsidian wailed.

I buried my face in my pillow.

Obsidian was hysterical. "MY VOMIT HAS TURNED BLACK! THIS IS NOT A TRADITIONAL SYMPTOM OF RABIES!"

Luca edged away from him. “What's that about rabies?”

Obsidian collapsed on the floor. “I never thought I'd die like this. Wretched. Surrounded by...” he shuddered, “...humans.”

Luca leaned over the edge of the couch and patted him on the back. “It's just the charcoal, Sid. It makes your puke turn black.”

“I want to go home.”

Luca turned to face the wall. “Need a blanket?”

“I'm fine,” Obsidian sniffed.

Soon, we were all three asleep.

THE LOVE LETTERS OF CAPTAIN HARRISON CRADDOCK

Helena, my life,

I don't understand what is happening. We arrived at Eveness to meet with Aresis as arranged, but when I opened the package, there was another book inside, and the Melodiac is gone.

Paxton must have switched it. He must have opened it on the mountain and somehow understood what it was and stolen it later.

There was that Klifrari girl who brought him down from the mountain. Maybe she knew what it was. She must have told him.

Or maybe she took it. When she was in my office. Maybe he showed it to her, and she took it.

Now I've lost my bargaining chip. I'm steaming, empty-handed, toward a meeting I can't run from. I must do something. I must find that Melodiac. Perhaps if I go back to Powderkeg?

Lock the doors. If you see anyone, hide in the cellars. I can't protect you without that book. I can't guarantee your safety.

I will fix this, my love. I will find a way. Whatever it takes, I will fix this.

I know you're confused. I know what I'm doing right now looks wrong, and I agree with your worries about what Aresis will do once he gets the Melodiac. But I don't think you can really understand how complex this is unless you're in the middle of it. I think to you, far away on the tundra, miles from any of this, it might seem clear, but it isn't. You can see a house fire from ten miles away, but you can't tell how it started, or how big it is, or what room it's coming from. And when you're inside the house that's on fire, everything just looks like smoke. You have to stumble around the best you can until you find an exit.

And if the exit is a second-story window instead of the front door, well, you have to jump.

Keep your chin up, and trust me.

I'm going to fix this somehow.

Crad

JAEL'S NARRATIVE

I awoke when the train jolted and began to slide to a stop.

Across the compartment, Luca sat pulling on his boots, his hair in disarray. I didn't see Obsidian.

"Sid wants to see us."

"Who?" I asked, sitting up and rubbing my eyes. My hair, which I kept in a curly fro and cared for with my own homemade hair oils and always bound up in a scarf before bed, was matted in the back and stuck to my sweaty neck. I felt disgusting.

"Obsidian. The Gravarian."

I climbed out of bed, trying to pat my hair back into shape, and followed him to the next car.

Obsidian's compartment was stark. Stripped wooden floor, bare walls, one table and chair, and no lights. He had one blanket on the floor, under which he huddled like a big, blue mountain.

"I have yet to succumb to your wretched plague," Obsidian moaned. And I've felt strange all night. Emotional. Weepy. Angry. Your hideous planet is corrupting me! This is our last stop for a while, and Aresis is stopped not far ahead, so we may as well get you some food so you don't die. Even if I must. You must get supplies for both of us without looking suspicious. The villagers must not know that there is a Gravarian on the train.

"I'll go," Luca and I said simultaneously.

We glowered at each other.

"I'd rather go alone," I said.

"I should go by myself," Luca said at the same time.

I frowned at him. "I'm a Klifrari, and you'll just slow me down."

"Well, I'm a Blockade Runner, and you'll just slow me down."

"You'll get lost. You have a terrible sense of direction."

"You'll look suspicious. After growing up sitting alone in caves, you're about as socially adjusted as a vole."

"At least I don't whistle or hum or drum on every flat surface I see. I can get the supplies without drawing attention to myself."

Luca snorted. "Klifrari don't have some magic gift of stealth. People ignore you because of the smell."

"What smell?"

"You know," he waved his hand in a circular motion in front of his face, "the boar fat."

"Maybe if you'd been a little more concerned about staying warm and a little less concerned about smelling like roses and lavender, then I wouldn't have had to drag your frozen behind off that mountain, and I wouldn't BE here right now!"

Luca smiled. "You bring that up a lot. Does it bother you?"

I turned to Sid. "I'm not taking him with me."

Sid covered his eyes with his arm. "I don't care. Work it out amongst yourselves."

"Alright," Luca consented, heading for the door, "you can go alone. Have fun lugging the supplies back on your own in the snow. I'm going to take a nap. In my warm, cozy compartment."

He slid the door open and hopped across the coupling, leaving the door open and the snow swirling in. Sid cursed at him.

I snatched the supply list from Sid, shouldered my bag, and marched out of the car.

The village was nondescript. It hung onto the river bank and seemed, over time, to be slowly sliding into the water. The streets were dingy layers of packed snow and ice. Not many people moved around, and supplies were scarce. It appeared many residents had left, fleeing from the rumors of Aresis.

It took me a few hours to gather even a quarter of what we needed. I was tired, hungry, and ready to return to the train, but I couldn't find any salt. Without salt, I couldn't preserve meat or properly tan hide. We couldn't live without it.

As I searched for salt, I rounded a corner and noticed a

young boy wearing white leather and a yellow and black plaid shirt. He was loading a saddlebag with mail.

"Excuse me," I called to him, "are you a Blockade Runner?"

He nodded and kept loading his bag.

"Can I send a letter with you to Rustypike?"

"It'll take a while," he said. His voice hadn't changed yet. "And I'll have to hand it off to a Klifrari to take it over the mountain."

"That's alright, that's fine. I just need to send a letter."

He held out his hand.

"Oh," I patted my jacket pockets, "I don't have any paper."

He rolled his eyes and handed me a small piece of paper and a pencil.

I scrawled a quick, very Klifrari message on it.

Birch,
I'm alive and safe. Will come home soon.
Jael

He took it, and I continued my shopping.

I meandered deeper and deeper into the dregs of the town, stopping at every shop, bar, alehouse, and yau hut. No one would sell me salt. As the cold and dark settled over the village, I gave up. I was about to return to the train when I heard a faint whisper of music in a dark alleyway.

I stopped and turned round and round, trying to pinpoint which direction it came from. It was almost as though the music came from beneath the town itself, like the snow was humming. I got down on my hands and knees and pressed my ear against the ground. I heard shouting. Stamping. Fiddle music.

A trash can four or five feet away from me jumped aside like it was haunted. I started.

Suddenly, beneath the trashcan, a piece of the street peeled back, a blast of light and noise burst out of a hole in the ground, and a man helped a woman climb out. They saw me, shut the street back up behind them, and scampered away.

I crept over to the trash can and tugged on it. Nothing happened. I tried to twist it to the left, then to the right, but it was fixed to the street. Frustrated, I kicked it. It hopped aside again, and a trap door opened beneath it.

A man put his head up. "Password?"

"What?"

"Do you have a password?"

"Uh...Melodiac?" I said.

His head disappeared, but the door stayed open, so I assumed I'd guessed right. I climbed down the ladder ten feet into a swirl of light and movement.

The room was large and square, with stone walls and a packed dirt floor. Lanterns flickered from four wooden beams that bowed under the weight of the ceiling. A little stove glowed orange in the corner. The sweet smell of yau and bacon and an undertone of sweat filled the room. People crowded around tables and a bar, but in the center of the room, people danced.

I'd never seen dancing before. They stomped, twirled, put their hands in the air, and moved their bodies. It looked natural. It looked joyful. It looked strange.

Those that weren't dancing clapped and smiled and talked amongst themselves.

And perched on the bar, leaning against one of the beams, with one knee bent and the other leg outstretched, was Luca. And Luca was where the music came from. His eyes were closed, and his fingers moved so quickly over the fiddle's strings that they blurred, and his head nodded with the rhythm.

I smiled, but I didn't know why. I felt happy, even though nothing had changed. A moment ago, I was tired and hungry and frustrated, but the music felt like warm water melting snow.

As I approached the bar, the jig came to an end, and everyone cheered. Luca didn't notice. He leaned his head back and began to play a slow song in a minor key.

Everyone went quiet. It seemed like the lights dimmed on their own, and the couples on the dance floor came together. Women leaned their heads on their partner's shoulders, and men perched their chins on their partner's heads; others went cheek to cheek. They swayed rhythmically. Everyone else fell silent.

The world suddenly felt very beautiful and very sad. And sad things seemed beautiful; the way wildflowers grow on graves.

I approached Luca, but he didn't see me. He was completely wrapped up in the music, and suddenly it was as though it wasn't coming from the fiddle at all, but like it was bleeding out of him. He was a living gramophone.

And then he began to sing.

Water silent, southward flowing;
Glacier sliding – ice toboggan.
Rest my Darling, feel the snowflake
Stardust falling on your lashes.

Watch the Northstar gently rising
In a sky of velvet darkness.
Now the bald moon hides his visage
All the wolves cry out in anger.

Moonlit morning, starry noontide,
Winter's endless blue horizons
Now my Darling, wake and join me
As we trek the track together.

Rise, my Darling, hear the loon call.
See, the summer days are coming!
Yet my Darling rises never
And I trek alone forever.

When he finished, everyone clapped, but this time with gravity. Luca opened his eyes and smiled at me.

"Where did you learn that song?" I asked.

"It's in the Melodiac. You translated it."

"But it didn't have music..."

"I wrote the music," he said.

He set the bow to the string and began to play a jig again. Laughing, everyone bounded back onto the dance floor.

"What is this place?" I asked.

"Never heard of a speakeasy?" He shouted over his own playing.

"No."

"Well, that's what this is. Except instead of selling alcohol, they sell music and spices and furs and things the Klifrari think only they sell."

"You shouldn't be here," I said. "It's illegal."

"Not illegal," he laughed, "just deeply frowned on."

"What if a Klifrari hears you?"

He shrugged and kept playing. The Melodiac lay open next to him on the bar. I leaned over him and picked it up.

"This is mine," I said as I slid it into my coat.

He shrugged.

"So all this time I've been trudging around town looking for salt, you've been here drinking cider and playing your fiddle?"

He finished the song he was playing and set the fiddle down on his legs. "You need salt? You should have asked me."

He reached into his jacket and pulled out a jar of white salt.

"Where did you find this?" I demanded.

"Here."

I took the jar from him and looked at the price tag. "We can't afford this," I said.

He laughed and picked up his fiddle again. "What, you think this music is free? It pays well to be a musician in times like these."

He set the fiddle to his chin again, but the trapdoor in the ceiling opened, and a man half climbed, half fell down the ladder.

"They're coming!" He shouted.

Chairs screeched, boots thudded, the room rocketed into chaos. People shoved each other, fell over each other, pushed each other up the ladder, and spilled out into the night above.

"What's going on?" I asked Luca. "Who's coming?"

Luca hopped off the counter and wrapped his violin in a leather sleeve. "Your friends the Klifrari must have found out about this place."

Above us, someone screamed. People were still desperately trying to get out the trap door, but someone was forcing their way back down the ladder.

"Where is the musician?" A voice in the crowd shouted.

No one pointed, but everyone looked at us. A little man in a red sweater, who was definitely not a Klifrari, swung down the ladder and his eyes locked on Luca and the fiddle.

"Get him!" He shouted.

A second man came down the ladder and ran toward us. Luca grabbed my arm and pulled me after him to the back of the room and through a door into a storeroom. There was a trap door in the ceiling but no ladder.

"Lift me up!" I shouted.

He hoisted me onto his shoulders, struggling a little because, even though I was a lot shorter than him, I didn't weigh much less. I pushed the trap door open, climbed out into the street, leaned back, and offered him my hand. He hopped up and grabbed it, and I hauled him up. Our pursuers came out of the other door at the same moment and chased after us.

We ran down the street until we hit a wooden slat fence. Luca clambered up it, doubled over the top, reached down, and gave me a hand. We both teetered a second on the top and then pushed off just as our first pursuer reached the alley. We tore down side streets, through people's houses, down alleyways. Luca had to slow down several times and wait for me to catch up. Just when I thought my chest would burst, we found ourselves on the edge of town, only a short run to the woods. I knew I was better off in the woods than in town, so we ran toward them.

We dodged through the trees, looking back over our shoulders until suddenly the woods ended, and the ground fell steeply away into the frozen river. I gasped and put my arm out to stop Luca from running off the embankment. He hit my arm and nearly knocked us both headfirst into the icy water,

We looked around for somewhere to go. To our right, the forest followed the embankment out of sight. To the left was a large clearing and in the middle of the clearing stood a gutted concrete fort spattered in graffiti. A few wagons dotted the open area between us and the fort, most broken under heavy tablecloths of snow.

Behind us, voices and crashing branches.

"Come on!" I said, getting to my feet and pulling on Luca's arm, but he hung back.

"I know this place," he said. "It's Old Eveness. The massacre site."

This gave me a jolt, but I was too wired on adrenaline to stop and think about it.

"Yes, and it looks like a great place to hide," I said as I turned and ran toward it.

Luca ran after me. "It's haunted!"

THE LOVE LETTERS OF CAPTAIN HARRISON CRADDOCK

Paxton is here, in this town, and he has the Melodiac. I knew he would make it out of Powderkeg. I told you he would! See, leaving him behind was the right thing to do after all, despite your doubts. Not only did it save his life, but now he is delivering the Melodiac right into my hands. This is my chance. I can get it from him and still hand it over to Aresis as planned. We are saved!

It seems Aresis isn't the only one after the book. There's this little man in a red sweater who wants it too. And Aresis brother, I hear. It's hectic.

I'm glad the salted pork is lasting you. Don't forget to melt snow for water and boil pine needles for vitamin C. I will be home soon. We will sit in our house and watch the cardinals build a nest in the holly bush outside our window like we used to, and we will forget everything behind us and look only to the future.

I just have to get through today.

Your most beloved,

Crad

JAEL'S NARRATIVE

It was dusk, and the fort lay in shadow – a grim, echoing row of single-story concrete buildings ranged in a semi-circle around a small, flat courtyard. In the center of the courtyard, a shredded flag waved tattered fingers at us. The windows gaped like dead eyes.

We flattened ourselves against one of the exterior walls.

"Who says it's haunted?" I asked.

"Everyone."

Luca flinched at a crashing sound in the woods behind us and took a deep breath.

"I don't believe in ghosts," he said stolidly and walked into the courtyard. I followed him.

"Are you scared?" I whispered.

Luca squared his shoulders. "Don't be ridiculous. Frankly, I'm insulted. I'm terrified. I think I'm going to pee myself."

"We can't spend the night here," I whispered.

"We could jump into the river and be smashed to pieces on the rocks."

"That doesn't sound so bad."

Luca straightened. "This is ridiculous! I don't believe in ghosts!"

An owl, somewhere in the ruins, hooted shrilly, and we both startled.

"Oh, bearhie," I bent over, my hand on my chest.

Behind us, the man in the red sweater and his entourage broke out of the woods.

"Give them the book!" Luca said.

"NO! And besides, they'd probably just take it and toss us off the cliff."

"Alright," Luca said, "we split up..."

I laughed.

"Ok, we stay together."

A breeze whispered past us. It was cold and wet and felt like fingers brushing the back of my neck.

I refused to look like a coward, so I scooted into one of the doorways. It was black as charcoal inside, so we had to run our hands around the walls as we searched for somewhere to hide, but the room was gutted, and all the doors were gone. We tried the second room.

Our pursuers came across the field toward the fort. One of them startled a cat, and it yowled. I grabbed Luca's shoulders from behind. He let out a yelp.

"SHHHH!" I hissed.

At the back of the room, we found a narrow opening that lead to a dark passageway.

Voices echoed off the buildings outside. Luca shoved me frantically in front of him into the passageway.

It was so narrow I had to turn sideways and scoot with my back against one wall and my nose almost scraping the other. I could barely turn my head. We scootched awkwardly down the passage for ten feet before I bumped into a wall.

"Why'd you stop?" Luca hissed.

"The passage turns a corner," I said.

"Ok, go on."

I took a step, but the ground disappeared, and I fell forward into the dark.

THE PERSONAL LOG OF OBSIDIAN, ONCE CROWN PRINCE OF GRAVARUS

I am somewhat recovered from the rabies. The humans have not yet returned to the train, and I'm worried. Not worried, actually. Concerned. About the Melodiac. Not about them. But about the Melodiac.

I've searched and searched, and they must have taken it with them. And I think Aresis is still here. I thought if I stayed here, outside town, I'd easily avoid detection, but I'm growing worried. It's the first and only stop after the last outpost, so it makes sense we'd converge here, but he mustn't see me. If he finds the humans and gets that Melodiac, it's over. I have to find them, and we need to run.

My future is in jeopardy.

Why did I let the humans keep the Melodiac? Why didn't I tell them about its importance? Why didn't I take it and leave them behind? I'm making amateur mistakes because I'm getting weak. Never name your pets! The next thing you know, you're letting them run around with no discipline.

Time is short. I must hurry.

JAEL'S NARRATIVE

"Jae! Are you Ok?"

I rolled over and laughed at myself.

"Jae?"

"I'm fine!" I said. "It's not far down. Actually," I stood up and felt for the top. The hole I'd stumbled into was only about chin deep. I could feel Luca's boots.

"Come down."

He lowered himself down behind me. The passage sloped downward, where it grew colder.

A low clatter echoed from further down the passageway. I took a step back and stepped on Luca's toes.

"Did you hear that?"

A shuffling sound, like feet on packed dirt, moved toward us.

"Yo! Who's there!" Luca shouted into the darkness. The shuffling stopped.

I whispered, "We should go back. Those people chasing us are probably gone by now."

"Come on. I'll help you up."

The shuffling started again.

"Go, go," I pushed him, "it's coming. Hurry!"

"I'm going!"

The shuffling sped up, then turned into rapid padding. A huge shadow grew toward us, bigger as it came closer.

"LUCA!" I shouted. "MOVE FASTER!"

Luca pulled himself up the ledge and reached back for me, but before I could grasp his hand, the shadow reached me. Something huge grabbed my hair and jerked me back. I shrieked, pulled my knife from my boot, and plunged it into something solid and soft, and the hand released me. Luca grabbed my arm and tried to pull me up, but the thing grabbed my foot and yanked. Luca fell forward, and I fell hard on my face as whatever it was dragged me down the concrete floor into a small room, where it dropped me and slammed the door.

I sat up, breathing hard, my eyes streaming from my impact with the ground.

I heard a fire crackling and made out its darting red light. I blinked, my eyes adjusted to the light, and I tried to take in my surroundings. I was in a small room with a fireplace set into the opposite wall. There was a table and some chairs, two beds covered in furs, and some colorful tapestries hanging on the walls. My attacker was a massive creature, taller than a man. She bent over the fire, prodding the coals with a metal poker.

"Who are you?" She asked in a deep female voice.

"What are you?" I shouted back.

"Confused," she replied and sat heavily in an armchair beside the fire. "What are you doing in my house?"

I got a better look at the creature and realized it was a female Gravarian, but instead of the typical dead-fish blue, she was pearl white. Her veins, black like other Gravarians, stood out, beautiful and striking against her almost iridescent skin. She wore a floor-length magenta dress decorated with yellow, green, and blue wooden beads. The beads clattered softly when she moved. She had long, silver-gray hair that brushed her waist. I'd never heard of a Grav with hair before.

"I didn't know," I stammered, "...I'm sorry, we were running away from...."

Something thudded against the door.

"Don't break it!" The creature shouted. "It's open!"

Luca pushed the door open and stood in the doorway.

Everything in this place felt surreal, almost as though I'd been sucked into an old legend. The ghostly Gravarian. The way Luca stood, indecisive, halfway between the dark and firelight. The corner hugging me, cold as a prison wall.

The Grav waved her hand dismissively at Luca. "Relax. I'm in a hospitable mood."

Luca stayed where he was.

"What are you doing in my house?" The Grav asked.

"We're running away from...someone," Luca said, edging slowly into the room.

The Grav swept to a dresser in the corner and rubbed a salve on her wounded arm. "My name is Ila, the Seer of Eveness. If you come into my hovel to hide from enemies, you must let me tell your fortune!"

Luca and I exchanged uneasy glances.

"I'm religious," Luca said.

"I'm not really into that kind of thing," I added.

"Come, you can do it together." She beckoned us over to a small, round table covered in a grimy silk cloth. "Let me look at you in the light."

"I think we'll pass," I said.

"If you don't let me read your fortune, I'll hand you over to the men looking for you outside."

Literally and metaphorically backed into a corner, we sat down at the table.

She reached up one thick finger and brushed my cheek.

"I can tell so much from a person's eyes and their skin, and whether they meet your gaze or shy away—also, the clothes. Your embroidery is beautiful – it says much. And the violin your friend has in his pack - that says much of him."

"How did you know about that?" Luca asked.

"I heard about you the moment you arrived. It's a small town."

"And how are you welcome here?" I asked. "In the actual location of the Eveness Massacre?"

"Who's telling whose fortune?" She snapped. "Now be quiet. As I was saying, you are both artistic, but in different ways. You are perfectionists toward yourselves and also toward others. Often, toward each other, but you're more alike than you realize."

Luca and I glanced at each other and then, suddenly awkward, looked away.

"Your skin," Ila continued, "is white and black…"

"Black and white, actually," I interrupted.

"You were rejected by your parents and sent to work with a Klifrari teacher named...Brag."

"Birch, actually..."

"…ah, yes, Birch. And Birch lives far away, on a mountain called..."

She squinted like she was thinking hard. "Pine..."

"Ram's Head," I said. "You're not great at this."

"But you have no tota," she said.

"I haven't passed my trial yet, and shouldn't you know that?"

"I was going to say Ram's Head." She turned to Luca, startling him, "your eyes are dark. Your heart hides secrets."

Luca furrowed his brow and tilted his head like he was trying to recall his secrets, but nothing was springing to mind.

The fortune teller lit a candle and turned her fingers in the smoke, making it curl between us. "You two are bound together through the bond of long friendship," she pointed at me, "but you desire more than friendship."

"We met a month ago."

"And you," she spun on Luca again, and he started again, "your heart belongs to another."

"Another what?"

"Another woman..."

"I don't know any other women."

"Then your friends..."

"Abandoned me."

"Your family?"

"Haven't seen them in years."

"Yes, but your father," she persisted, "was a farmer…"

"Clergyman."

"That's what I said, a clergyman who wanted you to follow in his footsteps, but you dreamed of adventure, which is why you joined the Blockade Runners."

I smacked Luca's arm. "She got the Blockade Runner thing

right!" I exclaimed.

"Yes, because it's pretty obvious," he said, opening his jacket a little and indicating his plaid shirt, "and I was conscripted."

"Well," she said through her teeth, pointing a finger in Luca's face, "I do know how you will die. You will die an agonizing death, bleeding out in the snow."

"Yuck."

"How does he die?" I asked.

Ila turned to me, her eyes flashing. "I said he'd bleed out in the snow."

"But what makes me bleed out?" Luca asked. "Like, do I get stabbed, or do I cut myself on a sharp rock or what?"

She was getting visibly annoyed now. "You'll be eaten, slowly, by ravenous dogs. One of them will only have three legs. That one will eat your EYES."

"I think she's cursing you," I whispered.

Somewhere outside in the courtyard, a dog barked, and Luca jumped.

I cleared my throat. "What's going to happen to me?"

She shrugged and waved her hand. "You'll marry a balding man named Bob, have seven children, and get fat."

"Tell us more about Bob," Luca whispered. I slapped him with end of my scarf.

The fortune teller tossed her hands in the air.

"I'm sorry," I cried. "You're just not very good at this!"

"You really just met? You don't smell like you just met."

"We just met."

"Ugh." She reached up and pulled her entire head of hair off. I let out an involuntary exclamation of surprise and grabbed Luca's arm. Luca leaned so far back in his chair that it tipped over backward and dumped him on the floor.

Ila tossed the wig on the table and rubbed her hands over a shiny, bald head.

"I need to make a living somehow. I've got more than my own mouth to feed. Now, tell me, why are you in my house? You didn't come to hear your fortune."

"We were running from some men who..." I hesitated, "want something of mine."

"It's really mine," Luca said, setting his chair on its feet again and sitting back down.

"No, it's definitely mine."

"I found it."

"What is it?" Ila asked.

"Just something priceless and precious to me that Luca keeps stealing," I glared at Luca, "even though he knows it's mine."

"You don't read mus..." he stopped himself, "uhh...the language the book is written in, and I already have all of the... passages...memorized."

"You do not!"

"Yes, I do!"

Ila's eyes snapped. "What did you say about music?"

"I didn't say anything," Luca said quickly.

"A book of music?"

"No," I pulled away from her. "It's mine."

"Let me see it, or I'll go out and tell the men outside that you're in here."

Luca nudged me. "Just show her."

"No!"

In a flash, Ila grabbed my arm, yanked me across the table, and snatched the book from my jacket.

"Ouch! Hey!"

She opened it and glanced at the first page. Then, with a shout that made my heart hit my collarbone, she flung the book onto the table like it was a red-hot stone.

"Get that thing away from me!" She cried. "How dare you... How dare you bring the Klifrari Melodiac into my house! How dare you bring one into this place!"

"I'm sorry!" I scrambled out of my chair, "I didn't know!"

"GET OUT!" She screamed. "Get out of here!"

"But I don't understand..." I began.

"GET OUT! Do you have any idea what they'll do to me if

they find out you have that? What they'll do to all of us? Why would you bring that here, of all places? To Eveness? To its birthplace? Especially when he is here. GET OUT!"

"Who?" I asked.

"Let's go," Luca grabbed my arm and pushed me urgently toward the door. I grabbed at the Melodiac, but Luca yanked me away too quickly. Ila snatched the book up and went for the fire.

"She's going to burn it!" I shouted.

"Doesn't matter. Let's get."

Just as Luca shoved me into the passageway, Ila called out to us. I dug my heels in.

"Don't listen to her," Luca said.

"Please!" She wailed. "Wait!"

"We don't want her explanations. We want to not get our arms pulled off. Come on!"

"I'll give your Melodiac back!" Ila called after us.

I turned, but Luca stood in my way.

"This is important to me!"

"And my arms are important to me!"

"Then stay here," I hissed.

"Jae..."

"I want my book back."

Luca sighed heavily and led the way back through the doorway.

Ila sat at her table, her head in her hands, the book open in front of her.

"Will you play me one of the songs from the Melodiac?" She asked quietly.

"No," Luca said, turning and starting back out the door.

"If you do, I'll tell you why they want it! I'll tell you why Aresis burned your home."

She'd struck a cord. We both froze.

Luca still hesitated. "The Eveness massacre site is the one place on Earth I won't play music."

Ila folded her hands. "I only want to hear the stork song. Then I'll tell you."

Luca looked at me. "If she murders us, I blame you."

He sat and took his fiddle from his pack, set the bow to the strings, and began to play.

The stork song was light, fragile. It trembled in the air like a shard of thin glass on the edge of a shelf. The music felt like sparkling spiderwebs blowing around me, entwining me softly. Memories rolled past me like a train.

My mother's voice from somewhere above me, "She can't stay here. What will we do with her?"

Steam swallowing my father's receding figure as I leaned out the train car window, the sill digging into my ribs.

Birch setting me at the base of a tree on an unfamiliar mountain, pointing to the stars, and walking away.

The Klifrari with their backs to me as I drank a cold cup of yau in Becky's.

At the table, Ila sat rigid, her back straight, eyes shut, her hands folded in front of her. She swayed slightly with the music. Suddenly, she smiled, and tears streamed down her cheeks. She put her hand over her mouth and sobbed.

I looked nervously at Luca, but his eyes were closed too.

The music faded, unfinished, through an unresolved cord.

Ila opened her eyes. "Thank you."

Luca nodded. He looked a little shaken. What had the music made him remember?

"The queen of Gravarus wants that book for herself," Ila said. "She's told her sons that whoever finds it first will be heir to the throne."

"Heir to the Gravarian throne?" I asked.

Ila stood and crossed the room. "Aresis and Obsidian are brothers. Both disgraced and disinherited by their mother."

"Brothers?" I gasped.

She tilted her head. "You know Obsidian?"

"No," I lied quickly.

Her eyes lingered on me for a moment; then, she turned away. "Whichever brother gets the Melodiac first will win the right to inherit the throne again."

"What if neither of them gets it?" I asked.

"Then their mother will pick some incompetent cousin to rule. It is very much in humanity's best interest that you get that book back to Obsidian and run."

"Why is Obsidian better than Aresis?" Luca asked as he gently wrapped up his fiddle and put it back in his pack.

Ila rolled her eyes. "Are you alive?"

Luca and I looked at each other.

"That should be answer enough. Now get out of here."

"What's so important about an old music book?" I asked.

Ila sighed. "Do you know what happened here, at Eveness?"

"The first Gravarians heard humans play music, and it sent them into a rage, and they killed everyone."

"It wasn't just any music," Ila said. "It was a song from that book. From that Melodiac."

"Which song?" I asked.

"I don't know."

We fell to silence for a long time.

"What did that song do?" I asked. "The one Luca played for you?"

Ila smiled. "It made me remember someone from my life on Gravarus. Now take that thing and go. And don't let Aresis get his hands on it."

We left her room and went out into the dark fort. We both wanted to return to the train, but now that word was out that we had the Melodiac, we weren't sure what to do. We found a spot in the woods where a tree's roots formed a little hollow cave and crawled inside.

I couldn't see Luca in the darkness, but I felt his shoulder pressed against mine.

Outside, among the shadows, raccoons and possums scuttled across the snow. Something howled, and I flinched.

"Are you normally this skittish in the dark?" Luca's voice, disembodied, asked from above me.

"I'm not skittish in the dark. I'm very comfortable alone at night."

"Why all the jumping?"

"You said this place is haunted."

We sat in silence for a while. I leaned my head against the frozen dirt and thought about the fire at Becky's, crackling and warm.

"I just want to go home," I said.

Luca snorted.

"What?" I asked, sitting up.

"The Klifrari aren't even nice to you."

"Birch is," I said defensively. "He took me in when my own parents didn't want me."

"Is that why you flinch any time I move my arm? Because Birch is so nice to you?"

"All Klifrari teachers hit their students," I said irritably, "It's normal. And you know what, I'm getting sick of you criticizing the Klifrari like you've got some kind of moral high ground. Like Blockade Runners are any better."

"Blockade Runners are definitely better! We serve a very important purpose, and we don't charge an arm and a leg for it."

"How old were you when you were conscripted?"

"What difference does that..."

"How old?"

"How old were you when Birch first hit you? Or left you alone on a mountain somewhere?"

"Don't dodge the question. How old were you?"

Luca sighed. "Thirteen."

"So, a child."

"I mean, I guess..."

"So, Craddock sent you into life-threatening danger when you were still a child. Sounds morally fishy to me."

"Craddock wasn't my captain back then."

"How old was Henry?" I asked.

"Stop it," Luca snapped.

"How old?"

"Stop! Don't go using my friend – my dead friend – as leverage. I don't want to talk about it."

We fell silent.

"I'm just saying," I said at last, "that your childhood wasn't much better than mine. Maybe Birch did sometimes hit me, but he also fed me and gave me somewhere safe to sleep, and stood up for me when no one else would. And maybe your captain cared about you and your friends, but, in the end, he left you behind."

Luca didn't say anything, but a tremor of tension hung in the air. I wanted to break it but couldn't think what to say.

Finally, he said, "Did Becky's ever get their window?"

"Yes," I said quickly, thankful for a subject change. "It's huge and clear as ice."

"Do you have the Melodiac with you?"

"I don't think playing music here would be a good idea."

"I could teach you how to read the notes."

"Really?" I perked up. "I have a tiny bit of paraffin. Maybe we could use that? If we scrunch into a corner, no one will see it."

I took the Melodiac from my coat, he lit the paraffin, and we huddled together against the roots.

He explained it all slowly and patiently. What sound belonged to each note, how the solid ones were one beat, the hollow ones two. He hummed the melodies. I flipped through and made him hum each one.

I swear the ghosts stopped to listen and watch us, a Klifrari and a Blockade Runner, bending over the crumbling book, finding comfort in each other's company in a bubble of yellow light.

The sun rose pale pink over the snowy countryside and found Luca and me still awake.

"So," I was saying in a sleepy, philosophical voice, "if the Gravarians are more highly evolved, wouldn't that mean that outlawing music is a good thing? The Gravarians don't use it, and they're advanced."

"I think that if they were advanced, they would write music," Luca said, "and poetry and stories. If anything, they've devolved."

"But isn't emotion kind of like weakness?"

"Of course not!" Luca cried. "Emotion is what makes us human. And besides, I don't think we evolved. If we did, then why do we make things like art, and music, and poetry? No other animals have those things."

"Birds sing," I argued.

"Not the way people do. And not for the same reasons."

"Then why do we have art and music and poetry? Why do we need them? Is it just so we can feel things?"

"No, it's because the Creator is an artist, and a musician, and a poet, and we reflect him. We do all those things to mimic him. Like children copying a parent."

"So now that music is illegal, and nobody wants to make art or write poetry, what? Are we losing our humanity?"

"I think the further people drift from reflecting the Creator, the more miserable they are. I think that they become cruel and selfish and cold, and yes, in a way, I think they do lose their humanity."

"Is that why you play music, even though it's illegal?"

"And it's why I play the fiddle and why I sketch and whittle and sing. If I didn't, I'd lose my mind. If we're not careful, we'll all end up like Sid one day. And if we end up like Sid, there's nothing to keep us from becoming like Aresis."

I humphed. "That's too extreme. The Klifrari have been without art and music for centuries, and we haven't turned homicidal yet."

"Is refusing a man blood for his wife after she's had a baby very far from homicidal? Or making him give you all his firewood to pay for it and not caring that his baby will freeze? Isn't that a kind of murder?"

"We have to eat!"

"Do you have to have a fancy glass window in Becky's?"

I couldn't answer him, but I resented that he was winning.

"Art doesn't feed you. Music doesn't keep you warm at night. They're a waste of time."

He touched the embroidery on my coat sleeve. “Why did you do this?”

“Because I was bored.”

“Exactly. You were bored, and you turned to creativity. Why?”

“I...well, because...there was nothing else to do.”

“Nothing? Couldn’t you have sorted something or cataloged something, or cleaned something? There was no work, anywhere, for you to do?”

I groaned. “Fine, I could have come up with something, but I was tired, and so...”

“And so you turned to creativity – art – as a kind of rest —something fun to do. You didn’t ask why; you just did it on instinct. Does that sound worthless to you?”

“Kind of,” I said.

He smiled. “Even if we are just meaningless dust blown here by chance, I don’t want to believe it. There’s no poetry in it. I’d rather believe I was made by hand by a loving Creator who knows me by name and put me here for a reason. Even if it’s not true, I’d rather believe that.”

We’d been at it all night. Launching ideas at each other like paper airplanes and seeing who could stay in the air the longest. My mind felt like a plant growing toward the light. The Klifrari never talked about such things. They debated the weather and predicted migration patterns and bragged endlessly about their youth.

Suddenly, Luca reached down and snuffed the paraffin.

“What is it?” I asked.

“I heard a noise.”

We sat with our ears straining.

“Maybe it's Sid,” Luca whispered.

“Obsidian?”

“Easier to say.”

“Don’t call him that.”

“Cap’n Sid.”

“Stop it.”

"Sid the Kid."

"Don't."

A faint rustle made my stomach tie in knots. Then footsteps shuffled just outside. Someone stood between us and the light of the faintly graying sky.

I pulled my knife from my boot. Luca already had his in his hands.

"They're here," the man shouted. "Just like she said."

Luca got to one knee, about to charge, but to our astonishment, the man reached into his belt and pulled out a shiny metal object. It glinted. I grabbed the back of Luca's jacket.

"Is that a gun?"

Neither of us had seen a gun before, but I just knew. I expected it to be large – as long as my arm, but this was a little thing, hardly bigger than my hand.

"Come with me," Gun Man said.

Luca hesitated, so Gun Man pulled a lever back on the gun. It clicked loudly. He held it overhead and...

Crack

I'd never heard anything so loud. I lost my breath. My ears rang.

Beside me, Luca dropped his knives.

A second man appeared a moment later. They tied our hands and put bags over our heads.

THE PERSONAL LOG OF OBSIDIAN, ONCE CROWN PRINCE OF GRAVARUS

After more hours than I care to mention stomping about in the snow until I could no longer feel my shins, I found a set of footprints and followed it to a train waiting about three miles down the tracks from my own train. I stood in the shelter of the trees and watched for a moment; then, I glimpsed a flash of Luca's garish plaid shirt through one of the carriage windows. I felt very pleased with myself.

I climbed aboard the train and flung the carriage door open. But instead of Luca and Jael running to me, confessing their own stupidity and praising my cleverness, I found about thirty human boys, all wearing clothes identical to Luca's and all armed to the teeth.

For half a second, we stared at each other much the way a nest of toothed verviles stares at you before they attack and chew your ears off.

Then the boys rushed me, and I fled for my life amidst a mad flurry of knives, hatchets, and other unnecessarily sharp objects.

Humans are so violent.

I ran madly through the woods until I reached the river and had no choice but to dive into the freezing water or climb a tree.

I opted for the river.

This was the wrong decision.

The current bowled me over, pulled me under, and turned me around in summersaults until I nearly drowned. Just when I thought it was over for me, I struck a log in the water and managed to crawl up onto it and then, very awkwardly, scootch along the log to the bank where I dropped, sprawling and humiliated, onto the snow.

I pray no one saw me. It was not the most graceful moment of my life.

But I am alive and hating humans with renewed ardor. I must press on and find them, though, because I need them.

Miserable prospect.

JAEL'S NARRATIVE

"Sixty-six, sixty-seven, sixty-eight," Luca mumbled under his breath as we climbed.

I didn't see the point in counting the stairs. They were taking us somewhere very high up. Probably to push us off. Why keep track of how far up?

"Eighty-one, eighty-two, eighty-three..."

A hinge creaked. We climbed a short ladder and emerged in an open room. I could tell from the way our footsteps echoed.

Someone yanked the bag off my head, and I blinked in dim, dusty light. We stood in a dark, square, stone room with one narrow window to the north, one to the south, and a small square hole cut in the floor, covered by a grate. I heard water running far below us. Two men and a woman sat on boxes. More boxes were stacked and arranged around the room.

"Oh," Luca said brightly, "I know where we are! We're in the Shadbone River shot tower!"

He leaned toward me and whispered, "If it's eighty-three steps up, how high is that? More than fifty feet?"

"What difference does it make?"

"How deep would you say Shadbone is?"

"Who cares?"

Luca looked around the room. "I wonder if they're using this place to make ammunition again."

"We are," said a voice from the staircase. A man emerged from a trap door across the room. He was short, with a balding head and a violently red cable-knit sweater. He crossed his arms and looked at us.

"Now, what are a Klifrari and a Blockade Runner doing together all the way out here?"

Luca and I exchanged looks, then launched into

explanations simultaneously.

"I'm going home..." I said.

"We're running from the Gravarian raiders..."

"... traveling on foot..."

"...just taking a steam train..."

"...planning to go over the mountain to get home..."

"...just following the river..."

"We're nobody," we finished together.

Red Sweater narrowed his eyes. "And what about the Melodiac?"

"What Melodiac?" We asked in synch.

"The one you were heard playing from in Eveness yesterday."

"The Grav took it," I said.

"We dropped it," Luca said at the same time.

We looked at each other, mutually irritated.

Stop talking, I mouthed.

You stop talking, he mouthed back.

"Shut up!" I hissed.

Sweater laughed. "Take their weapons. If they have any."

Gun Man patted us down and took my knife. He pulled four or five from Luca's belt, boots, sleeves, and rucksack. He took his fiddle, and Luca went a little white.

"Don't touch that. It's a custom piece."

Gun Man turned it over and squinted at the carved wolverine. "What is it?"

He held it by the neck and brandished it like a club.

Luca shouted. "It's not a weapon!"

"It's an instrument," Red Sweater said. "Isn't it?"

"No," Luca lied.

He held the fiddle out to him. "Play it for us."

"You'll need to untie me."

Red Sweater nodded to Gun Man, who took a knife and cut the ropes around Luca's hands. Luca turned and faced me for half a second, his back to the others, and snatched the Melodiac from my jacket and slipped it into his. He did it so deftly that I didn't realize what happened for a moment.

"Hurry up!" Red Sweater shouted.

Luca held out his hands, and Gun Man handed him the fiddle. He took it like a mother takes her newborn baby.

"Play!" Red Sweater shouted.

"The ropes cut off circulation in my hands," Luca said, sitting on the sill of the open north-facing window.

"PLAY!"

Luca shrugged. He set the bow to the strings, leaned back, and back, and back, and tipped backward out the window. One second he was there; the next, there was just his fiddle on an empty window sill.

For a moment, everyone stood, open-mouthed, rooted to the floor. Then we all ran to the window and looked down at the river rushing below us.

"Do you think he made it?"

"Could a person survive that?"

"Is the water deep enough?"

I had no thoughts, just white-hot panic. Now I was alone, and I didn't have the Melodiac. Was that good or bad?

"Sit her down on a box."

I was pushed down on one of the wooden boxes, and Red Sweater stood in front of me, his arms crossed. He was a tiny little man, short enough to look me in the eyes when I was sitting. He was rotund, balding, but somehow, despite his size, his unremarkable looks, his small eyes, short, round fingers, and hairy hands, he frightened me. He leaned forward, so close I could smell his breath.

"Where is the Melodiac?"

Suddenly I wondered if Luca had actually taken the book or if I'd just imagined it. I thought I felt it in my jacket still, pressing against my stomach like hot iron.

"I don't know what you're talking about."

"Search her."

Gun Man searched me for the Melodiac but returned empty-handed. I couldn't decide if I was relieved or upset.

Red Sweater straightened, but he was so short it didn't make much difference. "Do you know who I am?" he asked.

I shook my head.

"I'm Jasper Judd."

The name meant nothing to me and my face must have showed it.

Jasper Judd looked deeply offended. "I'm the leader of Underground Earth."

"I don't...I don't know what that is..."

"We are an organization that seeks to rid Earth of all Gravarians and restore order to the continent."

"But how..."

"Earth is not a Gravarian prison planet..."

I decided to stall him. "But, it is...literally."

"If we let them stay, then before we know it, the Gravarian queen will come for our resources and wipe out every living creature."

"What resources?"

"Solar power."

"I think that's a conspiracy theory."

"It is not a conspiracy theory."

I looked at the two men and one woman waiting quietly behind Judd. They were wearing identical clothes. They stood in the same posture, their facial expressions mirrored.

"Are these all your followers?"

"There are more!" Judd said in a voice that made me suspect there were not, in fact, more.

"I think you're a cult."

"Bold words from a Klifrari," the woman mumbled.

"I think you're about to get thrown out a window," Judd said.

I swallowed.

"The Gravarians will come after us with their hive mind and destroy us all," Judd ranted, "you mark my words! And anyone who doesn't believe that is old fashioned and stupid!"

"Your sweater is old-fashioned and stupid."

Judd gasped. The two men gasped. The woman gasped.

"Throw her into the river," Judd ordered.

The two men grabbed me under each arm and bore me toward the window. I kicked and twisted, but their hands dug into my arms.

"I can tell you where the Melodiac is!" I shrieked. "I'm sorry I insulted your sweater!"

They hoisted me onto the window sill.

"It's a beautiful sweater! I love it! I know where the Melodiac is! Please!"

They were braced to toss me out when we heard footsteps coming up the stairs.

That was fast, I thought, assuming, of course, that it was Luca.

It wasn't.

Up the stairs came a red-headed man with a beard.

Captain Craddock.

He went straight for Judd, grabbed him by his neck, and pressed him against the wall.

"Where is it, Judd? I know you have it!"

"The boy had it," Judd spluttered, "but he got away!"

"What boy?"

Craddock's eyes brushed over me, then darted back.

"Where's Paxton?" He asked me.

I pointed out the window.

Craddock almost smiled for a second, then he grabbed the front of my shirt and dragged me off the windowsill, and threw me onto the floor.

"You stole it!" He screamed in my face. I could only see his eyes, less than an inch from mine, sick with fury. "Do you know what you've done?" he grabbed my shoulders and pounded me against the floor. I couldn't catch my breath. Any second, I felt he would snap my neck. "Do you realize what you've done?"

I struck at him and kicked. He had his hands around my throat. Judd tried with all his little might to pull Craddock away from me.

"The Melodiac is mine!" Judd said through his teeth. "You can't have it!"

Craddock stood up and whirled on him. He looked like a bobcat with its foot in a trap. "Do you know what he'll do to us all if I don't give it to him? If I don't have it when he finds me?"

"Well, none of us can get it if the Blockade Runner has it and he's in the river."

"You're sure she doesn't have it?"

"Of course!" Judd spat. "What kind of idiot do you think I am?"

"Search her again."

The woman who worked for Judd approached me, but at that moment, we heard a commotion below. Craddock crossed to the window opposite the river and looked down but leaped back as though something had bitten him.

He cursed and rushed down the stairs. We heard him stomping, story after story, for a few minutes, and then the shot tower door slammed.

A moment passed. Judd and the others exchanged nervous glances.

Footsteps ascended the staircase again.

Finally, rescue! I thought.

The trap door opened, and up came a blue head, followed by another, and another, until four Gravarians stood in the room. They stopped and waited for the fifth – a huge grav with thick arms and a jutting brow.

"Where is Craddock?" The big Grav asked Judd. "We know he was here..."

His eyes rested on me. They were cold as ice, opaque, extraordinarily dark.

"A Klifrari?" he said.

Judd shrugged. "She's nobody."

The big Grav ignored him and crossed the room to me. "You wouldn't happen to be the Klifrari who ran off from the village with Aresis' Melodiac, would you?"

I was too frightened to speak.

“Where is the boy?” The big Grav asked.

Beads of sweat rolled off Judd's snubbed nose. “What boy?”

“I was told there was a boy with her. A boy with an instrument.” He looked at me. “A Melodiac without a musician isn't much good, is it?”

He turned to Judd. “The girl isn't any use to us. You may get rid of her.”

THE PERSONAL LOG OF OBSIDIAN, ONCE CROWN PRINCE OF GRAVARUS

This already lovely day spiraled out of control faster than even I could have anticipated, but it was educational. I learned three important things:

1. Humans can fall from great heights without dying.

2. A human falling from a great height makes a very funny noise, not unlike a train whistle.

3. When wet, humans turn blue, tremble, and look very small.

After a night of fruitless searching, I took a nap to renew my strength, built a fire to dry my clothes, and then resumed my search. I clearly don't have a clue how to find a lost human, and after hours with no success, I tried clapping my hands and whistling. (And no, I couldn't just walk into town and ask around. It's not as though humans are known for open-mindedness and hospitality. Especially here, in Eveness).

I skirted around town until I found human footprints in the snow and finally recognized the smell of my humans – a very distinctive mix of affection (which smells a little like strawberries) and irritation (which smells like rubber), heavy on the irritation. A dash of prejudice (an unpleasant odor reminiscent of stale rosewater). A whiff of arrogance (garlic). Strawberry-rubber-stale rosewater-garlic is hard to forget and easy to find, even when it mingles with the mass odor of boredom and frustration wafting on the breeze from the village.

I followed the scent to an abandoned concrete structure on the edge of the forest near the river.

And then a new scent hit me. Nearly knocked me clean off my feet. And suddenly, I remembered things I'd tried so hard to forget.

I remembered velvet nights and dove feather mornings and feelings that I shouldn't have felt. Skin white as the milky way galaxy. Eyes the color of aged copper.

Grief like cardamom and molasses. I remembered grief. And anger. I remembered the anger even better. It stung my eyes.

The grief and the anger flooded me, and that was what finally got my feet moving. I had felt too many things in those days, and I wasn't ready to feel them again. No, not me. I'm not a weak human, giving into every emotion that squirts in my brain. Love is just a chemical, and so is anger, and so is grief, and so is joy. All of them equally useless.

So I ran and I ran until I remembered that I was supposed to be looking for the humans.

I found their scent again and followed it to a stone tower built on the bank of the river. The river flowed under several feet of blue-gray ice, but just under the tower, a trickle of water from a nearby hot spring mingled with the current, melting the ice to just a thin skin on the surface.

As I approached the tower, I heard a shrill sound and saw someone fall from the very top of the building and splash into the water.

I instantly knew that was my human because that's just my luck. I couldn't pick up a sensible adult human who sits calmly in its compartment and smells decent. No, I pick up the lunatic humans that do things like leaping from unimaginable heights into freezing water.

I didn't slide on my belly across the frozen surface to rescue the human as it clung to the sharp, slippery edge of the ice because of any affection I may harbor for it. I did it because I need him to help me get my throne back. I certainly wasn't frightened or worried as I pulled it out of the water and dragged it back to the shore. And I gave it the shirt off my back because I need it to survive long enough to thwart my brother Aresis, not because the strange blue color around its mouth and the way its teeth chattered together frightened me. It didn't bother me at all. It's just that I can't have Aresis getting his hands on a musician and making it do whatever musicians can do.

And I agreed to go back and help rescue the female one because I worried the male one would get lonely, and loneliness smells like mold. That's all. I detest mold. My physician once warned me that inhaling too much loneliness can give one a lung infection.

Luca insisted we go back for the female right away, but I heard somewhere that if humans get cold enough, they die. There are so many silly ways humans die; it's overwhelming trying to keep track of them all.

Too cold.

Too hot.

Too little food.

Too much of the wrong kind of food.

Too many microscopic bugs in their system.

Too few of the right kind of microscopic bugs in their system.

They leak red fluid long enough, and they're dead; they don't drink enough water, and they're dead; they bump their head in the wrong place, and INSTANT DEATH.

AND YET this one can leap from the top of a tower of dizzying height and go plunging into icy water, and he's fine.

I wish I'd gotten a lower-maintenance pet.

I told him we needed to go back to the train and get him a change of clothes. He told me he didn't have a change of clothes and the best thing for him to do was keep moving. I decided to let him make that decision for himself.

Someone came to the tower and then left again, but we didn't see who it was.

Then, as we prepared to leave the cover of the forest, a group of Gravarians appeared a few yards to our left. We hid until they were gone.

"That's Aresis," Luca said (I know you're not supposed to name humans because then you get attached to them, but it's such a short, easy name).

He was wrong; it wasn't Aresis, but my buffoon cousin Gregorikus, who was banished with my brother for colluding in the failed assassination against my mother. It would be in Gregorikus' best interest to have Aresis on the throne, so I assume they are working together.

I despise Gregorikus. When we were children, he always tried to steal my gumtops, and he and Aresis plotted my assassination at least three times. Never succeeded as they are, apparently, atrocious at properly carrying out assassinations. Gregorikus has a big blue head with nothing but rusty metal clanking about it in.

Luca said he didn't have any weapons. I told him he could use his teeth since we both remember how adept he is with them. He asked if he could borrow one of my weapons, and I told him no. It would be too heavy for him anyway.

Besides, all I've got is a cleaver and one knife.

He asked for the knife.

I gave it to him, but it's as long as his forearm and weighs so much he can barely lift it.

We climbed the stairs to the tower, which took far too long since Luca insisted onto lugging my knife behind him and waited outside the door.

I counted to three, and we burst in.

Gregorikus had his foot on Jael's throat and was holding a very small human off the ground by its bright red sweater. The little human was kicking and spitting and Jael was squeezing Gregorikus' ankle and turning blue.

There were four other Gravarians in the room and three other humans.

When Gregorikus saw me, his big dull eyes brightened, and he dropped the little human and ran at me. I was only too eager for the opportunity to get my hands around my cousin's throat, but Luca, the idiot, jumped between us and tried to swing the knife I gave him. It was too heavy, so it swung him around, and he fell to the floor. But, by some comedic luck, Gregorikus tripped over him.

I stood for a moment in disbelief as the two of them kicked at each other and tried to get to their feet. Gregorikus pulled his cleaver from his back and flailed it awkwardly around. Luca would probably have lost his head if I hadn't stepped in, grabbed the back of his shirt, and flung him across the floor behind me.

I leaped at Gregorikus with glee, got my arm around his neck, and began to choke him, fulfilling years of childhood fantasies. He swung his huge, stupid head back and struck me in the face, stunning me. I fell, and he pounced on me. He pinned me beneath him, twisted the cleaver from my hands, took his knife, and laid it on my throat. I raged, and the smell of my anger filled the room. Gregorikus laughed, and his knife cut into my skin, but something struck him suddenly from behind. With a shout of fury, he twisted around and came face to face with Jael, who was holding a rather large gun. She had it backward and was swinging it about like a club.

For the first time since we entered the room, I remembered that I wasn't alone with Gregorikus. The other humans were gone, apparently fleeing in the kerfuffle, but Luca was being dragged back toward the window by one of Gregorikus' compatriots. Luca still clutched my huge knife in both his hands, and with a rush of strength, he swept it over his head at the Gravarian's arm and lopped it off at the elbow. The Gravarian shrieked and stumbled away, bleeding black blood on the wooden floor.

Luca grabbed a human knife from on top one of the boxes, flipped it in his hands with a smirk on his face, and darted at another one of Gregorikus' minions. The poor Gravarian couldn't react. Luca was a blur. Nightmarishly fast. It was over before the unfortunate fellow had time to scream.

Meanwhile, Gregorikus moved toward Jael, swinging broadly with his big cleaver. She stepped backward into a pile of boxes and fell, but she'd bought me the opportunity to get to my feet and grab my knife Luca dropped. Sadly, before I could decapitate Gregorikus as I wanted, he turned back and blocked me with his cleaver.

The third Gravarian ran to attack Jael, but she kept swinging the gun with such frantic madness he couldn't get close. The other Gravarian decided to take on Luca.

He made one good swing with his cleaver, which Luca dodged. With lightning speed, Luca grabbed the Gravarian by the wrist and pulled him forward, then cut his forearm, then his quad, bringing him to one knee, then sliced his throat.

Gregorikus and I, locked in a wrestling match on the ground, both stopped and stared in horror and astonishment. This little human, with his innocent-looking eyes and his boyish body, killed that Gravarian in less than a second.

I recovered myself first and struck Gregorikus' head with mine, dazing him a little. I got hold of my knife. He grabbed my cleaver from the ground, raised it, and probably would have cut my arm off at the shoulder, but...

Bang!

It was the loudest sound I'd ever heard. It split my ears and made my heart quake.

Jael stood shaking over her dead attacker, a smoking gun in her hands. Gregorikus and I were too startled to do anything for a moment, then she lifted the gun again and flailed it around. We all covered our heads and dropped to the ground. Gregorikus and his remaining compatriot got up and tried to run at her, but she fired again. This time, the projectile from the gun splintered a piece of wall inches from Luca's ear, and he dove for cover.

Gregorikus and his companion ducked down and tried to rush her a third time, but Jael fired at them again. This time, she hit Gregorikus' companion in the chest, and he dropped like a dead fish. Encouraged by her success, she strode toward Gregorikus, screaming like she'd gone insane and firing indiscriminately, hitting every bit of the room for ten feet around him. Luca and I were forced to take refuge behind boxes in terror for our lives. Gregorikus, who had fought trained soldiers his whole life, couldn't stand in the face of the sheer madness of Jael and her random aiming.

He was forced to retreat down the stairs. Jael kept shooting down the stairs at him until she ran out of ammunition, then she just stood there, clicking the empty gun at the empty staircase.

Luca crawled out from his hiding place, white-faced and panting, and approached Jael cautiously.

"Jae," he said as he came up behind her.

She spun on him, gun up, panting, her eyes wild, her hair flying, her whole body trembling.

"He's gone," Luca said, pulling the gun gently away from her. "All the bad guys are gone. It's Ok."

She looked around the room blankly, like she'd just awoken from some terrible nightmare, and then sank to the floor.

Luca sat down next to her.

"Deep breaths. That's it. Just take deep breaths."

"I'm sorry," she gasped.

"You're Ok. Just breathe deeply."

"Did I..." she looked around at the two dead Gravarians on the ground, "Oh, bearhie, did I..."

"You did good, Jae. You did good."

She took a few more heavy breaths, then got up, dusted herself off, and raised her chin. "Well, they deserved it."

JAEL'S NARRATIVE

The train sliced across the open tundra like a knife through cream. A white moon rose behind the distant mountains and looked like a halo over distant Ram's Head. I lay on my bunk, exhausted in every nerve. I wanted to sleep, but I felt wired. My muscles hurt, and a purple bruise the size of my hand bloomed over my shoulder. In the moment, I hadn't noticed how hard the gun kicked when I fired it. I noticed now. I also had a goose egg growing rapidly on my forehead. I couldn't remember how I got that.

Every now and then, I'd sit up and look at the gun lying on the couch on the other side of the room. I didn't have any ammunition for it, so it was just a glorified club now, but it made me feel powerful, equal. Gravarians who could snap me in half with one hand scattered before it. I just needed to learn how to hit what I was aiming at the first time.

Next door, Luca played a shrill, sawing song from the Melodiac.

I banged my fist against the wall. "Play something else! You're gonna give me an aneurism!"

Luca resolved the cord and then began another song. It was repetitive - three notes played loudly, then the same three played quietly over and over again until I thought I'd lose my mind. I hopped off my bunk, stomped out to Luca's door, and pulled it open without ceremony.

"Can't you play something else?" I asked.

"This is something else."

"Play something less annoying."

He rolled his eyes, flipped the page to a song decorated with an owl, and began to play. It was nervous and high, but I didn't feel like telling him to stop again, so I went down a car to get something to eat.

My head hurt, so with a syrupy consciousness, I sorted through a box of human food. In Eveness, I had bought a lot of ingredients but no prepared food except dry venison with the consistency of shoe leather. With no alternative available, I settled on a piece of the venison and shuffled back toward my compartment. As I passed Sid's compartment, Luca played a new song. A high, romantic air that reminded me of snowflakes on a breeze.

Sid's door was open, and he was sitting on his bedroll, looking off into the middle distance.

"You ok?" I asked.

"She was so beautiful, you know," he said in a yearning voice.

"Who?" I asked.

"I love her with all my heart and soul. I love her with everything I have. I never should have let her go. She was my sunset and my sunrise and the air I breathed and..."

Luca's music stopped, but I didn't notice. Sid shook himself, coughed, and looked at me.

"Do you need something?"

"You were telling me about someone."

"No, I wasn't."

"Yes, you were. Someone you loved."

Luca began to play the annoying sawing song again.

"I wasn't talking about anyone! Get out!" Sid sprang to his feet and lunged at me. "Get out! GO!"

He snatched a yau mug from the floor and hurled it at me. It struck the door and shattered the glass window. I ducked and ran down the corridor back to our train.

I bumped into Luca in the doorway.

"I wouldn't go down there," I panted. "Sid just flipped out and threw a mug at me."

"What did you do?"

"Nothing!" I cried. "He was sitting there, talking about some lost love of his, and then he just flipped out."

Luca passed me, walked to Sid's compartment, and put his head in.

"You ok?" I heard him ask.

Sid said something I couldn't hear, and Luca stepped out, looked at me, and looked incredulous. He ducked into the rations compartment, and I followed him.

"He seems fine to me," Luca said as he picked up the kettle from the stove and poured a cup of yau.

I crossed my arms. "A minute ago, I swear he threw something at me."

Luca touched the goose egg on my head with his finger. "I think you're concussed."

I slapped his hand away. "I'm not concussed!"

He shrugged and walked out into the corridor. I stayed a moment to think before I followed him.

"What were you playing?" I asked him as I entered his compartment behind him.

He held up the Melodiac. "The Goose Song."

An idea gripped me.

"Play something else."

"Like what?"

"I don't care, just anything."

He opened the Melodiac and played a cheerful, tumbling melody. I ran down to Sid's again and looked in the door. Sid saw me and burst into violent laughter. I'd never seen a Gravarian laugh. He had lots of teeth. It was unnerving.

He held his sides and rolled around the floor.

"Are you ok?" I asked.

"You're face is so..." he gasped between spasms of laughter, "so funny!"

"Ok..."

"And you're so...puny and weak!"

"I mean, I wouldn't say that I'm puny and..."

"And you're brain is so very small and ineffective!"

He curled up, laughing so hard I thought he might suffocate.

I ran back to Luca's compartment. "What song is this?"

"Bear cub."

I grabbed his arm and dragged him with me back to Sid's compartment. Sid was sitting calmly again, eating dried fish and looking out the window.

"Play another song," I whispered.

Luca looked concerned, like he thought I was cracking up, but he played the sawing, angry song again. Obsidian turned around slowly, his eyes locked on us, and his face darkened. Then he let out a shattering yell and ran at me, arms extended like he meant to get his hands around my throat.

"STOP, STOP!" I screamed.

Luca stopped playing and pulled me out of the doorway. Obsidian was running so fast that he careened through the door and into the opposite wall. Luca and I turned on our heels and ran and didn't stop until we were locked in my compartment.

When we'd caught our breath, we looked at each other. A smile spread slowly over Luca's face, and I knew we were thinking the same thing.

"The music makes him do things," I whispered.

Luca's eyes lit up like a mad scientist's.

"Try something else," I said.

"Which one? I don't want him trying to kill us again."

I took the Melodiac and found a song with a beaver penciled above it. "This looks safe."

Luca played it. It was soft, lilting, and made me think of a warm fire and a bright hearth.

I opened the door, intending to go see what Sid was doing now, but he was outside the door.

"Oh!" I cried and slammed the door in his face. Before I could lock it, he slid it open, wrapped me in a huge embrace, and patted my head.

"You're like a daughter to me," he whispered.

I looked over Sid's big blue biceps at Luca, who was still playing, his eyes the size of dinner plates.

"Beaver!" I whispered, excited. "Home!"

"What?"

"Stop playing."

Luca stopped.

Sid froze, looked down, and pushed me away with a shout.

"Get off me, vile human!"

"You came to me," I said.

He retched. "You could give me an infection! You're filthy! Look at you!"

He gagged and fled, wiping his hands on his shirt and mumbling indignantly to himself about grime and germs and rabies.

"This is a Klifrari Melodiac," I said to Luca after Sid was gone. "Klifrari use animals as symbols. Beaver means home!"

"And goose?"

I chuckled. "Love."

"Bear cubs?"

"Humor."

"This means that we can control Gravarians with this music!" Luca cried. "That's why everyone wants this book!" In his excitement, he grabbed my hands.

We grinned at each other like naughty schoolchildren dreaming up a wicked prank.

And our week of mischief began. Every chance we got, we tiptoed to Sid's compartment, played a song, and then penciled his reaction on the bottom of the coinciding Melodiac page.

Hare – Grav runs from us, screaming and hiding. Conclusion: Fear.

Mountain Goat - Grav suddenly became very adventurous. Climbed to the train's roof and tried to dive into a river. Also began eating all our human food. Conclusion: Courage and Adventure. Don't ever play again.

Lynx – snuck up on us from behind and bit Luca. Conclusion: Cunning. Don't play this one again either. Grav can be very sneaky. Sharp teeth. Terrifying.

Wolverine – Grav tried to kill us. Conclusion: Anger.

Stork – Just stood there and cried. Conclusion: Memory. Apparently, Sid had a pretty bleak childhood.

It was more fun than it should have been - sliding around the train in our socks, sneaking up on Sid, then scurrying away, giggling, to our compartments. I forgot about the journey, about going home, about Birch and Becky's and the tota in my pocket. I'd never had a friend before, and I'd never really had fun – careless, thoughtless, childish fun – in my life. I didn't know it then, but I lived an entire childhood of lost joy in that short week.

On the sixth day, I woke up perhaps for the first time in my life – slid open my door and nearly walked into Luca, who stood bleary-eyed and flushed in the corridor. Curls of sawdust clung to his flannel shirt.

"I was up all night," he said in a hoarse, gleeful voice, "and I just finished it."

I rubbed my eyes. "Finished what?"

He held out a little wooden flute.

"Does it work?" I asked, taking it from him and turning it over in my hands. It was cold and smooth like bone.

"It's not very pretty, but I thought you might like to embellish it yourself. I could teach you."

I was touched and embarrassed and pleased, but I couldn't think of anything to say, so stupidly I said, "I don't know how to play."

"I'll teach you."

I felt suddenly nervous. "I...I don't know. We're not supposed to..."

"And then," he continued, ignoring me, "we can play two songs at the same time and see what happens."

His eyes shone with such enthusiasm I couldn't turn him down.

"How long did this take?" I asked.

"Just last night."

I shook my head, smiling. He was some kind of genius, and

he had no idea.

"Let me get my coat. We'll go up top, and you can teach me where Sid won't hear us."

I bundled in all my warmest Klifrari gear: a coat lined with rabbit fur, a hare-skin hat, and gloves I'd knitted myself. Luca was waiting for me on the roof, wearing a poncho he'd made by cutting a hole in a threadbare blanket. He'd lost his coat when we escaped Powderkeg and he'd been shivering stoically ever since.

The world swept past us in a gray and white watercolor under a smear of pale blue sky. The flat tundra that stretched between the train and the mountains rushed beneath us like a swift river of snow, but the mountains, distant and yet so close I thought if I ran for an hour, I could reach them, stood still. Eternal. I'd lived on those distant gray peaks my whole life, so I'd never seen them from the valley. They brushed the sky and spanned horizon to horizon like they encompassed the whole world. I'd never realized they were so beautiful.

"Just piles of granite and ice," Birch would say.

But they weren't.

Seeing them like this, from a distance, how they pierced the clouds – it made something in my chest billow up like a flag caught in the wind. A joy I couldn't describe. A swell of pride and happiness. It was a feeling I wanted to share but couldn't put into words.

Luca looked over and grinned at me. His cheeks were pink and his eyes shone. Speed did something to him. So did music. So did mountains and tundra and cold, biting wind. I smiled stupidly back at him, and I longed to tell him how I felt. But I saw that he knew.

For the first time in my life, someone looked at me, and they understood.

Sitting on top of that train with him was a little like flying, a little like falling.

Luca held out the flute. "Let's get to it."

At first, when I blew into the flute, it squawked like an angry wood stork. Luca showed me where to put my fingers but had to explain again a minute later when I did it wrong. After an hour, I could blow a long, high *"squeeeeeeeeeee"* in a few different tones.

By the time the sun began to dip low behind the horizon, I could play a simple song.

"It'll be dark soon," I said, "so we should go down."

Luca leaned back on his arms and gazed at the landscape. Above the mountains, the sky glowed orange.

"What color is that?" I asked, pointing.

Luca looked at me with surprise. "Orange."

I felt ashamed and dropped my eyes. "Klifrari don't talk about color. It's just white snow, gray snow, and blue sky or gray sky. I've never really...noticed that color before."

It was like fire. Like new blood. Like life. Suddenly I had the word that described the way the mountains and the music and the speed of the train made me feel. These feelings were orange.

My eyes rested on Luca and, somehow, I felt like he was the color orange. Fire and new blood and life. Burning sunrises and sunsets.

"It's not common in nature," he said.

"Have you ever seen it anywhere else?" I demanded.

He thought a moment. "Foxes?"

"They're white."

"Not down in the valleys and warmer places. They're orange down there."

"Really?"

He laughed. "You've never seen an orange sunset before?"

"I have, but I've only ever used it to predict the weather the next day. I've never, you know, looked at it."

"Once," he said, "when I was living in the Ice City..."

"You lived in the Ice City?"

"I saw a flower growing through the pavement, and it was orange. It had five flat, heart-shaped petals and a tiny green stem, and it was that same color."

"I've never seen a flower in the wild. Only what Ama keeps in her greenhouse."

"I've only seen the one."

"When did you live in the Ice City?"

"I was born there. My family is probably still there. But when they took me away to be a Blockade Runner..." he sighed, "It's so far away. But I don't want to go back."

He swept his hand across the mountains and the sunset and the tundra. "There's none of this in the city. Just ice and greed and walls closing you in on every side."

It grew dark, and we climbed back into our car.

That night I dreamt of a tiny orange flower struggling through the crack in the packed ice, reaching desperately for the sun.

THE LOVE LETTERS OF CAPTAIN HARRISON CRADDOCK

My love, I am shattered. All my plans have collapsed. I am sick with fear.

We fled Eveness the day of the meeting and are going back toward the mountains across the tundra. I don't know what I plan to do or where I plan to go. Perhaps into the mountains. Maybe I can find somewhere we can hide. I think Aresis is chasing us. At the moment, We're running and we will run until I think of something to do.

The boys are slowing me down. I think we may need to split up. They're smart; they'll be fine. I want to keep us together, but they're hungry all the time and confused, and they won't stop endlessly asking where we're going, who we're running from, why we didn't wait for Paxton. They're becoming a heavy burden.

And worst of all, they're an obstacle between me and you.

I think I may be forced to contact Aresis and try to come to some kind of agreement. He will punish me. He will want to show me that I failed him, but I can guarantee our future if I am cunning enough.

Don't be afraid, my love. I will find a way for us to be together again soon.

Forever and no matter what,

Crad

THE PERSONAL LOG OF OBSIDIAN, ONCE CROWN PRINCE OF GRAVARUS

Humans are shamefully competitive. It doesn't matter what the topic; they compete. They compete ideas, skills, experiences. They compare scars to see who has the ugliest. My humans have argued hotly over which of them has gone the longest without sleep. I don't know why one would be proud of one's past deprivations, but they are.

Disgusting as it is, I'm growing a slight bit fond of them. They can be charming sometimes. They have funny little habits, like how the female one meticulously tidies her quarters, smoothing the covers on her bed each morning, disposing of rubbish in designated bins, keeping all her belongings organized and sorted. The male human's quarters, however, are entropy's playground.

The female has a great mass of curly hair, which she cares for with many oils and balms she has made herself. The male one has perpetually messy hair, and he has stopped shaving and looks very scruffy.

And he spends most of his time either playing music on his fiddle or whittling. He whittles constantly. And he draws – which is using charcoal to make a rendition of an object or person on paper. He's very adept with his hands.

Sometimes the train car is filled with the wafts of raspberry wine as the humans love each other more each day, and sometimes the rubbery smell of their irritation with each other makes my nose prickle.

I find this is the great mystery of mankind. They are both broken and god-like.

I have seen the male human, with the same hands, turn a

shapeless block of wood into a rendition of a tern in flight, make an instrument sing to break your heart, and cut a Gravarian's jugular in a single, untraceable movement.

What does humanity do to their children to make them this way?

But they are a deeply selfish race. Bent on their own way. It is not hard to believe that the ultimate show of love the Creator sent to them was self-sacrifice. That any human would die for another human is unthinkable. When I see that, I will believe that they are, indeed, made in the image of their creator.

These two love each other as far as they are able to give and get from one another, but I do not believe they would be capable of any significant sacrifice. That is where the reflection of the Creator ends. Once one human impedes on the comfort or the hopes and ambitions of the other, their relationship will break down. They will walk away.

That is the plight of all humans. They are bent on self to the point of self-destruction.

As for the journey, we are woefully low on supplies and getting rather hungry.

And the wood for the fires is running out.

Oh, and the humans are doing experiments on me.

It's annoying.

They're playing songs from the Melodiac, and the songs make me feel strange things and do things outside my control. It's so very, very irritating. They think I don't know, and of course, I do, but I don't know how to tell them I know what they're doing and I wish they would stop. I should have said something in the beginning. Now it's too awkward.

I'm hoping they will get bored eventually and find something else to break. The music bothers me less and less every day, as does the smell of human emotion. Some days I hardly notice either.

And that worries me most of all.

JAEL'S NARRATIVE

I always woke late now, a bad habit I'd picked up from Luca. We'd eat breakfast together in the caboose; then we'd play a song for Sid on Luca's fiddle, then scurry, laughing like naughty children, up to the roof of the train and sit wrapped in heavy blankets as a glistening landscape blurred by. Luca taught me how to read music. What the notes meant. How to coax the flute to song. I discovered with some disappointment that I had no affinity for music. I almost gave up a dozen times, but Luca insisted that I didn't need to be good at a thing to do it. It was enough to enjoy it.

Three songs from the end of the Melodiac, our belated consciences finally caught up to us.

We'd come to the Honeybee Song and the Buffalo Song. It was my first time playing for Sid. We crept up to Sid's compartment as he was eating his breakfast. I was nervous and excited and would have lost my nerve and escaped to my compartment, but Luca egged me on. I raised the flute and played.

The Honeybee Song was easy – just the same four notes played six times. I closed my eyes so I could focus. When I was done, I opened them. Sid sat rigid on the floor. I turned to Luca, but he shrugged.

I scratched my head and waited, but he didn't do anything.

"This isn't what I expected a song about a honeybee to do," I whispered. "Did I do something wrong?"

We watched Sid for five minutes, but he still didn't move.

"I wish he'd do something," I muttered.

Then, slowly, he turned toward me and stared at us blank-eyed.

"Why is he doing that?" I asked. "Sid, are you ok? Get up!" I shouted.

He stood.

Luca and I exchanged a look of alarm.

"Tell him to do something else," Luca said.

"Walk over to the door," I ordered.

Sid walked to the door.

"Jump up and down."

He jumped up and down.

"Spin around!" Luca said.

Sid stood still.

"He only listens to you," Luca said. "Tell him to...do a silly dance."

I giggled. "Do a silly dance!"

Sid began to dance and wheel around the room, swinging his arms. We laughed. He looked like a marionette on strings. Careening wildly around the room, Sid tripped and fell heavily, but he got to his feet again and kept dancing. He crashed into his little table, and it splintered beneath him.

My stomach soured. All the blood drained from my face. Suddenly, I just wanted it to stop.

"Stop!" I shouted. "Stop now!"

He stood still, one foot in the shattered remains of the table.

I turned to Luca, who had his fiddle tucked under his arm and was thumbing through the Melodiac. "How do I make him snap out of it?"

"I'm working on it."

"I want him to stop doing everything I say; it's creepy!" I cried.

"You're the one who knows what these mean!"

I snatched the book and turned to the last song – the Buffalo Song – and played it clumsily and too fast. Played well, it would have been a beautiful, soaring melody, but I was in a panic. As the last note stumbled from my flute, Sid jolted, like the marionette strings had snapped, and sat back down on the floor.

Luca and I ran back to our car and clambered to the roof of the train, where we sat in an unsettled silence, watching the great, white plains flying past us and the dark mountains standing still in the distance.

"What is wrong with us," I said at last.

Luca sighed heavily. "I think we kind of got caught up in the science."

"Or we might be horrible people."

Luca nodded.

"Do you realize what we've been doing?" I asked with rising horror. "We stole his free will. We're...we're just..."

"The worst people on the planet?"

"YES! Exactly. We are the worst people on the planet. I mean, isn't free will what makes us human?"

"Well, Gravs aren't human."

"It was still wrong," I snapped.

"No, I agree." He turned toward me, "but it's good to know. There's a song that makes the Gravs do whatever you tell them to do. It might be useful someday."

I shivered. "I don't think...I don't know if I could do that. It doesn't seem right."

"You just did it like five minutes ago."

I glared at him.

"Is free will really a good thing, anyway?" Luca asked. "If humans didn't have free will, maybe we wouldn't have destroyed the earth, started an ice age. Don't we use our free will for evil more often than good? Don't we use it to make self-pleasing choices most?"

"Can good and evil even exist without choice?"

"We'll come clean to Sid and apologize," Luca said.

We fell silent and popped our collars against the wind. Luca wrapped his arms in his poncho and shivered. Below us, in the valley, something rippled across the plains in a mist of snow. I held my hand above my eyes and tried to see what it was. A brown line like an eel, miles long, undulated across the planes. As the train leveled out and we got a little closer, I made out fur coats, bristled manes, curved horns. I gasped and jumped to my feet.

"Luca, look!"

Thousands of buffalo dashed across the tundra, snorting and puffing like a living train. They moved like water, almost like flight, and kicked up a snow cloud that rose to the sky. Looking wasn't enough for me. Instead, I wished, oh, how I wished that I could write a song, or paint a picture, or pen a poem about this moment.

They ran parallel to us for a while and then bent away toward the mountain.

My eyes stung. I grabbed Luca's arm in my excitement.

"I thought they'd gone extinct!" I cried.

Luca's eyes swam. "So did I."

We watched them until they were just a sliver of bronze on the white horizon.

THE PERSONAL LOG OF OBSIDIAN, ONCE CROWN PRINCE OF GRAVARUS

The humans came to my compartment last night. They looked guilty, like small children caught tormenting the family pet. It made me feel rather smug.

"We have something to tell you," Luca began, "and we're really sorry about it."

"Don't tell him we're sorry yet," Jael whispered to him.

"I wanted to preface it, so he knows from the beginning."

"But that's not what we agreed you'd say!"

"Well, I changed my mind in the heat of the moment!"

I interrupted them. "You've been experimenting on me to see how the Melodiac affects Gravarians."

The look of shock on their faces. It was a beautiful moment.

"I don't know what came over us," Jael said. "It's like we were different people."

Ah, how distinctly human to blame any bad action on their fallen nature. How adamantly they defend the concept of free will when they are behaving themselves only to cast it aside like a lump of hot coal the moment they misbehave.

"We're sorry," Luca said. And he looked it.

I'd always known he was the more emotionally developed of the two of them.

"Can we make it up to you?"

"You know that I need the Melodiac, I assume?" I said.

They looked at each other, but I didn't understand their expression.

"I must take it back to Gravarus and give it to my mother, and then she will make me the crown prince once again. And that would be very much in Earth's best interest. I would not mine Earth's resources or use it as a prison planet anymore once I am king. If I don't get it, Aresis will, and you do not want him to be king."

Then Jael asked a question I had hoped she wouldn't think of.

"Why does your mother want it?"

"That's not the problem at the moment."

"It's a problem for me," Jael said. "One of these songs makes Gravarians obey everything the player commands without question. Won't that make her supremely powerful?"

"Yes," I said, "but better her than Aresis."

"I don't know that," Jael said. "She's the one who first sent prisoners here. She doesn't seem like she cares much about us. Your mother seems dangerous to me."

She had a point, and I disliked it.

"But I will be king when my mother dies," I argued.

"When will that be?" Luca asked.

"Not long. Maybe a hundred years."

They laughed, but it wasn't a happy laugh. "We'll both be dead by then."

Humans and their pathetically short life spans. I know it's the radiation from the sun, but really? Eighty years? They couldn't hold on a decade or two longer? I think it's all in their heads.

"Well, we can't keep the Melodiac here on Earth for Aresis to get," I said. "And I have to claim my right to the throne, or else someone else will get it, and they'll certainly turn Earth into a giant solar farm."

"Solar farm?" Luca said as though he didn't know.

"Our planet's sun is dying, and Earth's sun is still quite healthy. It's the nearest source of solar energy. My mother has long dreamed of using it as a solar farm, but there are impediments."

"What kind of impediments?" Jael asked. "Is it because it's a prison planet?"

I laughed. "Of course not. You don't know?"

"Don't know what?"

"Earth is a wildlife preserve. It's protected in our planet's charter."

"Wildlife as in bears and birds and things?" Jael asked.

"No, silly," I said, laughing still more. "Humans. You are the wildlife."

JAEL'S NARRATIVE

Sid crossed the room and looked out the window. Luca and I sat on the floor of Sid's compartment because he had no furniture, leaning against the wall.

"I don't like being wildlife," I whispered to Luca. "Do you? I feel very...dehumanized."

"Well, it's not like we look at the Gravs like they're people either, so I guess it's fair enough."

"But what do we do now? We have the Melodiac, and we don't want anyone to get it. Should we destroy it?"

Sid returned and stood over us, his hands clasped behind his back. "I say we use it."

"Use it for what?"

"Use it on my mother. If we can control what she does with it, we can make her hand over the crown to me."

"Are there moral problems with that?" Luca said, looking at me. "Didn't we just decide it's wrong to make someone do things they don't want to do?"

"Bit late to ask that question, isn't it?" Sid said. "It does seem better than my mother turning Earth into a giant solar farm and killing all the humans."

"But I thought it was protected in the charter..." I began, but Sid shook his head.

"It won't matter what's in the charter if my mother has control of the minds of all Gravarians. She can make them change the charter, or ignore the charter, or burn it. No one can object. Our planet is run by a queen or king and a very strict set of rules. If you break the rules, the high council will have you deposed. But if she controls the high council..."

"But it's not as though I can teach Sid how to play songs from the Melodiac," Luca said. "And I can't travel to Gravarus, can I?"

Sid shook his head again. "It's not as though I can just bring a human home on the shuttle."

"See? So what are we going to do?"

"What if we had a recording of the music?" Sid asked. "Would that work?"

"A what?"

"You know, a Remembering Box."

Luca and I looked at each other to see if the other knew what he was talking about. Neither of us did.

Sid got up and left the room. A moment later, he returned with a little black box.

"Say something," he said.

"Uhhhhh," I looked nervously at Luca, "Luca's got brown eyes."

Sid pushed a button on the top of the box, and I heard a voice coming out of it.

"Uhhhhh...Luca's got brown eyes."

Luca's brown eyes lit up.

"How did it know that's what I said!" I demanded, reaching for the box. Sid pulled it away.

"That was your voice."

"No, it wasn't. I don't sound like that!"

Luca laughed. "You sound exactly like that."

"My voice is deeper!"

"That was you."

"But how..."

Sid ignored me. "The point is that this box will remember the song. If I bring it with me, I can use it on my mother."

"And we're sure that will work?"

Sid shrugged. "Test it out."

Luca played the Bee Song while I held down a red button on the top of the box. When we played it back, I held the box, and Sid obeyed my every command. Then Luca played the Buffalo Song, and Sid snapped out of it.

"There," Sid said resolutely. "We have a plan. We'll continue to the launch site, where I'll catch a shuttle back home, and soon all of this will be over."

Luca came to my compartment that night, looking guilty.

"We need to make it up to Sid somehow," he said. "He's been so nice to us, and I feel so guilty."

"What do you suggest?"

He grinned like a little boy. "Christmas."

"I don't celebrate Christmas."

His face fell. "Why not?"

"Klifrari aren't religious. We don't have any holidays..."

Luca crossed his arms. "No holidays? What's the point of working hard if you never get a break?"

"They're a waste of time..."

"A waste of..." he was almost too disgusted to argue. He turned around like he was going to leave but turned back in the doorway and burst, "Christmas is not a waste of time!"

"It's an excuse to be lazy..."

He held up his hand. We are celebrating Christmas on this train. I suppose if you don't want to engage in the religious part of it, then you can... I don't know...celebrate another year of not being swallowed by the abyss of existential dread. But there will be a tree and there will be presents and we will make good food and, so help me, you and Sid are going to like it."

I stared at him. "Klifrari just don't celebrate holidays..."

"Then lucky you're not a Klifrari yet."

I shrugged. "Ok...so, how does celebrating Christmas work?"

He reached out, grabbed hold of the emergency brake, and yanked.

THE PERSONAL LOG OF OBSIDIAN, ONCE CROWN PRINCE OF GRAVARUS

The humans are acting very absurd. They have brought a giant coniferous tree into the train and set it up in the compartment next to mine. Then they got smaller coniferous trees and put one in each of their compartments and insisted on putting one in mine. I don't understand why.

They spent the day gathering pine cones, and Jael taught Luca how to weave thread into snowflakes. Seemed like a waste of time and yarn to me.

Then she taught me how to do it, and I just can't stop. I've made a ridiculous number of little thread snowflakes. It's immensely satisfying, and I have no idea why. We have hung them everywhere – from the ceiling, the locks on the windows, the walls. There are piles of them all over my compartment.

Then, when we had made enough, we hung them on the branches of the tree. This was a delicate task, as the thread snowflakes had to be spaced appropriately to satisfy the humans' obsessive sense of symmetry.

Luca played some songs on his fiddle that didn't make me do anything alarming, and Jael sometimes played her flute poorly. Some of the songs were rather pretty. My favorite had a part that said:

A thrill of hope
The weary world rejoices
For yonder breaks
A new and glorious morn

Humans have a remarkable capacity for faith. Especially young humans.

Luca then wove an ancient story about the son of the Creator, who came down to Earth as a human child, born in a stable to an unwed young mother. And when he was ready, he died to cover all the terrible things the humans have done. All the betrayals, all the cruelty, all the pain.

Apparently, the trees they dragged onto the train symbolize everlasting life.

The humans dubbed yesterday the beginning of Christmas and said that we had seven days to come up with gifts for each other.

A gift, I am told, is a thing you give to someone else because you like them and you think they'll like it.

We had stopped the train so that Jael could hunt for supplies. She wasn't gone a day and a night but brought back a deer and about ten rabbits. Maybe more. We processed the meat together (she taught us how). Then she took the hides, spread them out on the train's roof, and salted them. She's been very busy up there doing something clever with them.

Meanwhile, Luca has been boiling nails on the stove.

I think the humans have accepted me into their pack, and I don't know how to feel about it. It's nice, and they're fine, but you know they die so easily, it's probably not a good idea to spend all this time with them. It's not as though I need companionship to survive. It's not as though I'm lonely.

Today was Christmas.

Luca and Jael awoke me at an obscene hour and dragged me into the rations compartment, where they had put their gifts under the tree.

Luca gave Jael a piece of paper with a painting of an orange flower on it. It was a very realistic-looking flower, if not a little more poetic looking than a real one. Apparently, he'd boiled the rusty nails down and made orange paint from it. She's not a very expressive person, but Jael looked the happiest I'd ever seen her, and she said it was "beautiful". I could tell she really liked it because she handled it very gently, like it was made of thin glass.

Then Jael gave Luca a big package. When he opened it, his jaw dropped, and he looked utterly stunned. From the brown paper wrapping, he pulled a thick buckskin jacket lined with rabbit fur.

"Did you make this?" He asked.

Jael looked like she might burst. Like she was holding in a geyser of joy and pride.

"It's incredible! Look at the stitch work."

"It's the kind of stitching you use on wounds, which is kind of weird. But it's the best I know."

He pulled it on, and it fit him perfectly and looked warm. He'd been shivering in his blanket poncho for a while.

She also made him a red scarf and a pair of gloves.

Luca gave me a piece of wood he'd carved to look like a buffalo.

"It's a symbol of freedom," he told me, "so you'll always remember that you have free will."

Jael gave me a bright red sweater. When I say bright red, I mean the most violent, eye-scalding shade of crimson you can imagine. But it's warm, and it feels nice on my skin. She made it herself, which is touching.

I gave each of them a small Gravarian knife. They were in awe of how smooth and sharp the blades were. Of course, Jael cut herself thirty seconds after I gave it to her. I hope this wasn't a bad idea.

We made a mess helping Jael bake gash cakes and rosemary bread. When the food came out of the oven, we ate together in the glow of the little pot-bellied stove. We sang songs (I tried singing, but it doesn't come naturally to me). We ate excellent venison and stayed up late sitting by the tree feeling warm and comfortable. Luca told the Christmas story again and then a tragic story about a very old man who was very sensible with his money and encouraged his employees to work hard and never slack. Everything was nice for him, and he lived a life of simple practicality and never wasted anything until three meddlesome ghosts broke into his house and manipulated him into believing that it was his responsibility to relieve the poverty of everyone around him simply because he had been shrewd with his finances and they had not. So he was forced to change his ways in order to get a good night's sleep. He had to buy food for his employees and pay for their medical expenses and suddenly became popular with all the people in the town. I thought this story supremely sad, but the humans seemed to think that the old fellow was better off in the end.

All night, the snow swirled past the windows. Luca's fiddle sang.

Tonight, I almost wish I were human.

THE LOVE LETTERS OF CAPTAIN HARRISON CRADDOCK

I have made another deal with Aresis. I agreed to work with him in the coming weeks and help him find the Melodiac. I told him about the shortcut I learned about in Eveness, so we can get ahead of his brother and cut him off at the next outpost. Aresis needs the Melodiac, and he needs Paxton because Paxton's a musician. He promised you and I would be safe as long as he gets what he wants. I think our future is secure.

We're lying in wait for Obsidian's train now. It should be here tomorrow.

Oh, but Helena, I was punished for my failure at Eveness. Severely punished. I can't write about it. I couldn't stop it. It was my only way to secure our future together.

A necessary evil.

I have begun to seriously think and sincerely hope that there is no Creator. Isn't that a relief to think about?

No great tribunal.

No Hell.

No final judgment.

No eternal punishment for the wicked or the mistaken or the confused.

Have you thought about it? If there's no Creator, then who determines good and evil? Can't we decide for ourselves?

If there's no measure of goodness, then who can say I'm not good? I'm trying to make my way in the world just like everyone else, acted upon by the random gyrations of fate. I protect what I love most, isn't that goodness enough?

If, when all this is over, I have protected you and perhaps even Paxton, then won't I have fulfilled some universal law?

And if there is a Creator, isn't his standard for goodness too high to bother about anyway?

And don't tell me about redemption. I don't want it. It's too far out of my reach. Once you've veered off the knife's edge of 'goodness,' then the fall is too swift to stop. I am cascading downhill. I can't slow down now. Why try?

I have one goal now, and I will hold to it. I will be with you again, and that will be Heaven for me. To not see you will be my Hell. And whatever happens in between is simply my Purgatory.

Wait for me. It will be over tomorrow.

Crad

JAEL'S NARRATIVE

We planned to stop for water and supplies at a little outpost twenty miles west of Fool's Bridge. But when we pulled into the station...there was nothing left. Charred buildings swam in black smoke, the station still crackled and burned, and a train lay derailed with hollow, smoking cars sprawled behind it.

We switched to a second track that avoided the wreck. As we came around, we pulled within inches of some of the smoldering cars. Luca and I pulled open the big sliding door on the side of the rations car and leaned out so we could see.

Snow fell, and the flakes sizzled when they hit the burnt wood. We could barely make out the writing on the engine, but one word was still visible.

Powderkeg

Luca looked like he might jump out, but I grabbed his sleeve.

"What are you doing?"

"It's Craddock's train," he said, yanking his arm away. "Aresis must have caught up to them."

"That's impossible. Aresis was behind us."

He hopped out of the train car and ran back toward the wreck.

Grumbling under my breath, I pulled the emergency break and ran after him.

The outpost burned quietly behind us, and in front of us, between the tracks and a line of woods, stretched an open meadow about thirty yards across and covered in snow. I found Luca in the center of it, trembling, surrounded by bloody bodies. We hadn't seen them from the train because they had melted into the snow. He turned round and round, murmuring something to himself.

I came up beside him and looked at the nearest body, hoping

my suspicions were wrong. But it was his unit. I could tell from the plaid shirts.

"Fifteen," Luca whispered to himself, "sixteen, seventeen..."

"Maybe someone got away," I suggested.

"...twenty-eight, twenty-nine, thirty."

He sank to his knees and put his head in his hands.

"Is it everyone?" I asked.

"All but Craddock," he replied in a cracked voice.

I didn't know what to say. The Klifrari regarded death with indifference, almost coldness. Birch taught me that death came for everyone as part of the ebb and flow of nature. It was natural, almost romanticized. But in that moment, as I stood so flanked in by it I could smell its rank breath, all the Klifrari words felt as empty and pointless as a shout for help from the bottom of a crevasse. I put my hand awkwardly on Luca's shoulder. "There's nothing you could have done..."

Luca startled me with a cry of pain and anger that made the tendons in his neck jut out, his face flush purple, his eyes go bloodshot. He pounded on the frozen ground with his fists until there was blood on the snow. Horrified, I dropped down in front of him and grabbed his wrists.

"Stop!" I screamed. "Stop it! What are you doing?"

He pulled his hands away.

"Look, we need to go," I said. "It isn't safe here."

I reached for him, but he flinched away from me.

"Go back to the train. I'll be there in a minute," he said.

"No, I want you to come with me. We need to go."

"Jae," his nostrils flared, and he almost shouted, but he took a deep breath through his nose and said in a trembling voice, "please. I'll come in a minute."

I was eager to escape from the blank staring eyes and the bloody plaid and the twisted faces, so I turned and walked away.

The sun had dipped below the horizon and lit the sky torn flesh pink.

Halfway to the train, I noticed movement at the edge of the woods. Dark figures milled around, pulling something large and gray toward the meadow. And then there was a flash, and a spray of dirt and a concussion lifted me off my feet before I heard the "boom".

I'd heard this same gun at Powderkeg but never actually seen it. The whizzing sound the shells made left me paralyzed for a moment, then something stung my ear, and I smelled burned flesh, and my mind snapped into gear. I got to my feet and sprinted for the train. Sid stood in the open door of the rations car and reached out for my hand, but before I took it, I looked over my shoulder, expecting to see Luca close behind me.

But he wasn't.

He still knelt right where I'd left him. Shells from the big artillery gun tossed dirt over his head, but he stayed rigid in the snow, staring down the blue wall of Gravs as they marched out of the trees. I couldn't understand why he didn't run, and then it occurred to me that he might have some wild, despairing idea of dying with his friends. I was so enraged by this that, for a moment, I forgot to be scared.

"Luca, come on!" I screamed.

He didn't seem to hear me.

"SKIN YOU!" I bellowed. I turned around and ran back for him.

I made it as far as the wreck before another shell sang overhead. I flattened myself against the hot wood of a burning car and shielded my face with my arm as a shower of dirt and pebbles pattered against my head. The air cleared, and I got to my feet again and started across the field. After no more than ten steps, an explosion hurled me into a fresh gash in the ground. I skidded on my hands and knees. My palms burned. There was so much noise, so much smoke. My brain flooded with sound and smell and terror. I curled up in a ball and covered my ears with my arms, but I could feel concussions through the frozen dirt below my body. Above me, brown smoke flashed like I was inside a thundercloud. I didn't know which way was forward and which was back. With trembling limbs, I felt my way to the top of the ditch and shouted for Luca.

A breeze picked up and peeled back a layer of smoke, and I saw him, about six yards ahead of me, slashing at a bearded man with such ferocity the man stumbled back, startled, with fear in his eyes.

Craddock lived. All the boys died, but somehow, he survived.

"Paxton," Craddock shouted, "I don't want to hurt you!"

"Is that what you told them?" Luca screamed. "Is that what you told the boys?"

"It was join Aresis or die."

"Then you should be dead!"

Luca ran at him, but he didn't have his usual control, and Craddock caught his arm and flipped him onto the ground.

"Paxton, stop!"

Luca let out a furious yell, twisted his arm, and sent Craddock flailing into the snow.

Beyond them, I noticed a figure growing closer behind a scrim of smoke. He broke out in an eddy of swirling brown. This was the Gravarian from the shot tower. He raised a crossbow.

"NO!" I screamed, rushing out of my hiding place. The Gravs were surprised and turned toward me. Luca took advantage of the split second and dashed at the big Grav, cutting his forearm. He went for the kill, but Craddock came up from the side and hit Luca in the side of the head with his fist, and Luca crumpled. The big Grav stood over him and raised his cleaver.

THE PERSONAL LOG OF OBSIDIAN, ONCE CROWN PRINCE OF GRAVARUS

It's not as though I've never seen artillery fire before. On Gravarus, I've commanded artillery legions that could flatten an Earth city in a blink.

But there's nothing like that on Earth. Not for four hundred years or more. And none of the Gravarians sent here have sophisticated weapons. They're prisoners. My mother allows each one a cleaver as a courtesy and sometimes a crossbow, but nothing noisy. And our artillery on Gravarus is silent, so the noise and smell of human weaponry can be difficult to acclimate to.

So when I heard explosions, I was surprised. Not really worried, of course, just surprised. I was also surprised that Aresis got ahead of us. The redheaded human must have found him a shortcut. I knew that if we kept our heads down and hurried, we could skirt around the wreck, dodge the artillery fire, and avoid Aresis altogether. His train was on another track entirely. Idiot didn't even block the tracks.

But humans are unpredictable, stupid things. For some indiscernible reason, Luca had leaped from the safety of the train and ended up right in the middle of the smoking field. And then, in an act I still cannot comprehend, Jael ran after him.

For the first time since I lost my birthright, I felt fear.

And I still can't understand it. Have I developed empathy? Heavenly stars, I hope not.

Perhaps it was weakness, but I left the train and followed the humans. It took a moment in the smoke, but I found them soon.

Gregorikus, the great muttonhead (this is a human insult

I've become fond of. It means your mind resembles the cooked flesh of a sheep), stood over Luca with a cleaver in his hands, presumably about to cut him in half.

I don't know what I was thinking. I wasn't thinking. I was angry.

Who gave Gregorikus the right to cut my human in half?

I stepped between them and blocked his blow with my blade. Gregorikus recognized me and laughed.

"You stink of human, Obsidian," he sneered.

"And you smell like Aresis' lap dog."

I pushed him back, and he came at me swinging, but I ducked under his blows and twisted behind him.

Gravarian warfare is hard-hitting and heavy, not fast a superfluous like human fights. We move slowly, and we swing our weapons with great force. I stepped back and raised my blade with the intent of finally taking off Gregorikus' head, he stepped back and raised his cleaver, most likely with the same intentions, and we were about to strike down at each other when there was a little blur of movement and Jael darted under Gregorikus' weapon, slashed at his leg, forcing him to fall to one knee, then slashed his weapon arm, forcing him to drop his cleaver. She would have struck at his throat, but he swept at her with his arm and carried her off her feet. I moved to follow up my advantage, but the artillery piece, which I'd almost forgotten, began firing again.

Jael dragged Luca to his feet, and the three of us ran back to the train, got aboard, and held on as we whipped around a bend, away from Aresis.

JAEL'S NARRATIVE

The moment we were out of danger, a wave of anger settled over me, and I turned on Luca and shoved him away from me into the wall.

"You almost got us both killed!" I shouted.

"I didn't ask you to chase after me!"

"You just stayed in the middle of a battlefield!"

"The only thing crazier than staying on a battlefield is following someone onto a battlefield."

"Don't!" I held up my hand. "Just...don't speak."

"That was Craddock, Jae."

"I know!"

"He betrayed everyone! He let Aresis murder my unit! I couldn't let him get away with that!"

"So you decided, why not let him murder me and all my friends? Sounds like a good idea!"

"Aresis did murder all my friends."

That stung. I felt foolish for chasing after him. "Do you know..." My voice scratched and, to my horror, furious tears stung my eyes, "that you're a RECKLESS IDIOT, AND I SHOULD HAVE LET GERGORI-WHATS-HIS-NAME HAVE YOU! When we get to Fool's Bridge, I am going home."

"Jae, you can't..."

"My name is Jael."

"...you can't just leave!"

"If all your friends are dead...no, listen, you said 'all'...

"I didn't mean..."

"No, you said 'all'..."

"That's not what I meant..."

"...then I don't see why you care what I do."

"Come on. Now you're just being snotty."

"I am not being snotty!"

"Yes, you are."

"No, I'm not."

"You are."

"I'm not. I've never been snotty in my life."

"Maybe not until right now, but you're being extremely..."

"I AM NOT!"

Luca raised his arm, and I flinched.

"Bearhie, Jael, I'm not going to hit you! I'm just..."

He put his hand to the side of his head and brought it back with orange blood on his fingers.

"Why didn't you say something?" I shouted.

"Right. Sorry. Pardon me. You know when Craddock cracked me over the head? Well, you'll never believe this, but it's bleeding."

"Don't be snarky."

"Don't tell me what to do."

"I'm not telling you what to do. I've never told you what to do. I'm telling you what not to do. There's an important distinction."

I bandaged his head, sent him back to his room, and told him to stay there.

And he did.

For two days.

A black cloud settled over the train. Sid complained that the train stank of cardamom and asked me over and over again to fix it. But I didn't know how to fix it. Besides, we were getting close to Fool's Bridge, so I forced myself to dream about Becky's and the look on Birch's face when I returned alive. I whittled away the lonely hours in the rations compartment. I stockpiled gash cakes, venison pies, herb butter, cheese scones, and yau. Then I made sure there were plenty of salves and ointments and wrote out directions on how to treat wounds, breaks, and fevers. I cleaned and folded all my spare bandages, then cleaned and folded them again. Deep down, I knew I'd lose sleep over every little thing I forgot to do. I knew I'd lie in my bed and wonder if Luca and Sid were well-fed and healthy and eating enough vitamin C to keep their teeth in their heads.

On the third day, I awoke to find the train had stopped. Outside the window, the lights on Fool's Bridge flickered in the blue dawn.

Finally.

I stuffed my few belongings into my rucksack. My coat, my hat, my gloves. I left a generous pile of dry herbs. I lingered a moment in front of the painting of the flower. I couldn't take it with me. I couldn't leave it.

I walked out the door without it, then went back, pulled it from the wall, and slid it into my jacket.

The corridor was dark, but Luca's frosted window glowed orange. I knocked timidly, and it slid open. Luca leaned between the door and the wall. His hair stuck to his forehead, and his eyes were heavy and purple underneath. He looked thinner.

"I'm heading out..."

I felt awkward because I couldn't forecast how this was supposed to play out. Would it be emotional? Would it be stilted? Would there be yelling? Crying? Or worse, nothing?

"I'm glad we found each other," I said, looking down at my toes. "It's been interesting."

Luca rumpled his hair at the back of his head. "Look, Jael, I'm sorry about what I said yesterday..."

"It's been three days, Luca."

He looked disoriented. "Really? Anyway, I didn't mean..."

"No, it's ok. I'm sorry too."

"It was just hard to see them..."

"I know."

"I wish you could stay."

"Yeah, but I have to go back."

He swallowed. "Sure, yeah, I get it."

We stood in uncomfortable silence for a moment. Then he pushed the door back and held out his hand. I shook it. He cleared his throat and sniffed, and I waved weakly at him and turned away. I felt his eyes on me all the way down the corridor;

something inside me urged me to turn and look back at him, but I hardened my shoulders and kept my eyes ahead.

Outside, it neither snowed nor rained, but cold moisture hung in the air and pierced through my coat and into my joints and nerves. I checked my bootlaces, adjusted my hat, and turned my collar against the wind. I went over my next steps: cross the bridge, climb the pass, back to Ram's Head, Birch. Becky's. Home.

The moment I stepped on the bridge, the train whistle called out to me in dismay. My boots made a hollow sound on the wood planks. I shivered and tried to imagine walking into the yellow-lit Becky's and meeting the eyes of the Klifrari as they hunched over their tables. But instead of laughing faces, I remembered withering scowls. Even if I made it back, I'd need Birch at my elbow to get me inside. They still wouldn't let me past the door without a tota.

I'd go back to the way things were, creeping behind Birch, hoping to be accepted because of him.

It would be frosty still.

Silent still.

No one would call me "Jae".

I stopped in the light of one of the torches, pulled the painting from my coat, and stared at it for a long minute.

The train huffed. I'd nearly crossed the bridge by now, but I watched the train as it picked up speed. As the passenger car passed me, my eyes followed the warm light in Luca's compartment window as that familiar longing flooded me. The same longing I felt every time I tried to get into Becky's.

My feet began to run before my mind decided to. I sprinted back across the bridge. The train swept past me, faster and faster, as I reached desperately for a handrail. The snow slid under my boots. I almost lost my footing, but as I tripped forward, I made a last reach.

THE LOVE LETTERS OF CAPTAIN HARRISON CRADDOCK

My love, how are you? I feel as though my letters are always about myself, and I so rarely hear about you. You can go out of the house now if you want. You're safe.

It was a tremendous sacrifice—a horrible loss. But I didn't know it would end this way, and it bought me safety. Bought you life. It's done. There's no point agonizing about it, is there?

Perhaps, someday, when I am back in the quiet with you, living a life so separate from this one and so far away, maybe then the nightmares will forget to come.

I'm in the inner circle now. I've shown that I'm dedicated to seeing Aresis with the Melodiac, whatever the cost, as long as it means you are safe.

So far, the smartest thing I've done is to buy the allegiance of the albino Gravarian at Eveness. She told me first that Paxton had the Melodiac and that they were with Aresis' older brother, Obsidian. She told us about the shortcut. And since she joined us, she has helped us a great deal. She knows people who will help us, and already our plan is underway. Aresis, Gregorikus, and I leave today to travel to our next destination. Ila continues by train to meet Obsidian. All is going well.

But tell me how you are, my love. Write me a letter even if you don't know where to send it, even if I never get it. That way, it will feel more like you're talking to me.

Keep the house warm and sleep as much as you can. Dream of me when you sleep and know we'll be together again soon because even winter comes to an end.

Don't seeds need to die before they sprout? Don't the deer shed their antlers? Isn't loss the cycle of nature? And yet, can't we hold on with white knuckles to what we know we can't stand to lose? Isn't love its own morality?

Soon now,

Crad

JAEL'S NARRATIVE

It rained outside. Harder than I'd ever seen. Perhaps the great thaw was coming after all. Perhaps Earth's great spring would come.

I sat in my compartment and tried to embroider, but my eyes ached in the darting light of the seal fat lantern. Next door, Luca plucked at his fiddle. No music, just plucking. I hadn't seen him since I got back on the train. I'd knocked on his door and told him I'd decided to stay, but he hadn't responded. That was two days ago.

The incessant plucking was driving me mad. Didn't he eat anymore? Didn't he sleep? It was past midnight, and I couldn't stand it. I threw off my blanket and stepped out into the corridor. I wanted to tell him what Birch told me when I heard that my father died: "Buck up. Grief takes too long, and we don't have that kind of time."

I remembered the coldness that flowed through me when he said that. A coldness I felt still.

I slid Luca's door open, words already perched on my tongue.

He sat on the floor, his back against the wall, and looked up at me with dry eyes. His face like granite. He was icing over, like a mountainside after a thaw becomes smooth, impenetrable, and unscalable.

Grief, left alone, turns to ice.

All my words fell dead at my feet. I stood in the doorway, frightened by his look and my own helplessness. What words could ease this pain? I didn't know any ointment for a broken spirit. No herbs I could grind down with my pestle and mix with oil could soften this wound.

Then a woman's instinct, long smothered under Birch's

influence, like a quilt crammed into a box, rose in me. I crossed the room, got down on the floor next to him, and wrapped my arms around him. I put my hand on the back of his head and pressed his face into my shoulder. I expected him to resist, but he melted into my arms.

"I'm sorry," I said softly.

He nodded.

"About your friends. About everything."

He sat silent for a moment, then he wrapped his arms around me and sobbed into my shoulder. Heavy sobs, violent and rasping. He gripped fistfuls of my jacket and hung on as though he were falling off a cliff, and I was holding him up.

I held him and let him cry.

Abandonment and loss held us together—arms reaching across a ravine.

THE PERSONAL LOG OF OBSIDIAN, ONCE CROWN PRINCE OF GRAVARUS

Aresis murdered all of Luca's friends. It seems he did it to tie up loose ends and punish the red-haired human captain for not holding up his end of the deal. The human captain is still alive, so apparently Aresis has something over him. This is how Aresis operates. He finds something to hold over you, and he exploits it. Wrings every drop out of it.

Luca is very sad.

No, I am not experiencing compassion for the human, and, no, I do not feel any sense of empathy because someone I loved, like, for example, my father, was murdered in a shocking manner when I was a child, forever shattering my sense of security and tarnishing my childhood innocence to the point that I am no longer able to establish a relationship of trust with anyone in my life. That never crossed my mind. But the train stinks of grief, and it's unpleasant. And Jael is not quite so enjoyable to be around as Luca, and she's been sponging up some of his sadness which has been miserable for everyone.

She initially got off the train, but then she got back on. I cannot understand why. She had wanted to get off the train at Fool's Bridge since the first day, but she changed her mind.

Humans are fickle.

It's been several days since my last entry. Luca is not so sad now. We all eat dinner together, which is enjoyable, and they tell me about human things, and I tell them about Gravarian things. They think Gravarus is very strange and funny, and I think Earth is very primitive.

They can't understand why most Gravarian technology doesn't work on Earth because they are a little stupid. I'm not going to explain it to them anymore. In the end, I told them that all of our weapons are too heavy to transport into Earth's atmosphere. This is partially true, so they are partially satisfied.

Earth is a mess, and I've told them so.

Much of the non-human wildlife is carnivorous and will kill you.

Many of the plants are poisonous and will kill you.

Humans kill one another quite frequently and for no reason.

Weather patterns will kill you.

Some of the rocks, if touched, will kill you.

Gravity will kill you.

Bacteria will kill you.

It's a marvel the human race has made it this long.

We have one human settlement to pass before we reach the launch site. I will take the Remembering Box back to Gravarus, use it against my mother, become king of Gravarus, and be sure Earth is no longer used as a prison planet.

I will put funds toward rebuilding Earth's economy. I want to see it thrive again. I want to see Jael and Luca living somewhere safe.

I plan to leave the Melodiac with the humans. They will take it into the mountains and hide there until my return.

And I will return once I am king.

And I will go back to Eveness, to the place where I smelled that smell, and I will find her again.

And perhaps we will be together again.

JAEL'S NARRATIVE

On our last morning together on the train, I woke up feeling different. Unsettled. Like I was standing on cracking ice.

After I poured a mug of yau, I met Luca on the little deck at the back of the caboose. Most mornings, we talked about whatever meandered into our heads. The intersection of music and poetry with theology and philosophy – or what we, at that age, thought was the intersection of music and poetry with theology and philosophy. We were like small children, learning to toddle and calling it a sprint. Both of us desperately wanted to experience and understand things like music and poetry and sunsets and orange flowers growing out of icy sidewalks.

I'd come to love these mornings playing intellectual badminton with him while the cold stung our cheeks and noses.

But today, I knitted quietly at a white scarf. Luca sketched rapidly on a sheet of paper, and we didn't say anything for almost an hour.

"What are you sketching?" I asked at last.

"You," he said.

"Why?"

"Because you're pretty."

My cheeks warmed. "No, I'm not."

"Then why am I sketching you?"

I knitted more quickly and listened to his pencil *scratch, scratch, scratching.*

"When this is over, what are you going to do?" he asked me after a moment.

"I guess I'll try to get my tota, become a Klifrari, bring blood bags over the mountain. Someday, I'll become a Lithna."

He nodded.

"What are you going to do?" I asked.

"I guess I'll join another Blockade Runner unit. There's one not far from our stop, and they'll take me in."

I don't know why this surprised me, but it did.

"Isn't it dangerous?" I asked.

He shrugged. "I don't really think about it."

"But isn't there anything else you want to do?"

"Not really. I don't know how to do anything else."

"What?" I smacked him with the scarf I was knitting. "You know how to do everything! You're the most talented person I've ever met."

"Yeah, but talent doesn't feed you. Work does. And besides," he rubbed the tattoo above his right thumb, "I need one more point on the antlers before I've fulfilled my conscription."

Something like panic began to rise like a strangling vine from my stomach up my throat, and suddenly I felt like I needed to get away from him – run back home where I didn't care about anyone enough to be really hurt by them. Because what if Luca did go back to Blockade Running? What if some Gravarian got him with a shaft through the throat one day, and there was nothing I could do about it? That could happen. That probably would happen.

The train jolted with a clang and began to slow down. Sid sauntered onto the deck.

"We're here."

"Already?" I asked, feeling a little sick. "But I thought it would be tonight..."

"I'll be there tonight, but I'm dropping you two off here. You can take the pass through the mountain back toward Rustypike, remember?"

That was what we agreed on, but it seemed too soon. I wanted more time. This journey, which I'd been so reluctant to begin, so eager to end, had turned into the happiest weeks of my life.

"Since I have the song I need on the Remembering Box, it would be best, I think, to keep the Melodiac here," Sid said. "I fear taking it back to Gravarus that it could too easily fall into my mother's hands. Hide it somewhere safe until I return."

That was all the goodbye we got from Sid. He just patted us each on the head and returned to his compartment.

We climbed off the train and looked at the endless gray forest in front of us.

"This would be my area of expertise," I said, just as Luca said, "This is my rodeo."

We scowled at each other.

I put my hands on my hips. "Hiking through the woods. That's what Klifrari do."

"Slowly," Luca laughed.

"Only when we have Blockade Runners slowing us down."

"Blockade Runners are trained for speed."

"Not when you're stranded on a mountain in a blizzard needing stitches, which, I might add, I gave you for free, which broke Klifrari code and my wallet."

"Left a scar," Luca said, trotting ahead of me into the trees.

"Slow down!" I called after him.

"See! What did I say?"

We walked for a few miles. Luca seemed comfortable enough. He whistled a song from the Melodiac, occasionally stopped and stared at a tree for a few seconds, made a sharp turn, and walked on. I would have contested, but he was going the right way, which was out of character for him.

"Have you been here before?" I asked.

"No, but I memorized all the river routes..."

Luca's voice trailed off, and he sped up.

"I say we stop here and camp for the night," I said.

"Nah, let's keep going."

"Remember that time I took you over the mountain, on my trial, and I failed, and that's why I'm here today with you instead of sitting peacefully by a warm crackling fire with my mentor and my tota enjoying a cup of hot yau."

"Why is your tota enjoying a cup of hot yau?"

I threw a snowball at his back. It struck him between his shoulder blades. He turned on me slowly, bent down, gathered together a handful of snow, wound up like a pitcher, and threw it overhand. It hit me between my eyes.

"No face shots!" I shouted, wiping my face with my sleeve.

Luca made another snowball and followed up his advantage. "This is how Blockade Runners play. Can't keep up?"

His second shot hit my shoulder. I got him in the side of his neck, and he whooped as the freezing water dripped down his collar. He started pelting me, making snowballs and throwing them faster than I had time to dodge or bend down and make more. With a squeal, I turned and ran, laughing, into the trees as the hard clumps of snow burst against my back. I darted behind a small pine tree and waited for him. When he was about a foot away, I jumped up, caught a branch, pulled it down, and then let it spring back as I stepped aside. The snow fell off the heavy branch and showered down on Luca's head. He shouted, shaking the white powder from his hair, then ducked his head, ran at me, and tackled me. We crashed into the deep powder and lay for a minute, laughing and shivering as ice dripped into our clothes and stung our skin. Luca had his arm across my waist, and when he noticed, he looked a little abashed and rolled away from me onto his back. I turned my head, our eyes met, and our expressions froze. Snowflakes drifted softly down from the trees, caught on the breeze, and danced around us as if to music. My breath caught in my chest.

Something in the pine tree above us rustled and caught Luca's eye. A barn owl, with his heart-shaped face and speckled wings, watched us with fathomless onyx eyes. But I wasn't looking at the owl; I was looking at Luca as he gazed up at the bird the way a master craftsman looks at another artist's work.

"Look at how perfect it is, Jae," he whispered.

I still looked at him. "Yeah, it is."

I rested my head on the pillowy snow and forced my attention toward the owl. "Did you know," I whispered, "that their faces are shaped like that so they can catch sound and hear better?"

"That's fascinating."

The owl flapped its wings and flew away through the trees. Luca sat up and got to his feet, then he took my hand and pulled me up after him.

"See," he said, smiling, "you're glad you ended up here with me instead of with all those stuffy old Klifrari, admit it."

"It could have turned out worse," I said.

As the trees cast long, black shadows, I made a dry fire under a little knot of pine trees. Luca sat down and looked mournfully into the flames.

"We don't have any food."

I stood up. "We're twenty feet from a river."

"Ok?"

"Ever heard of a fish?"

"I have heard of them, yes."

"Ever eaten one?"

"Yes, but they're in the river, and we're on the land."

"How do you think they get from the river onto your plate? Magic?"

"Fishing poles. Which we don't have."

"Please," I rolled my eyes. "Since Klifrari are so slow, we know how to catch our own food instead of having mommy pack us a lunch before we go."

"Fish are basically a vegetable."

"Better than nothing."

He shrugged and followed me to the river.

We whittled down two sharp spears from tree branches, and I walked into a small pool where a warm current had melted the ice. Luca found his own pool about ten yards downstream. I crouched over the water, my spear up, waiting for a fish to swim under me.

The water ran around my legs, so cold it made my feet ache, then itch, then lose feeling altogether. A few fish darted around my legs, avoiding my shadow. I waited, poised, for one to swim into that perfect spot beneath my spear.

A rumbling snort startled me. A huddle of bushes rustled and dropped heavy clumps of snow. A branch snapped. Some birds took flight in a flurry of feathers and complaints, and out of the woods ambled a mountain-sized grizzly bear.

I glanced over my shoulder at Luca. He had his back to me, bent over the water, waiting for a fish.

The bear walked to the edge of the water and waded lazily in. She splashed closer until she stood only a few yards away. I almost could have touched her deep fur, but she didn't see me because her left eye and ear were missing.

I'd heard stories about this bear. They called her Old Yuma. She'd lost her eye and ear to a Klifrari Vayda, who she ultimately ate. Klifrari Vayda had both dreams and nightmares of killing Old Yuma, but no one tried anymore because, with each legend, she grew a little bigger, a little more fierce, until killing her seemed impossible.

I backed away quietly, hoping the dimming twilight hid me. Just as my foot sank into the slushy snow on the river's edge, Luca let out an ear-splitting "Whoop!"

Old Yuma's head shot up like a hound dog on the scent.

"I caught one...WHOA!" Luca was so startled by the bear he fell backward into the water.

"Don't run!" I shouted. Just as I said it, Old Yuma came at me.

"Run!" I screamed.

I scrambled out of the river, but the bear was right on top of me. She swiped with a paw the breadth of my torso and carried me clean off my feet. I hit the ground so hard I lost my breath. When I rolled to my back again, Old Yuma stood over me, five feet at the shoulder, large as a horse, her little amber eye staring into mine.

I wasn't at all resigned to my fate. I started to shriek like a terrified child. Old Yuma opened her great mouth, and...out of nowhere, something wet and slimy slapped her muzzle so hard it sent a ripple down her whole body.

She hesitated, aghast at the indignity of it all.

I looked up and saw Luca standing just above me, holding a big salmon. He followed up his advantage and slapped Old Yuma with the fish again. She recovered from the initial shock and let out a roar I felt in my gut. I wiggled out from under her, shot up from the ground, and we both took off into the trees. Luca tossed the fish behind him.

Old Yuma took two steps, stopped, bent down, and sniffed at the fish.

We didn't stop to see if she ate it. We ran until our sides split.

THE PERSONAL LOG OF OBSIDIAN, SOON CROWN PRINCE OF GRAVARUS

I left the train with some regret. I'd found it rather comfortable in the end. The shuttle departs from a Gravarian settlement on the edge of the river, and I arrived by nightfall. I kept the Remembering Box tucked under my red sweater.

I got a lot of looks for the red sweater, but I'm not the one banished to a prison planet, so I don't much care what these Gravarians think.

The shuttle is a rusty, clanking ship, looking not unlike an egg. It flies to Gravarus with whoever is allowed to leave, usually no one, and comes back packed full of fresh prisoners.

I went to the clearing station, where they did a genetic scan to prove I'm not trying to escape Earth.

Like most everything Gravarian, the settlement is unfussy. And, being constructed out of scrap by Earth inmates, it's just a lot of shanties and muddy streets.

Like all Gravarian populaces, it's very quiet. After months with noisy, smelly, laughing, talking, scampering humans, the quiet actually bothered me. No emotions on the breeze. No one feeling anything.

They scanned me in, and I was about to step onto the shuttle when I turned and nearly had a heart attack. Ila herself. Ila, beautiful and tall – taller than me. Ila with her eyes like the light reflecting off the stars. When I saw her, I wanted to throw myself into the sea.

"If it isn't Obsidian," she said in her imperious way.

"If it isn't Una," I replied, hoping that if I pretended to forget her name, she'd forget our past.

"Don't play games with me. I know you remember me."

"Vaguely. I went to a grieving room after they exiled you and forgot almost everything."

She came closer to me and spun the tassel on my shirt around her finger. She is the color of snow. She smells of raspberry wine – the smell of love. Sweet, rich, and intoxicating.

"You didn't go to a grieving room," she said softly. "You didn't want to forget."

I looked away because I feared she would see the truth in my eyes – that I did not forget her. That my mother gave my birthright to Aresis because I was a disgrace, and so I pretended to forget, but I never did.

"I was your wife not long ago, you know."

"It was long ago. More than a human lifetime."

"You know," she said, "marrying you ruined my life. For the first few decades, I thought you would come for me, but you never did. You abandoned me and pretended I didn't exist. Did you think that would go unatoned?"

She slid a long knife out of her sleeve and touched it to my throat. "I asked myself, 'what kind of king would leave his wife to rot in exile? 'And so I decided to join Aresis and help him get the throne. I know the humans have the Melodiac, and you have a Remembering Box."

"And you think I'll just give it to you?"

"I do."

"Or what?"

"I'll kill you and take it anyway."

"You couldn't kill me, Ila," I said, leaning closer. "I'm the only person who has ever made you feel anything. And isn't that what you miss? Feeling things?"

I slipped the box from my pocket, pressed the rewind button until I felt the vibration stop with a click, and then I pressed the red button.

"I was going to come back for you," I said. "When this was over. I would have come back."

She pressed the knife against my throat until the edge bit into my skin.

"This sweater is the silliest thing I've ever seen," she hissed.

"So is your wig," I replied.

She snatched the box from my hand and pushed the playback button.

"So is your wig," it said.

She looked up at me, her mouth open.

"You recorded over it?"

I smiled at her, feeling very, very satisfied with myself.

"Fine," she said, her lips tight. She pulled her wig off and tossed it in the mud. "Then we'll get the Melodiac from the humans."

JAEL'S NARRATIVE

We followed the trail until it was too dark to see. As we sat down and tried to make a fire, I smelled venison and heard the low thrum of voices coming through the trees.

We followed the sound and smell until we came upon an overhang of rock jutting out of the hillside and a group of seven or eight fur-clad men and women sitting around a fire and lounging on the ground. A big woman with a gray fox fur around her neck stood and came to greet us.

"Welcome, travelers!" She cried, smiling with blackened teeth. "I'm Hetta Hiliak. If you're looking for a guide through the forest, we're the finest. Or if you're looking to buy, we have furs and leather and wooden wares."

"I'm a Klifrari," I said. "We're looking for a place to spend the night."

I knew Hetta Hiliak. She was a Klifrari matriarch, esteemed almost at highly as Birch. He edged her out just slightly because he owned Becky's and because he was Lithna, which garnered more respect than Hetta's job as a Laidish.

Hetta's smile melted off her face like wax before a fire. "I recognize you now."

She turned back toward the others.

"You're not a Klifrari," she said over her shoulder. "But Birch told me to help you if I saw you."

"You've heard from Birch?" I said eagerly, following her toward the fire.

"Yes, he got your message, and a Blockade Runner brought a message from him for me. He must have guessed you'd come this way."

She sat down with the others. They ignored us.

"Birch has been busy back in Rustypike. He's pressured the

council, and they've agreed to let you repeat your trial."

"They have?" I cried. "That's wonderful! As soon as I get home..."

"They want you to do it now."

"Now?"

She glared at me. "Now."

"But I'm...do they want me to bring blood over the mountain, or..."

She poked the fire with a stick. "Old Yuma has stopped all the Berablotha from using this route over the mountain. She's here in the valley by the river to feed for a few days. If you want to win your tota and the respect of the Klifrari, the council wants you to kill Old Yuma."

All the blood drained from my face. My stomach went sour. My knees felt weak. Luca grabbed me by the shoulders and steered me away from them.

"Who is Old Yuma?" Luca asked.

"The bear is my tota," I stammered.

"The big bear we just ran away from? They want you to kill that?"

I nodded.

"This isn't fair. They're using you to get rid of something they should get rid of themselves."

I was dazed. "I'm not a Vayda. Why would they ask me to kill something like this? I don't kill things; I heal things. And I can't kill a bear. It's my tota."

"Exactly! Exactly. Don't do it, Jae. This isn't right."

"This doesn't make sense."

"Good. Let's just keep going and wait for Sid. We're already behind schedule."

"But this is my one chance," I said. "I have to." I pushed down my panic. "I have to do this. I have to."

"No, Jael, listen. What makes you think they'll suddenly accept you when this is over?"

"They will..."

"Because if they wouldn't accept you before..."

"No, they will..."

"Why would they suddenly..."

"Because this is how I earn their respect."

"Do they treat everyone who fails their first trial this way?"

I disliked the question."I know what you're doing."

"I'm trying to help..."

"You're afraid of abandonment. You're trying to talk me out of this because you don't want me to become a Klifrari and leave you behind."

Luca's face reddened. "No," he said in a clipped voice, "I'm trying to protect you because I am actually your friend."

"Then you should want what's best for me."

"WHICH ISN'T GETTING EATEN BY A BEAR!"

"Skin it, Luca, I will not let you be the reason I fail another trial!"

His lips tightened, and he took a step back.

"I'm going," I said firmly.

He put his hand to the back of his head, and I flinched.

"SEE!" he cried. "That is why you shouldn't do this. Because the Klifrari treat you like dirt."

I shouldered my rucksack defiantly.

"You won't make it to meet Sid," Luca said, with a terrible realism in his voice.

"Yes, I will."

Luca looked down. "You know you won't."

"Wait for me here."

His face tightened, and I thought he might cry. "You know I can't. Even if I do wait, you'll go back with your people and I'll go and find mine. Besides, I should hide the Melodiac."

"Let Sid and the Gravs figure it out amongst themselves. Wait for me, and we'll go home together. The pass is just a little way from here. We can go home. We'll keep the Melodiac, or, no, we'll send it to Sid with a Blockade Runner."

Luca shook his head. "If you do this, I'll take the Melodiac and hide it somewhere safe. Then I'm joining the Blockade Runners at Hellspite."

"Why?" I pleaded. "Why can't you just wait for me?"

"Jae, come with me now and forget the Klifrari. What have they ever done for you anyway?"

"These are my people!"

Luca couldn't have looked more stung if I'd slapped him. He began to back away.

"I'll come find you when I'm done," I said.

We stood in silence for a while. Then, to my shock and horror, I burst into tears.

"Skin it, Luca," I sobbed, "don't go to Hellspite. That's on the other side of the Blockade of Grav settlements. If you go there, I may never see you again."

"Now that Powderkeg is gone, it's the closest I can get."

"But..."

"Don't do this trial."

"You know I have to do this. I'll regret it forever if I don't."

He reached out and took my hands in both of his. "Hey, hey, it's ok. We knew we'd have to part ways eventually, right? It was bound to happen. In the end, you're a Klifrari, and I'm a Blockade Runner."

I threw my arms around his neck, and he held me tightly. I pressed my face into his shoulder and felt his hand on the back of my head.

"Take care of yourself," I said.

"I will. You too."

"I'll come find you at Hellspite."

"I'll look out for you."

I stepped back, and without thinking, I stood on my tiptoes and kissed him. He leaned into it, put his hand on my cheek. For a moment, I came dangerously close to changing my mind.

I let him go, turned on my heel, and willed myself forward. I didn't look back until I felt like I was a safe distance away. By then, he was already gone.

THE PERSONAL LOG OF OBSIDIAN, ONCE CROWN PRINCE OF GRAVARUS

Ila has always been a domineering little widget. Even when we were married, she drove me half mad with her constant need to make the rules and break the rules.

She blames me, I know, for her banishment but was it I who let the secret slip to a servant who then told Aresis?

As soon as he found out, Aresis knew he could use my unsanctioned marriage against me. When my mother disowned me and banished my pregnant wife to Earth, Aresis laughed.

I hear his laugh many nights in my dreams.

"Where is the child, Ila?" I asked her as she pushed me, knife in my back, toward the shuttle. "What happened to our child?"

"He is in Eveness."

I turned toward her, ignoring the knife, which cut me a little when I turned. "The child lives?"

Ila looked offended. "Of course, the child lives! Perhaps I wasn't a good wife, but I'm a very good mother."

"Can I see him?"

"No! How do you think Aresis bought my allegiance? He knows about the child, and he threatens him."

I lifted my chin. "No one will hurt any son of mine. We will go and get him and take him to my mother in Gravarus. He is the heir to the throne, and all this foolishness about the Melodiac means nothing."

I told her to gather whatever she needed for the journey to Eveness, but she wavered.

"The child is here," she admitted. "A man with a red beard, who Aresis bought, found me in Eveness. He told me he'd kill my son if I didn't show him the shortcut through the tundra. I had to bring him with me."

"And what if you don't bring him the box?"

"You know what will happen."

I demanded that she take me to the child, and she led the way to a small shanty only a few feet from where we stood.

Inside, sitting at the table, studying a Gravarian text, was a child in early adolescence.

His skin was white like his mother's, and he seemed much older than I'd imagined. He looked up at me with large blue eyes. Ila crossed the room to him and put her hands on his shoulders.

"Creed, this is your father."

The child regarded me with quiet curiosity. Then he got up from his chair and walked across the room to me.

I knelt so I could look into his face and reached out my arms.

"Do you know how to embrace, my son?" I asked him.

He stepped into my arms and laid his head on my shoulder. Something inside me changed forever in that moment. A piece of granite long lodged in my soul shattered.

Ila made us food, and we sat at the table and ate as Creed chatted happily to us about his reading, about his playtime with another child he liked, about the sound the shuttle made when it took off every morning and night. Ila and I watched each other across the table.

After dinner, Ila sent Creed to his bed, and we sat by the fire.

I asked her what Aresis' plan was for the humans. She asked which humans, and I told her my humans.

"Originally, I was to bring him the Remembering Box, but you erased it. He has his own, but now he will need a musician to play music into it, and he will need the Melodiac to claim the throne."

"And when will he expect you back?"

"Soon," she said. "When I don't arrive on time, he'll go after the humans."

"What should we do?" I asked her.

"You know," she said, looking up at me with her large eyes, "that song does not simply give you control of one Gravarian. It gives you control over any Gravarian who hears it. It creates a kind of hive mind so that you can command large numbers of Gravarians at once."

"Aresis could have his own personal army."

"He could own the minds of every Gravarian on Gravarus or on Earth."

She was not reckless and wild as she was when I knew her before. Now, I saw she was wiser and more cautious. Yet still brave.

"You take Creed to your mother and make her end the search for the Melodiac. I will intercept the humans."

JAEL'S NARRATIVE

I backtracked for half the day and made camp by the river. I caught a fish and cooked it for dinner, but I wasn't hungry. My stomach was queasy, and I felt cold all through. Deep inside, I felt like I was sitting on a cliff's edge, buffeted by heavy gusts of wind. When I fell asleep, I dreamed that I was kneeling in the snow on Ram's head. Below me, in the valley, I saw Rustypike Outpost, Becky's, and Birch, but behind me, on the wind, I heard the faint wail of a fiddle.

When I awoke, it was still dark. I cut three big salmon mouth to tail and laid them on the bank, hoping Old Yuma would smell them and come around. The sun rolled slowly across the sky. A deer came to the water and drank. A raccoon emerged from the bushes and washed his quick little hands. A mink scuttled across the ice with a small fish in its mouth. At one point, a smaller grizzly came to the water, caught a fish, and vanished again into the woods.

I turned my mind away from Luca and Sid and the warm train and bent it on a strategy. How does one kill a twelve-hundred-pound bear with nothing but a hunting knife and a lifetime of spite?

I began to make a javelin, and while I did it, I came up with ten or fifteen very bad plans. The worst included getting her up a tree and stabbing her in the eye.

I could try Luca's method, which always worked: cut the leg, cut the arm, cut the throat.

How high up is a bear's throat, anyway? Could I reach it?

Eventually, I laid out an eight-step plan.

One: confront the bear.

Two: get the bear to chase me to tire her out.

Three: climb a tree. She'll follow.

Four: jump out of the tree and circle behind the bear. Stab her with the javelin.

Five: bear will fall. Spring onto bear's back and cut her throat.

Six: bear dies.

Seven: get tota

Eight: stride into Becky's and finally get the respect I deserve.

But I remembered Birch once telling me that grizzlies can run faster than a dog, almost as fast as a horse, which meant I probably couldn't outrun her and get up the tree, so the plan died a horrible, bloody death right between steps two and three.

The trouble with bears, besides the fact that they'll eat you alive, is that they don't kill you with one paw swipe – they absolutely ravage you. They bite you, drag you, claw you, tear your muscles out, snap tendons. I had one strike to kill Old Yuma or die in nightmarish pain and terror.

I made up a fire again, built a hide out of pine boughs, and watched the salmon slowly freeze to the river's edge.

Darkness fell, and I began to worry.

That night I dreamt of Hetta Hiliak throwing my tota in the fire.

"You never found the bear!" She cried. "You will never earn a tota!"

Morning dawned cold and sunless, with the smell of rotting fish on the breeze. I took my carved javelin and inspected it. Was it strong enough? Was my aim true enough? Could I down her with the javelin and finish the job with the knife?

With a growing sickness in my stomach, I ran through it in my mind. How it would play out. The part of the neck I'd have to strike.

My mind wandered. I thought about Luca and Sid, but mostly Luca. I remembered things about him I hadn't thought about before, like the calluses on the tips of his fingers, a little chip in one of his bottom teeth, the little, spasmodic way he rumpled his hair at the back of his head when he was thinking.

The sound of rumbling, happy snorts broke into my reverie. I opened my eyes and saw Old Yuma, her rear to me, quietly eating the salmon by the river. Her copper fur was frosted with gray, and she moved heavily like her massive size had begun to be too much for her old bones.

My heart stopped beating. My position wasn't ideal – cornered in my hide. If she turned and saw me...

Old Yuma swung her head around and sniffed the air. Her beetle eye fastened on me, and she released a long, misty blow. I slowly closed my hand around my javelin and waited for her to charge.

But she didn't.

She stood, mountainous and heavy as a train car, and blinked lazily at me. She looked tired and old. Like she'd had her days of chasing down big prey and had her fun eating humans, and now she just wanted to sit on rocky river beds and eat salmon someone else caught for her.

My conscience struck me. What was I doing here? Birch taught me that to kill an animal without a use for its meat or fur was murder or, at the very least, a terrible crime. Why would the Klifrari task me with this? This wasn't me; I was a healer – a Lithna. A Berablotha – a bringer of life. And if not one of these, I was at least a Yushta – an herbalist and a lover of all living things. Would the Creator smile on this destruction of his creation?

And the bear was my tota. A symbol of solidarity and belonging. How could I earn a bear tota by killing a bear?

I sat still for a long time, waiting for her to move on. If she left, my dreams could lumber off with her. I couldn't ever show my face in Rustypike, and I'd never get my tota. I pictured Ama the Yushta, her hair blowing in the heavy smoke of some potent herbal brew. The dark of her cabin. The sickening smell. The loneliness of being neither a Klifrari nor a villager. The people coming to her window with their open sores and rattling lungs and rotting flesh.

I was no Messiah. I couldn't live among the lepers.

Old Yuma was turned away from me now. I took my javelin with one hand and my knife in the other, crept out of the hide, and edged toward the river, giving the bear a wide berth. She tore contentedly at her fish and ignored me. When I'd reached the river, I stopped. Old Yuma lifted her massive head and looked at me again. Her eye caught on the javelin, and she rumbled.

I planted my legs.

Old Yuma let out a huge, lung-rending roar and charged me with long, rolling strides.

Her size. Her speed. Her massive sound. I knew I couldn't survive this. I threw my javelin at her, and it stuck in her shoulder. She attacked, so big she blocked out the sun. I turned, ran past her, then threw myself into the river, but she crashed after me, swiping, and one of her giant paws caught my shoulder and spun me around. As I fell, the water roiled and plunged me downriver into violent rapids. Before I could take a breath, angry water dragged me under.

I somersaulted, striking rocks and ice flows until I thought every bone in my body was broken. I didn't know which way was up anymore. I clawed at the water, desperately hoping to find the surface. I struck a rock, and the water crushed me against it. The water pressed into my mouth and eyes. Slowly, I dragged myself across the front of the rock until the current pulled me off and whipped me away down the river.

Suddenly, the current slowed, and I bobbed to the surface, coughing, spluttering, and bleeding. The river flowed more calmly here, dotted with tall gray ice flows. I swam to the bank and lay with my face in the icy rocks, hurting in every nerve.

I gave up. There would be no tota. No Becky's. No Klifrari life for me. Everything I'd learned and all my knowledge for nothing. I felt caught like a hare in a trap. They had set me up for failure. I couldn't win this battle.

Someone touched my arm and, in my delirious half-madness, I thought it was Luca. I rolled over and looked up at the translucent white skin of a familiar Gravarian. I couldn't remember her name.

"Aren't you the fortune teller?" I asked.

She took my arm and lifted me to my feet, but my knees buckled, so she picked me up and tossed me over her shoulder.

She brought me back to her hide, laid me on a pile of furs, and tended to my gashed shoulder and bruises. At first, I tried to tell her how to do the stitches, what to put on the bruises. When I saw that she knew what she was doing, I began talking. Maybe because I was so tired or because it kept my mind off the pain. A floodgate opened, and I poured my soul out to Ila, the fortune-telling Gravarian. I don't know why. Perhaps her silent, ghostly presence – there but not there – made me feel like I was talking to an imaginary thing. A fever dream.

When she finished tending me, she sat near the opening to the hide, put her hands on her knees, and listened until I'd spread all my grief and frustration before her like a picnic of old anger and disappointment.

When I finished, she waited a few minutes before she said anything.

"The Klifrari weren't always as they are now," she said.

I huddled under the furs she'd piled on top of me and waited for her to say more.

"In those days," she continued, looking over me like she was watching it play out in the air above my head, "a Klifrari wasn't a Lithna or a Berablotha or a Vayda; she was all of those things at once. A Klifrari could do anything, endure and overcome anything, and they were compassionate. They would charge small fees, a bundle of firewood for a set bone, or a single beaver fur for a hundred stitches. Helping people was sacred to them. And the ancient music bound them together. Klifrari Melodiacs were common, and every Klifrari child was taught their melodies. But when the Gravarians first began to arrive, life became hard. The Klifrari began to grow more mercenary, and then...Eveness."

"What really happened," I asked, "at Eveness?"

"I remember I was only a few days on Earth. I was with a few others around the fire when we heard this music and...I don't know what happened. I felt rage and helplessness, and I was rushing toward the village with murder on my mind, but I didn't know why. And then...I just stopped. The others went on. And they massacred that village. I don't understand what happened. I don't know why I stopped. I had this warmth inside me still, from what I'd had before I was exiled, and it felt like..." she paused, her eyes boring into the dark above my head, "...it felt like a candle driving out the dark."

"What did you have before you were exiled?"

She looked at me, a little dazed. "I was in love with the queen's son."

"Aresis?" I asked.

She pursed her lips and rubbed her hands together. "No, Obsidian."

I gaped at her. "You were in love with Sid?"

She smiled a little. "I had his child."

"What happened?"

"When the queen found out, she sent me to Earth. Gravarians aren't supposed to feel passion or love. But I let myself feel it, and Obsidian let himself feel it, and that is why Obsidian was disinherited, and I was exiled."

"What happened to the child?"

"He was born after I came here."

"After Eveness, the Melodiacs were destroyed?"

"Yes," she sighed. "Most of them were destroyed, and music was outlawed. No more song, no more instruments. Humans forgot how to sing. They stopped making art. There was no more color. No more song. They're not much different from Gravarians now."

I pondered this for a moment.

"How did you find me out here?" I asked.

"I've been following Obsidian since I met you at Eveness," she said. "Craddock sent me to get the Remembering Box from him, but...Obsidian wiped it."

"What does that mean for us?"

She considered the ceiling a moment, probably trying to

find the right words. "The song isn't in the Remembering Box anymore. Now that my son is safe, I've decided to switch sides."

"Then what is Sid going to do?"

"He is going to Gravarus with our son in the hopes that his mother will accept him as her heir in place of the Melodiac. She will probably reject him, but perhaps it is worth a try. It's no more dangerous for my son there than here."

"What about Aresis?" I asked. "If he sent you to get the box and you didn't get it, then what will he do?"

"He'll want it, of course, but that's why I'm here. To help you and to take it somewhere safe, where Aresis won't find it."

I felt warmth in my cheeks. "I can take care of myself. And I don't have the Melodiac."

Ila looked disappointed. "Where is it?"

"Luca has it. He kept going."

"Then we must meet him and get it before Aresis gets it."

"I have to finish this thing," I said. "But Luca will be near the pass by now."

"I can find him." She looked me up and down and shook her head slowly. "You cannot kill that bear with your bare hands. You know that."

I laid my head down on the furs. "I do."

"I will help you."

"It's no good. I'm not allowed help. Even this is breaking the rules and should disqualify me."

She humphed. "And are they not breaking the rules?"

"What?"

"Killing a she-bear is not an accepted trial for a Berablotha. And they're requiring you to kill your own tota, which is against the rules. They aren't allowed to do this to you, and they know it. They are counting on you getting killed by that bear. You must beat them at their own game."

I stared at her. "I can't...I can't cheat."

"You can and you will."

She reached behind her, pulled out something small and heavy, and wrapped in a hide.

"This will help you. But you mustn't miss."

I sat up, and she laid it on my lap. I unwrapped it.

It was my gun.

"Is this..."

"It might kill the bear," she said.

"Where did you get it?"

She smiled. "From Obsidian. You've used it before, I think."

"Yes, I did."

"Well, if you're absolutely set on being a Klifrari..."

"Of course I am..."

"And you're sure?"

My temper flared. "Everyone always acts like I have some great second option to turn to. Like I have a choice to be something other than a Klifrari..." I threw my hands in the air. "Luca doesn't understand! The Klifrari are all I know. I've lived among them since almost before I can remember! How do I do something else? How do I live another way? Whatever you think of them, whether they're mercenary or greedy or cold, they're all I've got, and they're all I know, and I must, I must be one of them and nothing, nothing will stand in the way of that. Not Ama, not Old Yuma, not the Melodiac, NOTHING."

"Not even Luca?"

"Not. Even. Luca."

"Nothing will change your mind?"

"I will not jeopardize this chance. I don't care if that bear eats me, I will drag myself to Becky's, and I will bleed to death on the front porch before I give up my tota."

Ila looked at me, taken aback, and I felt a little embarrassed.

"Well, then," Ila said, "you'll need two of these, I suppose."

She handed me a second, smaller gun. "The big one you can use far away. The smaller one you can use from up close. They may not work. Use a knife if you have to. And don't struggle."

I felt deep nausea in my stomach as I thought about the size of Old Yuma.

"That bear is so old she may be too lazy to kill you," Ila said as an afterthought.

THE PERSONAL LOG OF OBSIDIAN, FATHER OF THE CROWN PRINCE OF GRAVARUS

The shuttle arrived in the evening, though the days and nights bleed together on Gravarus, and one can hardly tell the difference. The copper buildings, still rich and shining after all these years because of the diminished oxygen, shone old blood brown under the light of the dying sun.

Creed looked frightened and shrank against me. I almost forgot that this was his first time on his native planet. I held his hand tightly as we walked to the palace.

The royal palace is a series of copper domes fitted with slat windows facing the anemic glow of the setting sun.

My mother's chamber is at the very top of the tallest dome. We waited outside for so long Creed began to fall asleep beside me. Finally, a handmaiden invited us in.

My mother's chamber was dark. She sat by the window on a settee, looking out at the city. She had diminished since I last saw her — withered until she was little more than paper flesh hung loosely over crackling bones. She wore a gray vervile pelt robe that threatened to absorb her into its heavy folds.

"Did you bring me the Melodiac?" She asked without turning around.

"No," I said.

"Then why are you here?"

"I don't need the Melodiac. I have an heir."

She turned now, and her eyes, large like Creed's, were not surprised. Her fur hat slid a little when she turned, and she had to push it back onto her wrinkly bald head. It was rather comedic and a little pathetic. I had honestly forgotten how hideous she was to look at, and I wished I had warned poor Creed, who would probably have nightmares for the rest of his life.

"I know you have an heir, Obsidian," she said. "I've known since I banished your illegitimate wife to Earth."

"But this is your grandchild," I said.

I knew my mother was cold and evil to the marrow of her bones, so I'm not sure why I believed she would instantly develop a maternal instinct she's never had in her before.

"I didn't ask for an heir; I asked for the Melodiac!" She said.

"But since I have a child and Aresis does not..."

"You're such a fool, Obsidian!" She hissed, standing and tottering toward me. "I never cared about who inherits the throne. You, your brother, that child, your wretched wife, the street sweeper, I don't care! I only used the throne as a motivation to get the Melodiac. That is what I want."

"Why? So you can have the perfect army to conquer Earth?"

"Well, I suppose when someone strikes you in the face with the obvious, you begin to see it."

"But Earth is protected and..."

"Our planet is dying!" She cried, gesturing at the shadowy city outside the window. "We run on solar power, and our sun is going out! We need Earth to keep us alive!"

"But the humans..."

"I don't care about the humans, and you shouldn't either."

"But the Creator made them in his image."

She laughed. "They say that, but the image is so marred you can hardly see it anymore. It is practically blotted out."

For some reason, this made me angry. "That isn't true!" I said. "There is much of the Creator in some of them. Even broken and marred, the smell of love and joy clings about them still, and they cannot shake it off. I only wish we could be more like them."

"Oh, we were once, a long time ago."

I didn't understand.

"We were humans once," she said, looking at me with disdain. "Still are, I suppose; just this planet has altered our genetics so it's hard to see. You might say we're a different race or clan from the humans on Earth, but we descended from Adam and Eve just like all of them."

I didn't believe her. Absurd. Insane.

"We came to Gravarus thousands of years ago when we thought Earth was too inhospitable for life, before the Age of Ice."

"But if we're humans, why does the music do what it does?"

She looked exasperated. "Emotion, Obsidian, is the bane of humanity. And music is the sound of emotion. We spent thousands of years training our minds, the minds of our children, to block out all unwanted chemicals and signals that cause love and grief and joy and anger. So, when music plays, and it unlocks those chemicals, and it makes us feel things we've been taught not to feel, well, it has a very potent effect."

"But if humans on Earth are our own blood..."

She sat down wearily. "Obsidian, you bore me. Go back to Earth and bring me that book, or I never want to see you again."

JAEL'S NARRATIVE

I left at first light and went back to the river. It had been on my trial three days now — four since I left the train. I wondered what Luca was doing. If he was over the pass yet.

Don't think about Luca, I told myself, *think about your tota. Think about Becky's.*

I spent an hour stuffing my coat sleeves with pine needles and strips of leather from my rucksack, hoping this would make me seem larger and maybe pad me out if I was bitten.

I found Old Yuma wading in the water, waiting for a fish. When she saw me, she looked annoyed.

With shaking hands, I planted my feet on the bank and raised the rifle. Old Yuma shook her shaggy barrel head and splashed across the water toward me. I pulled the gun into my shoulder, lined up the sites, and fired. The stock struck me so hard it knocked me flat on my back. I hit the ground, and for a second, I couldn't tell where Old Yuma was. Then her shadow fell over me.

The fear hit me like a lightning strike.

I reached for the pistol, but Old Yuma came down on me, her mouth gaping, her black, dripping lips curling away from her teeth. I rolled into the fetal position and covered my head with my arms.

Play dead, Birch had always told me, *and wait it out.*

Her mouth closed on my right arm. I bit my tongue to swallow a scream. I knew if I screamed, she'd shred me to ribbons.

Her teeth tore my heavy coat and ripped into the rags and dry pine needles I'd crammed in my sleeves. She rocked her head back and forth, biting me, and I felt her teeth pinch my skin. She batted at me with one paw. The blow was so powerful it lifted me into the air, and I crashed face-down into the dirt. She placed her big front paws on my shoulders and ripped my coat open. I was pinned—her weight crushing me. I couldn't breathe. For a moment, she tore at my coat, making little grunting snarls. Then she stopped biting and sniffed the back of my neck.

I closed my eyes and held my breath. Every hair on the back of my neck stood on end. My nerves were on fire. Every muscle in my body tensed. A tear slipped from my eye and slid down my cheek, but I kept my nerve.

She snuffled around my ears, then the back of my head. I could hear her slobbering mouth smacking and the tickle of her wet tongue. Then she stepped off of me.

Without meaning to, I gasped for air. Old Yuma, about to turn and walk away, turned back toward me. I scrambled to my feet and, thoughtless and mad, tried to run. Something in her must have snapped. She rushed me, clawing, batting with her huge paws, biting. She plowed me down, tore clean through my clothes, and her teeth sank into my left arm. The pain surprised me, and I screamed. The scream gave her more energy, and she began to worry my arm. There was dirt in my eyes and mouth, and I had no thoughts, just this blur of panic and pain.

Somehow, my hand, grasping desperately in my jacket, found the little gun. Old Yuma, her teeth deep in my shoulder, lifted me and slammed me into the ground. I took the gun, rolled halfway, and fired.

I missed.

All I could see were teeth. She let go of my shoulder and went for my throat. I pressed the gun against her big head and pulled the trigger again and again and again. I didn't even hear the gunshots. Blood spattered me. The bear didn't seem to care. She put her mouth around my throat and trapped the gun between my body and hers. I pulled the trigger one last time.

The shot burned my chest. Old Yuma lurched. I was still holding my knife in my injured arm. I struck at her neck with the knife viciously until she collapsed. Her weight smothered me.

I wriggled out from under her and crawled away, crazed and

half frantic, my knife still in my left hand, the pistol in the other.

Behind me, the bear lay in a pool of blood on the riverbank.

I wanted to run away, but I needed proof to take back with me. I crawled down the river bank and huddled under a tree to recover my composure. I trembled so violently my teeth rattled. A manic energy made me want to scream or jump up and down. I couldn't let go of the gun and knife, even though I wanted to.

Gradually, I began to calm down. I felt pain now, and my arms began to cramp. I looked over my bleeding left side and couldn't believe my good luck. Puncture wounds, no broken bones. She hadn't torn anything but skin, and my heavy coat saved me. Only my shoulder worried me. It bled heavily, and I couldn't lift my arm.

I looked at Old Yuma, dead on the bank of the river, and I tried to feel victorious. I'd done it. I'd completed my trial, but I just felt tired and...something else. Was it guilt?

I limped over to the body to cut off a claw to take back with me, so I could prove I'd done it.

Up close, Old Yuma was big as a mountain but gray all over, and I noticed now that her teeth were dull, a few missing. She was thinner than she'd looked from a distance and older than I'd realized. If she'd been in her prime, I'd have died in seconds, but her old teeth couldn't shred muscles and tendons as they had in her youth.

Poor old bear.

I pressed my face into her deep, furry neck and sobbed. The forest fell silent until, overhead, a crow took the message back to the forest, shrieking out the news.

Old Yuma is dead! The queen of the forest is dead!

THE LOVE LETTERS OF CAPTAIN HARRISON CRADDOCK

Darling Helena,

I woke up in a panic this morning because I've forgotten the color of the curtains in the kitchen. Are they green, or are they blue? Why can't I remember? And I think my memory of you is even getting a little blurry. It's like you're slowly receding into the distance. I can't tell you the fear that gives me.

I swear, nobody can do their job anymore. I have wasted more flint, furs, and wax candles, and, I'm telling the truth, the literal shirt off my back to get that Melodiac, and I still don't have it! My hands itch to strangle the old woman I hired to get it. Skin all the Klifrari. They're worthless. I will have to do this thing myself, or Aresis will skin me. He says I am a wasted investment. He says I've failed him at every turn. He says I'm not worth the stench. But none of this is my fault! You see that, of course, my love; I know you do. None of this is my fault. From the very beginning, this has been Paxton's fault. Stupid, slippery Paxton, constantly sliding away at the last second like an eel. Always skipping around with his brainless music and his reckless ideas. Jumping out windows and climbing on strange trains. He's ruining my life.

But don't worry, I'll fix this. I'm putting pressure on someone, and he's about to break. He'll get me the girl, and she'll lead me to Paxton. They're too dumb and moonstruck with each other to stay apart for long. Those two and their idiot puppy love nearly ruined everything. But they split up so the girl could go earn her tota. I should have known. Real love requires sacrifice, you know, and that one isn't ready for any real sacrifices.

Our love has made me sacrifice everything, hasn't it? I look in the mirror, and I don't know myself. I wouldn't recognize my own voice in a crowd. I used to think I was one type of person, and I find I'm another. I'm someone I wouldn't have spoken to a year ago, but are the kitchen curtains green or blue? Why can't I remember?

I can't stand this much longer. If I don't get home to you soon, I think I'll lose my mind.

Yours forever,

Crad

JAEL'S NARRATIVE

Eventually, I gathered myself together and went up the bank to my hide. I tended all the wounds I could reach and bound everything in clean bandages.

With trembling, bloody hands, I tied my tota around my neck. I closed my eyes, took a deep, happy breath, and ran my fingers over the little bear on the leather string. How smooth it felt. How right.

When I was done, I returned to Old Yuma and meant to take a claw, but it felt wrong. She'd ruled this forest for longer than I'd been alive. I couldn't leave her to rot here.

So I stripped the skin from her carcass, rubbed it down with salt and a special Klifrari curing oil, and laid it out to dry in the sun.

Then I fell asleep.

I awoke, hardly able to move. I unwrapped my wounds and doused everything in alcohol and peroxide. It burned as though I'd set my whole body on fire and made me grind my teeth in pain.

My muscles were made of dry wood, my skin felt too small, I had a bad lump on my head I'd only just noticed, and I had to hike over the mountain today.

It was snowing and sleeting when I left the hide. I took Old Yuma's pelt in a bundle on my back. It was heavy and chafed my wounds as if she was biting me again from beyond the grave. I took both guns, using the rifle as a walking stick.

At first, the walk was easy, but I struggled as it grew rocky and steep, and the air thinned. I'd lost blood yesterday, and my head spun. My internal compass guided me because I was too tired to lift my head. I watched my boots stepping one over the other in the snow. My face stung. The snow whipped me violently. My coat was full of holes.

When it was too steep to walk, I climbed, hand over painful hand, dragging myself over rocks and snow.

Finally, as the sun began to set behind the snow, I came to the cave.

Crawling on my hands and knees, I built a small fire and collapsed behind it. I had nothing to eat or drink, so I spread Old Yuma's pelt out and wrapped myself in it. It was stiff still, but better than nothing. I realized suddenly, and with a piercing sadness, that this was the same cave I brought Luca to when we first met. We'd sat right here, by the fire, and he'd played on his fiddle, and we'd argued about music or some silly thing. I couldn't remember now. How long ago had that been? A month? A year? A hundred years?

I huddled behind my anemic fire and shivered. The dark outside seemed bigger, the mountain more isolated, the wind more ghostly than it had then.

This, I told myself, *is my last night as an outcast. Tomorrow will be different.*

The next day I began my descent. I hadn't eaten in two days and could barely bend my knees, but I kept going—breath after breath, step after step. Years later, it seemed, I finally saw Rustypike nestled in a crook in the mountain, and above that was Becky's. I dropped to my knees in the wet snow and could have wept for joy. With my last inch of determination, I pulled myself up and stumbled down the hill toward Becky's.

Finally, the moment I'd dreamed of. They'd let me in. They couldn't stop me now. I took the little carved bear from my collar and stepped onto the front steps.

But before I made it to the door, Birch appeared and ran to me.

"Jael!" he cried. "Did you do it?"

I nodded and stumbled toward him.

He reached up and held my face between his scratchy hands.

"You look pale."

"It was a hard win with the bear."

"I see you're wearing your tota now."

"I am," I said, smiling weakly.

"I didn't approve of the bear thing, but I knew you could..." His eyes traveled to the gun in my hands. "Better keep that hidden, just in case."

"Shall we go in and get a drink?" I asked.

"Let's go up to my cabin first and see to your bites."

I felt the bitter cloy of disappointment. "But I was hoping we could go to Becky's first."

Birch put his arm around my shoulders. "You're dead on your feet. We'll see to the bites first."

He pulled me away. I looked longingly over my shoulder at the orange glow in the windows. "I'm not sure I have the energy to..."

"We'll come back."

I felt lightheaded and sick, so I followed him to his cabin, walked through the door, and dropped onto the cot.

"I'll get you some water and yau. Are you hungry?"

"I feel sick."

He brought me a small plate with a piece of bread and some venison jerky. "Eat that. It will help."

Fighting the rising nausea, I ate slowly and swallowed deliberately. My head was filled with sludge, and I wanted to slide into a heavy sleep, but I was so tense I felt like the slightest touch would make my tendons snap. I watched the fire, determined to stay awake. But the weariness overtook me, and I soon fell fast asleep.

When I awoke, cold light came through the papered windows, and steady sleet pattered the window pane. I couldn't remember where I was and looked around in a panic.

"Luca!" I shouted.

Birch hobbled in through the door holding an armful of wood. He lowered his arms, and the logs rolled into the woodbox.

"Headed to Becky's for a drink," he said, turning back

toward the door.

I sat up and put my fingers into my thick mess of hair. "What time is it?"

"Headed to Becky's," he said.

I stood stiffly and looked blearily around for my coat. Birch grabbed it from a peg by the door and held it out to me. I pulled it on and followed him.

As we trudged through the snow toward the yau hut, I felt dreamy and heavy in my limbs. I pinched myself. I'd wanted this for so long. I needed to be able to feel it in every nerve.

As we approached Becky's, it was already getting dark again. Before we stepped onto the porch, the door swung open. I expected a flood of light and sound, but it was silent. A big Gravarian walked out the door, followed by a man with a red beard.

Gregorikus and Craddock.

The Grav looked at me and his nose crinkled like I smelled foul. His eyes traveled from me to Birch, and his face hardened, almost as though he were irritated, and he strode off the porch and into the dark.

I felt an overwhelming confusion. I thought I was hallucinating. I hoped I was hallucinating.

My hand found Birch's arm.

"How did they get here?" I blurted.

Birch clapped his mittened hand over my mouth and pushed me around the side of the building. I dragged his hand away from my face.

"He's here!"

"I know, I know."

I pulled him toward the trees. "We need to get out of here. We can make it to the cave on Ram's Head by tomorrow..." My mind fumbled around like a child chasing a wayward ball. "We'll hide there and send word to Sid somehow that he's here, and then..."

Birch stopped and stood firm. I walked a few steps before I noticed and turned back to him.

"Birch, we have to go! Now!"

He knelt and tied a broken strand on his snowshoe.

"Birch!"

Something horrible was happening. My stomach tied in knots.

"We'll have to intercept Obsidian and Luca and tell them..."

Birch finally looked up at me. "It's already taken care of. We're safe..."

"But what about..."

"Aresis won't hurt us..."

"...Luca and Obsidian need..."

"...because all Aresis wants is the Melodiac and the boy with the fiddle..."

"...but he's going to..."

"...and so that's what I agreed to give him in exchange for our safety."

"WHAT?"

For a moment, the world stood still. The snowflakes themselves seemed suspended in air.

"You've made a deal...with Craddock?" I cried. "With Aresis?

"Craddock says Aresis just wants the book and the boy."

"But...how could you...what if...bearhie, this isn't possible..." I began to cry, but a firm look from Birch made me press my panic down the way you push a frantic dog into a crate.

"You're Klifrari now," he said. "We look after our own."

"You let me take my trial to get me out of the way so they could turn Luca over to Aresis," I said in a weak voice.

Birch fitted his snowshoe onto his foot and stamped his feet a few times.

"Does Aresis have Luca?"

Birch walked past me toward Becky's, but I caught his jacket and swung him around to face me. He lost his footing and fell to his knees.

"Jael, I'm an old man..." he cried.

"Tell me where they are."

"Remember who you are now, Jael."

"Tell me!"

His face set like granite.

"It doesn't matter," I said, letting him go and backing away, "I'll find him."

I took three steps and then turned back. "Did you ever even want me to be a Klifrari?"

"Of course I did, but this was the only way I could convince the council to let you take your trial."

Birch grasped a tree and tried to stand, but his knees wobbled. He foundered around in the snow.

"Help me up, Jael."

For the first time, I didn't see him as I had when I was a child – a white pine standing straight and defiantly alive against the wind and the snow and the cold. Suddenly, he was just a feeble old man who couldn't find the strength to get from his knees to his feet. Like Old Yuma, he was imposing from a distance, but up close, he looked tired and toothless.

I walked to him and pulled him to his feet. He nearly fell forward, but I steadied him. We didn't look at each other. Neither of us said anything.

I left Birch and went back to the cabin for my rucksack and supplies. Mentally, I worked through everywhere in the outpost they could be hiding Luca. How long had it been since I started my trial? Four days? Five? I sat down on the hearth with trembling hands and grappled with reality and hope. Was it even worth looking? Would there be anything left to find?

Someone knocked heavily on the door. I didn't move. If Birch wanted to warm up, he could go to Becky's. I had nothing to say to him.

The knocking grew more insistent, then the latch snapped, and Craddock burst into the cabin.

"Where's Luca?" We demanded simultaneously.

Craddock began to rummage around the room. "I know he's here."

"He isn't," I said.

Craddock grabbed me by the front of my coat, pressed me

against the wall, and then held a knife against my cheek.

"Tell me where he is," he hissed, "or I'll..."

I yanked the gun from my belt and would have shot him, but he grabbed my hand and pushed it aside as I pulled the trigger. The gunshot rattled the walls, and Craddock leaped back with a shriek.

"Put that down!" He shouted.

"See these," I tilted my head so he could see the scratch marks on my neck from Old Yuma's teeth. "I've killed worse things than you with this thing." My hands shook, and I think I sounded a little mad. "You think I'm scared of you and your little knives?"

Craddock dropped his little knives and backed away.

"Tell me what you did with Luca and the Melodiac," I said, "or I'll blow your brains out."

"You don't have the nerve," Craddock said. "Your hands are shaking."

"If I get close enough, it won't matter if my hands shake," I laughed, taking two long strides toward him. "And you have no idea the things I have the nerve to do."

I dragged the hammer back with both my thumbs.

"Alright, alright!" Craddock held his arms in front of his face. "I don't know what happened to them. The albino Gravarian woman caught up to him and warned him, and he got away."

"Ila?"

"I don't remember her name."

"What did you do to her?" I demanded.

Craddock looked embarrassed. "She got away too."

I jabbed the gun at him. "You're lying. I want to know where Luca is."

"I thought he came to find you!"

The sight of him made me sick. "Why are you helping Aresis? After everything..."

Craddock's eyes suddenly burned, and he snapped, "I didn't have a choice."

"But he killed all those boys. And Luca..."

Craddock held up his hand. "Don't..."

"He was like a son to you..."

"Stop."

"And you've betrayed him! You betrayed everyone!"

"No!" Craddock said. His voice cracked. "Luca betrayed me!"

"What are you talking about? You left him behind."

"All of this...all of this...is his fault!" His voice rose until he was spitting. "He's ruined my life! Both of you! You're ruining my life, and I didn't have a choice! I had no choice!"

I lifted my chin a little. "We all have a choice."

Craddock laughed bitterly. "You're so superior, but you don't understand. Sometimes, the 'right' thing, the 'moral choice'...the consequences are too horrible..."

The door behind him burst open, startling me so badly that I pulled the trigger. A little piece of the door frame splintered off and showered wood down on the intruder's head. Craddock took advantage of the distraction and dove headfirst out the window.

Luca stood in the doorway.

"You almost killed me!" He shouted. "Where did you get another gun?"

I ran to him and threw my arms around his neck. "I can't believe you're here! How did you get here?" I cried.

"I ran," he said. "Everyone keeps forgetting that I'm a Blockade Runner. Running is my thing."

"But Birch said that Hetta handed you over to Craddock," I said, holding him at arm's length and looking him up and down.

Luca snorted. "Do you think I would hang around with your creepy cult? I knew they were up to something, so I took off the second you were out of sight. Ila found me yesterday and told me to come find you and hide the Melodiac until Sid returns."

He looked at me and frowned. "You look awful."

"Killed the bear," I said.

"Liar."

"No, I did it. I have her pelt and everything."

"I don't believe you."

"I did! I can prove it!"

He took my chin gently in his hand and looked at the bites on my neck. "Are you...are you ok?"

"I've felt better. Do you have the book?"

"Yes."

I shut the door behind him. "The Klifrari made a deal with Craddock and Aresis, so we'll have to find our own way out."

"Gravarians don't like high elevations, so if we can get to that cave on the mountain, we can stay safe."

"Should we destroy the Melodiac?" I asked. "Then no one can use it to activate the hive mind?"

"True, but no one can undo the hive mind either."

"If we memorize the songs?"

"What if we get killed?"

"Ok. But we need to go."

I didn't want to take the open mountain path back to the cave, so we took the long way through the woods and past the glacier to an indirect pathway up the back of the mountain.

We were only a few minutes walk into the woods when we came to a narrow gulley, flanked on one side by the glacier and on the other by a steep, rocky incline. We started through it but stopped when we saw someone standing in the narrow exit.

"Oh, no," I whispered, "it's Craddock."

Behind us, Gregorikus and four other Gravs barred our escape. I turned toward them and drew the pistol, but someone stepped up behind me and twisted it out of my hand.

I whirled around, and my stomach bottomed out. Birch stood between me and my escape, aiming my gun at Luca. I looked at him in horror, but I couldn't think of anything to say.

Craddock and the Gravs tied our hands and led us out of the gulley and around the glacier toward the outpost. The train tracks ran through the trees here. A dozen yards from the trees, a Gravarian sat beside a small fire, illuminated in the darting red glow like a squatting demon.

We had met Aresis at last.

"Untie their hands," he said. His voice was very soft and

a little high. He stood, and I was surprised to find that he was rather small, very human-like in his build, and he was missing his left eye and ear. He reminded me of a little maimed greyhound.

"Give me the book," he said.

Craddock took the Melodiac from Luca's rucksack and handed it to him. Aresis licked his thumb and flipped through it calmly until he found what he was looking for.

"They say that you can play this," he said to Luca.

Luca nodded slowly.

"Then do so, please."

Aresis took a little black box from his shirt.

"Is that a Remembering Box?" Luca asked.

"It is."

Luca knelt in the snow, took his beautiful, hand-carved fiddle from his rucksack, and gently unwrapped it. He held it for a moment, looking down at it with love. Then he stood and took it by the neck.

"Now play the Bee Song, please," Aresis asked.

Luca lifted the fiddle to his chin and laid the bow to the strings. One note sang out before Aresis held up his hand, and Luca stopped.

"Please note that Gregorikus and I have stopped our ears with cotton, so don't imagine you can play the wrong song and make us go mad. Craddock will be sure you do the right thing."

I looked at Luca. All the confidence had gone out of him, and his face was white as the snow. He backed away from Craddock, took the fiddle again, held it by the neck, and swung it against a tree. It exploded in dozens of tiny shards.

The Gravs forced us both to the ground. Aresis got his knee into my back and crushed my head against the ground with his hand. I screamed in pain.

"You forget," he said sharply, "that you have this as well."

He dug around in my pockets until he found what he was looking for. He held my flute in front of my face.

Craddock pulled Luca to his knees and stuck the prick of his knife under Luca's jaw until the blood trickled onto his collar.

"If he will not play, I'm sure you will," Aresis whispered.

"We had an agreement!" Birch shouted, hobbling forward. "You said you would not hurt her."

"And I will not," Aresis said. "But Craddock will kill him."

Aresis leaned down, his full weight pressed against my temple. I thought my head would crack like a melon under a wagon wheel.

"Now, play the song."

"I don't know it," I spluttered.

"I think you do."

I looked across at Luca. He tried to shake his head, but it made the knife prick him, and he inhaled sharply.

Aresis sighed. "Kill the musician, the girl, and the old man. We'll find another who knows."

"NO, NO," I shrieked, "I'll do it!"

Aresis pulled me up and held the remembering box close to my face. All the blood rushed to my head, and my vision blackened for a moment.

"You have three seconds."

"Alright, alright."

I took the flute and began to play, but my mind was blank. "I can't remember it," I stammered. "I can't remember how that one goes."

"I think you can," Aresis whispered.

I looked at Luca in a panic.

"Hum it for me," I begged.

"Jae, I can't..."

"Skin you, Luca, how does it go?"

Aresis held the Melodiac in front of me.

My eyes ran over the notes a few times, then I held the flute to my mouth and played the song softly, a little off-key. The Gravs, except Aresis and Gregorikus, swayed a little. Their eyes glassed over, and they stood rigid and blank, the same way Sid had on the train. When I finished, Aresis took the Remembering Box and handed it to one of his followers.

"Bring the girl and the old man. Put them on the train."

"No!" I screamed. One Grav grabbed me, but I struggled against him, kicking, clawing, and biting.

Craddock tried to tie Luca's hands, but Luca brought his elbow back into Craddock's face, stunning him and sending him stumbling backward into the snow. In a flash, Luca took a knife from his boot, ran at the Grav holding me, and cut at his arm. The Grav didn't notice the pain or the black blood dripping off his elbow. He swung his heavy weapon at Luca, but Luca was too quick. He dropped to the ground and slid in the snow, slicing the Grav's ankles so he fell silently to the ground, still holding me. I wriggled out of his weakened arms. Luca, already on his feet, held out his hand to me, and I reached for him, but someone struck me hard from behind and knocked me into the snow.

I rolled over and saw Birch standing over me, brandishing a walking stick.

Gregorikus hauled me to my feet and grabbed a fistful of my hair. I couldn't move my head, and he twisted my arm behind me until I thought he would break it.

Craddock tackled Luca, and they scuffled for a minute, rolling over and over. Craddock was heavier, but Luca had speed and youth on his side. He hit Craddock in the cheek with his elbow, knocked him aside, and then sprang to his feet. Craddock stood up slowly, wiping blood from his mouth. They faced each other with about ten feet between them and paused. In the struggle, they had both dropped their knives.

We all noticed it at once.

Something glinting in the snow.

Luca's knife, equidistant between them.

Luca and Craddock braced like runners at the starting line.

"I don't want to do this," Luca whispered.

Craddock let out a puff of breath. "Neither do I."

I thought they'd straighten and step away, but they remained as they were. For a moment, the world stopped turning; the wind stopped blowing, and we all held our breath.

The train shrieked and cracked the silence between them.

They both dashed at the knife. Luca reached it first, but, for a fraction of a fraction of a second, he hesitated, and Craddock snatched it from under his fingers. They collided.

I felt a grating scream in my throat, but I didn't hear it.

Luca doubled forward with a shout of pain.

Craddock caught Luca as he fell and lowered him gently into the snow as though he were laying a child in bed.

"Why?" Luca gasped, grabbing Craddock's elbows.

With one hand still on the knife handle in Luca's stomach, the other behind Luca's head, Craddock blinked tears out of his eyes.

"For Helena?" Luca asked.

Craddock nodded.

"Get off me," Luca cried, pushing Craddock away. "Get away!"

Craddock stumbled back with a sob and sat in the snow, covering his mouth with his hand.

With a sudden, puppet-like flail, Luca yanked the knife out of his stomach and slashed at Craddock, who lurched back in a spray of blood. Luca lunged at him again, but Craddock caught his arm and snapped it over his knee, and Luca dropped.

With all the raw energy of horror, I lurched away from Gregorikus, leaving him with a handful of my hair, and threw myself on Birch. He fell as easily as a scarecrow. I pulled the gun from his hand, turned, and shot at Craddock. A piece of bark shattered off a tree two feet away, but Craddock ducked away from Luca. Gregorikus charged at me, but I turned and fired at him, forcing him to dive behind a tree. Then I turned and shot at Craddock again.

This time my aim was true. He spun around and fell into the snow, cursing.

A hand clamped down on my wrist, and Aresis twisted the gun out of my hands.

Bleeding from his shoulder and the deep slash in his torso and swearing profusely, Craddock floundered around until he found his feet. Aresis handed me over to Gregorikus, who dragged me toward the train.

"No!" I shrieked, doubling over in Gregorikus' arms and kicking. "Let me go! Luca!"

Gregorikus pulled me toward the train. I dug in my heels, grabbed at passing trees, swung my head wildly.

"Let me go, skin you!" I shrieked, clawing at his arms with my fingernails. "LUCA!"

Gregorikus grunted and hooked his elbow around my neck. I wheezed. My head swam. I slapped his forearm and pulled at it, but he tightened his hold, and darting black flies appeared in my vision.

Ahead of us, the train puffed eagerly, ready to go.

Gregorikus dragged me into a car and tied me to a metal ladder bolted to the wall. Birch climbed in after us and sat calmly on the floor.

When all the Gravs were gone, I turned to Birch.

"Cut me loose!" I begged. "They have what you promised them, so now I can go!"

Birch shook his head. "You're safer here."

"Skin you, Birch, I have to go back!"

Birch took a cigar from his jacket, struck a match, and lit it with unsteady, arthritic hands. The car lurched and began to move. Outside, the train whistle wailed as if in pain. With a scream of fury, I yanked on the ladder with all my might. It budged a little.

"If you don't untie me, I'll pull this from the wall, even if I break my wrist."

Birch's eyes followed a trickle of blood down my forearm. I braced my legs against the wall and pulled with all my might.

"Don't struggle, Jael. I won't let you go."

"TRY AND STOP ME!"

I pulled with every ounce of panic and horror anger steaming inside me. The ladder shuttered. Outside, the ground flew past us, every second whisking me further away from Luca. Frantic, I lurched and yanked. The rope burned my skin, but the ladder groaned and snapped away from the wall. I fell flat on my back as the rungs separated from the sidebars and clattered to the ground. Birch approached me, but I picked up one of the rungs and brandished it.

There was a brief standoff. Birch trying to decide if I'd hit him or not. Me, blinking dust from my eyes, bracing myself in case I had to.

"I know you're about a hundred years old, but we're not on the same side anymore, so I will hit you with this," I warned.

Birch's hands fell to his sides. "I just wanted to protect you."

"So you betrayed me?"

"I kept you safe!"

"Did you see what they did to my friend? Bearhie, Birch, they killed him!"

"I'm sorry, Jael, but it's over."

"Then let me go," I held my hands out to him, pleading. "Just let me go back for Luca."

Birch looked at my bleeding, bound hands, then into my eyes. "Why? He's dead. There's nothing you can do."

I walked to the open door.

"Jael!" Birch shouted. "What are you doing?"

I jumped.

The ground came fast and hard. It struck the air out of me. When I stopped rolling, the train was already past me, trundling into the darkness. I lay still for a moment, gasping for breath. My shoulder ached, and my left knee stung. I felt blood trickling inside my pant leg. My hands were still bound, so I got to my knees and elbows, then stumbled, splaying awkwardly, to my feet.

Behind me, the train squealed, and its wheels spat sparks.

Soon, they would be after me.

I ran along the tracks until I reached the woods again, then I followed Craddock's blood trail and footprints back to the gulley. A cloud covered the moon, and I couldn't see, so I stumbled and groped through trees and around boulders calling for Luca. After what felt like hours, I found him, bloody, lying where he fell.

"Are you alive?" I panted, lifting his head from the snow.

I felt his hand grasp my elbow. "How did you get here?"

I pulled his coat open and tried to see the wound, but it was too dark.

"How bad is it?"

"I think it's bad," he said.

"Don't worry, I can stitch it and get you blood, but we need to hurry. Do you still have that knife?"

Luca held it up. "I'll cut you loose."

"You'll cut my hand off."

He shook his head. "I won't."

I held my hands out, and he carefully cut through the ropes. All his movements were sluggish, but I was afraid to hurry him for fear he'd slice off one of my fingers.

When he was done, I helped him sit up, unwound the scarf around his neck, and tied it tightly around his ribs. It was the red one, the one I gave him at Christmas.

"We need to get out of here." I felt frantically around in the snow. "I need to find that gun. Oh God, where is the gun?"

My fingers, wet and bloody, stuck to something cold and metallic. I grasped the gun, shoved it into my belt, and returned to Luca.

"Can you walk?"

"Maybe. With help."

I pulled his arm around my shoulders, and we struggled to our feet. He leaned against me heavily, and I staggered under his weight. I didn't know where to go. Back to the cabin? Off into the woods? We stumbled through knee-deep snow for a few minutes before I realized we were going in circles.

It was so dark. All the trees looked the same. The wind whistling past me kept changing directions. If I took much longer, Luca would die. Even now, he was bleeding, on his feet, half frozen.

For the first time in my life, my internal compass failed me. I turned round and round, the trees blending into a black wall between me and the sky. I felt my chest tighten, and my breathing came quick and short.

I sat Luca against the trunk of a pine tree, walked a little into the woods, and tried to get my bearings.

"There's no way out, there's no way out, there's no way out," screamed a voice in my head.

"Oh God, what do I do?"

My face and hands tingled, and I sat in the snow, clutching my chest.

I was five years old again, and Birch had just left me alone in the forest. I could hear his footsteps crunching away, leaving me with the wolves and foxes and owls. The cold pressed down on me, sharp as broken glass.

Get your bearings, Birch had said, *from the stars, from the trees, from the weight in your gut. When everything fails, go south.*

Go south.

I pulled the lace from my boot and wrapped it around my two hands, leaving a length between them the span of a tree trunk. I used it to bite the bark as I shimmied up a tree. I got as close to the top as I could and looked out for constellations, but there were none. There was no moon, and the sky was masked with clouds. Tonight, everything failed me—even the stars.

I slid down the tree and sat frozen with panic.

"Oh, God," I whispered, "how do I get out of here?"

Then I heard running water. The glacier.

I ran back to where I'd left Luca.

"How are you holding up?" I asked, feeling for the scarf. It was soaked through.

"Um, I don't know," he said. "Jae, be honest with me. Am I dying?"

"No," I said with forced cheerfulness, blinking back sudden stinging tears, "you're going to be fine! But we need to keep moving, ok?"

I dragged him up again, and we staggered forward, but it was too optimistic. He couldn't keep his feet, and he fell. I managed to get him to his knees.

"Luca, try to stay awake. Please," I pleaded. "Just a little further. Just a little more."

He steadied himself on a tree, and we made it another ten feet before he fell again.

The sky began to fade to a cashmere gray, and I could almost see. Luca leaned against a white pine and shut his eyes.

Behind us, in the forest, I heard breaking branches and feet crunching on snow.

"He's sent a party back to clean up loose ends," Luca muttered.

I got down on my knees in front of him. "We've left a trail. They'll be able to follow us..."

"Go without me."

I almost laughed. "What?"

"I can't go on, Jae," he said. "Go on without me."

"I'm not leaving you."

"We don't have a choice."

"No."

"Jae!" He grasped my arm. He was shaking and pale. "You know the Buffalo Song."

I suddenly felt angry with him. "No, I don't."

"Yes, you do. I know you remember. You can stop Aresis."

"I don't care about that right now. I have to save you!"

"You don't have to save me."

He put his hand on my cheek and rubbed a tear away with his thumb. "This isn't about you or me anymore; this is about humanity. We aren't like Craddock and Birch. We can't trade thousands of lives for one. It isn't right, Jae."

I wanted to scream at him. To make him understand. Why was he so stubborn?

"This is different," I choked.

"It's not."

"I can't do it."

"You can."

"What difference does it make?" I cried. "Aresis has the songs too. He won. It's over."

"If you stay here, we'll both die. This is the only way out of this, and you're the only thing standing between Aresis and the rest of humanity."

I knew he was right. I couldn't bear it, but I knew he was right. I touched my forehead to his and held his face between my hands. "I love you more than anything."

"And I love you."

I tried to turn and run, but I couldn't let go of him.

"Go, Jae!"

I heard the Gravarians crashing through the woods.

"I can't do this," I sobbed. "Please, don't make me."

"GO!"

I wept and clung to him, but he pushed me away.

"Go! Now! Go!"

I took off my coat, wrapped it around him, and handed him the gun. "Try to stay warm."

"Ok, now go."

I kissed his forehead. "Hang on. I'll come back for you."

"Go!"

"I'll come back. I promise."

I took one last look at him, then shut my eyes and ran.

For a few minutes, I tore blindly through the trees with no idea where I was going.

Soon, I heard running water. The glacier rose above me, blue like a frozen shard of sky. A little trickle of water ran from a narrow crack in the ice and along the ground in a shallow rivulet.

Two quick gunshots rang out of the woods, then a shout, and a third gunshot. I stopped, my stomach turned, and I vomited. I heard a commotion nearby, and I glimpsed a Gravarian coming toward me through the trees.

I crawled to the crack and peered into the narrow opening. It was a little wider than my shoulders and tall enough to crawl on my hands and knees. I felt sure it would lead me through the glacier, and the Gravarian wouldn't be able to follow me.

I crawled in. My shoulders brushed ice walls on either side. I groped, my knees slipping, my pants tearing on jags in the ice.

I'd made it six feet when I heard someone scrambling behind me.

I looked back and could barely see Gregorikus' silhouette crawling in after me. He reached out, and his fingers brushed the soles of my boots. Panicking, I scrambled forward, but my head hit a wall. I felt along it frantically, looking for the opening.

Gregorikus pounded at the walls with something sharp and metallic. It clanked, and I heard the glacier groan. With trembling hands and short breath, I ran my hands over the ice until I found where the tunnel continued—a low opening, barely tall enough for me to fit into lying down. If the glacier shifted, it would smear me across bedrock like an ant under a shoe.

I rolled onto my back, my arms above my head, and wiggled into the tiny slat. I felt a crack in the ceiling with my fingers and pulled. I tried to push with my feet, but the ceiling was so low I couldn't bend my knees. I wriggled my body forward, inch by inch, and the walls around me moaned. The glacier was an old man, weary, trying to turn over in bed.

As the tunnel grew tighter, my nose scraped the ice above me. I could smell my own breath. Water dripped into my eyes. Ridges beneath me cut into my back. My chest felt crushed. My breathing too fast. I couldn't move back, and I could barely move forward. Any moment, I would be pinned.

I couldn't breathe.

It was pitch black.

I lay in a frozen coffin.

I was buried alive.

I panicked. I couldn't thrash around, and I couldn't scream, so I just dug my nails into the ice and screwed up my eyes, and let out a silent shriek. I began to sob, and for a moment, I indulged myself. Then I realized that I was still stuck, crying or not crying, and I was running out of oxygen faster this way. If I didn't hurry, I'd suffocate.

In my mind, I imagined Birch giving me his coldest look.

"You're a Klifrari," he would say, "and Klifrari are made of ice and stone."

I started struggling forward again, sliding millimeter by millimeter. Then, suddenly, my fingers felt a ledge. I gripped it and pulled. There was a great, painful scraping, and I broke free. I felt a burst of cold air and tumbled into the pale light of dawn and landed on wet snow.

"Yes!" I shouted hoarsely. I turned over, buried my face in my hands, and praised God with every fiber of my being.

Behind me, Gregorikus swore and screamed and pounded against the ice. He was too broad to follow me.

I lay in the snow for a moment, filling my lungs with the sharp, cold air. I wanted to lay there until the snow covered me, and I slept peacefully forever under an endless white blanket.

But something inside me pulled me to my feet again, made my weary legs move.

All the adrenaline was gone now, and dredging exhaustion racked every nerve. Sprawling, stumbling, grunting with every step, I kept moving. I couldn't give up. I wouldn't give up. My mind was in a cloud; I didn't know where I was until I found myself leaning against the door frame of Birch's cabin.

I snatched the percolator from the stove and took a long gulp of cold yau, and a little of the fog lifted from my head. I took the rifle I'd left behind, went around back and found the dog team, tied them to the sled, and started back toward the gully.

It felt like hours since I'd left Luca, but from the sun, I calculated it had been less than an hour. Perhaps only twenty minutes.

Luca lay in a red puddle. He had the pistol in his hand and ten feet away lay two dead Gravs.

The woods stood silent. Snowflakes fell like ash.

With numb, blundering fingers, I felt for his pulse and found a light, thready beat in his neck. I dragged him onto the sled, and the dogs carried us smoothly and quickly through the woods to Becky's.

A few Klifrari eyed me nervously through the shimmering glass window as I left Luca on the porch and pounded on the door. Ced, the bouncer, opened the door a crack and peered out at me.

"No admission without a tota," he droned.

"I have a tota!" I shouted.

He slammed the door.

Cursing him, I pounded again. This time, when he looked out, I held up my tota.

He stepped aside. "You can come in but not your friend."

"But he's with me."

Shaking his head, Ced slammed the door in my face.

Boiling with anger, I hammered on the door with my fist until the entire building shuddered. "Let me in! I'm Klifrari!"

Nothing.

"Just let me speak to someone!"

No response.

With a scream of fury, I came back onto the porch and punched the wall. A sheet of snow slid off the roof.

I looked down at Luca, whose face was now the color of the gray sky. Through the window, I glimpsed a few Klifrari looking curiously out at us.

I saw red.

I picked up a rocking chair and hurled it through the window, sending glass and customers scattering. I waited a second for them to get out of the way, then climbed in through the broken window.

The room went dead silent. Everyone stared at me with their mouths hanging open. The bouncer strode toward me, but I held my tota out at arm's length.

"I have a right to be here!"

"It's alright, Ced," Hetta Hiliak came around the counter. My spirits sank when I saw her and my tattered courage failed.

"I'll...I'll repair the window," I faltered.

"No, no," she said. "Ced shouldn't have kept you out."

"I need blood and medical supplies."

"For yourself?" She asked.

"For my friend. He's dying."

Hetta sniffed and turned back toward the kitchen. "I'm

afraid we cannot treat him unless he's Klifrari."

"What?" I stammered. "That's not the rule..."

"That's the rule now."

"I have my tota now! You're obligated to help me!"

"If you needed blood, then yes."

"I'll pay you!"

She snorted. "With what?"

"I'll pay you later, with interest."

"If you're not going to buy a drink, then leave."

"But Hetta..."

"Go."

"Please!"

"Go!"

Reeling, I returned to the porch.

Inside, a hum of conversation began to grow again. Glasses clanked. A few people laughed.

I struck the log walls with both my hands and screamed.

Everything I cared about was melting away like snowflakes in blood. Something in me cracked like ice on a waterfall. Taking the rifle from the sled, I climbed back through the broken window, snatched a mug from the hands of a big man in a bear jacket, jumped onto a table, and threw the mug into the fire. It shattered loudly, and the fire blazed out, catching everyone's attention. The room rumbled, but I held up my hands and looked at them with such anger they fell silent.

"I have two things I would like to say!" I shouted. "First, I rescind my tota! I no longer want to be a mercenary, heartless pile of bearhie like the rest of you!"

I ripped my tota from my neck and threw it in the fire. "Second! Birch is gone, he's probably dead, and I am his heir. That means that this yau hut now belongs to me. I am collecting on two years back rent right now."

I turned toward Hetta. "I will accept payment in blood and medical supplies."

"And I will not give them to you," she said slowly. "What gives you the right to come in here and break things and..."

I racked the rifle. "Get off my property or I'll blow you off."

Most of the people in that room had never even seen a gun before. They fidgeted and cast uncertain glances at each other.

Ced came toward me, followed by two big men. I held the gun up, tensed my shoulders, and fired it into the ceiling. It was so loud it made my ears ring.

Half a beat of silence, and then the room erupted. Chairs scraped, tables overturned, people shoved each other out of the way and fell out the door and broken window. In seconds, Becky's was empty.

Once the air cleared, I dragged Luca inside and left him on the floor by the fire while I ran into the basement and found the blood cabinet. It was locked, but I used the butt of the gun to break it open. I grabbed three bags, a suturing kit, and a roll of bandages.

With ragged breaths and quivering fingers, I prepared the needle and started the transfusion. Dark blood flowed through the thick tube and into Luca's arm.

I checked his neck for a pulse.

All my breath left me. There was no pulse.

I checked his wrist.

"No, no, no, no," I rolled him flat on his back, put my palms on the center of his chest, and pushed with all my weight until I felt ribs crack. Then I pumped.

One, two, three, four...

My arms ached.

...seventeen, eighteen, nineteen...

My shoulders felt like they might seize.

...twenty-eight, twenty-nine, thirty...

Anger filled me up like a flooding river rises to your chin, your nose, the tips of your ears.

I breathed air into his mouth and pumped again.

One, two, three, four...

I felt disoriented. Was this my trial? Had I done my trial?

...fourteen, fifteen, sixteen...

Had Old Yuma been real or just a phantom?

...twenty-eight, twenty-nine, thirty...

I felt his neck again. Still nothing.

Killing the bear was easier than this.

One, two, three, four...

Killing is easier than saving life.

...fourteen, fifteen, sixteen..

My shoulders hurt so badly I had to bite my tongue against the pain. I felt the punctures opening all down my arms. Hurting again. Bleeding again.

...twenty-one, twenty-two, twenty-three...

Why was this so much harder than the trial?

I checked his neck again and still felt nothing. I breathed into his mouth.

One, two, three, four...

I would make him live.

...ten, eleven, twelve, thirteen...

I would cram the life back into him.

...nineteen, twenty, twenty-one...

"Dear God!" I screamed, "Make him breathe!"

...twenty-eight, twenty-nine, thirty...

"Breathe, skin you!"

I felt his neck a third time, and this time, I felt a light, thready pulse.

My hands trembled. My elbows could hardly bend. I tried to start another transfusion, but my vision was blurry, my hands were made of wood.

I couldn't find a vein. My eyes filled with tears of exhaustion, of frustration.

Oh, God, I can't do this.

I took a deep breath, then let out a long sigh. I closed my eyes. I'd done this a hundred times. This was my gift from God. I was born to be a healer, a steady hand, a skillful touch. Perhaps I couldn't be a Klifrari, but this...this I could do.

I relaxed, put my head between my knees, sent up an inarticulate prayer. Breathed.

My vision cleared, my hands steadied, the blood flowed into

Luca's body. I took up a needle and began to suture.

When I finished, I took the bearskin and threw it over us.

That night, Old Yuma's heavy pelt kept us alive, safe from the cold.

THE PERSONAL LOG OF OBSIDIAN, ONCE CROWN PRINCE OF GRAVARUS

I left Gravarus because there was nothing to be done but travel back to Earth and bring my mother that wretched book. I hoped that Ila got it from the humans and we could make this quick. In every way, we are back to square one and are now separated, which plays right into Aresis' hands. I am a massively stupid being. I am the stupidest of all beings. I am, as humans would say, a nincowpoop.

Of course, things were bound to get worse. Things always get worse. The moment we stepped off the shuttle on Earth, Ila met us and told us that everything had gone very wrong. So wrong, it seemed, she wasn't confident there was anything we could do to fix it.

The last she knew, the Melodiac was in Aresis' hands, and Aresis had both humans. Aresis was on his way here on the train, meaning to take the book to my mother and win my birthright. Again. And I'm sure he has the same plan I did, to play the song for my mother and become the hive-mind leader of Gravarus. Add to that, of course, the minor detail that he also plans to destroy every living thing on Earth.

I can't allow that.

Maybe Earth doesn't deserve a second chance, but neither does Gravarus.

Upsetting as it may be to think about, I now have more on Earth than on Gravarus. My wife, my son, Luca and Jael. And so, I suppose I am really more of an Earthling than a Gravarian now. And I want Earth to survive because I want them to survive, and I think I almost want all humans to survive. If nothing else, Christmas should survive.

We were standing outside the shuttle, discussing what to do next, when I noticed a little human man in a bright red sweater dart behind a nearby shanty.

Humans are never in Gravarian settlements, except when Blockade Runners try to sneak past, and even then, they won't come into one.

I felt uneasy, so I steered Ila and Creed away from the shuttle toward Ila's shanty. We were four or five steps away when there was a flash, a boom, and the shuttle exploded into a thousand little shards.

I pulled Ila and Creed to the ground and tried to shield them from the burning debris raining down on us.

When the air cleared, we sat up. The shuttle was no more than a pile of twisted metal.

"Someone else doesn't want Aresis leaving Earth," Ila said.

"The train!" I cried, springing to my feet. "He might be after the train. What if the humans are on the train?"

I don't know what I planned to do. I left the settlement and ran toward the tracks. As I came around a curve in the line, I saw humans, one in a distinctly bright red sweater, pushing wooden boxes onto the tracks.

The rails began to tremble. I couldn't see the train because of a bend in the line, but I knew it was coming.

"DON'T!" I shouted, waving my arms. "THERE ARE PEOPLE ON THAT TRAIN!"

The humans scattered into the trees. Then the engine burst around the corner and shattered the boxes.

The explosion knocked me off my feet. There was the concussion, then an aching groan as the heavy engine tipped slowly over and thudded onto its side. I covered my head with my arms and curled into a tight ball. Bits of flaming wood shattered tree branches above me and fell sizzling into the snow.

When the air cleared, I sat up and looked around. The engine lay smoking, and the two cars behind quietly burned. I ran to the wreck, fearful of what I might find.

I found an old man dead under one of the cars.

A few dead Gravarians.

No sign of Aresis.

A man with a red beard lay about twenty feet from the wreck, flung against a tree by the explosion. He bled from his shoulder and torso and was severely burned. His face was smeared with blood and soot, and he blinked rapidly. I approached him cautiously.

"Are you the brother?" he rasped.

"I'm looking for the two young humans."

He closed his eyes and let out a long, shuddering sob.

I knelt beside him, and he reached his hand out, clutched my sweater, and pulled me close.

"Take this letter," he said, cramming a piece of paper into my hand. "Please, I'm begging you, and mail it for me. She must get my last letter, or she'll never know how hard I tried."

His eyes bulged and his body convulsed. "She needs to know that she must run."

"What happened to Aresis?" I asked.

"Aresis escaped the explosion," Craddock rasped. "He saw smoke coming from the settlement and he guessed that the shuttle was destroyed. Now he will go from settlement to settlement, uniting the Gravs on Earth until he has an army of his own. He will purge all the humans, and then, when there is a new shuttle, he will return to Gravarus and take the throne."

"If I play the Buffalo Song, will it set everyone free?"

Craddock nodded. "If he hears it, the hive mind will break. Or if you kill him."

"I will defeat Aresis," I said. "Then she will have nothing to fear."

Craddock clutched me desperately. "Do you promise?"

"I do. Now tell me what happened to the humans."

He coughed. "The girl one...she got away, I think."

"And Luca?"

"Aresis said I had to do it or else he would..." he coughed again and struggled for breath, "...he would kill my wife."

"Do what?" I asked with rising horror.

He looked up at the sky. "I cannot die! I have to live! Skin you, Paxton, you did this to me!" His face twisted in anger. "This is his fault! If Helena dies, her blood is on his hands!"

I shook him. "What did you do!"

"I think..." he looked at his wounds and then looked back at me with confusion. "How did this happen? Who are you?"

"What did you do to Luca Paxton?"

"Who?"

"Luca!"

"I did it for Helena," he said.

"What did you do for Helena?"

"It was all for Helena."

His eyes glassed over, and his body went limp.

JAEL'S NARRATIVE

I awoke to cold and the pale light of morning. A snow drift slid quietly through the broken window. I threw the pelt off and tried to get to my feet, but my arms wouldn't obey. The muscles in my shoulders had completely seized, and I couldn't move anything above the elbow.

I panicked. I needed to patch the window. I needed to set Luca's arm (skin me for not doing it last night), I needed to make a fire before we froze to death or caught pneumonia.

The thought of pneumonia sent ice through my veins.

Blood clots.

Dehydration.

Gangrene.

Blood poisoning.

I imagined every possible complication stalking us, striking us down.

With short, awkward movements, I managed to make a small fire while shots of pain streaked up and down my arms and shoulders.

I couldn't see the bites on my back. I couldn't reach them. I had to do something about them, or they'd kill me. Then I thought of Ama. I did my best to make the fire warm. I tucked the pelt around Luca as tightly as I could. It took five minutes just to get the snowshoes on my feet.

It was a short trip to Ama's cabin, but I waded deeper into guilt with every passing minute.

Birch's voice shouted in my head, "You're being dramatic! Walk it off! There is someone else relying on you, and you need to take time to deal with a few scratches?"

But what if I get an infection? What if I get sick? I have to keep going, or we'll both die.

"Then what are you doing up here, crying to the Yushta like a baby harp seal?"

I almost turned back, but by now I could see Ama's cabin. I stumbled the last few feet and fell against her door. She pulled it open and stood in the doorway for a moment, her head tilted a little to one side, listening to my heavy breathing.

"Hello," she said, smiling, thinking I was a customer, "you sound like you're in pain. Tell me, how can I help you?"

I dropped to my knees, grasping her elbows as I fell. She knelt with me, and her hands were strong with compassion.

"Ama..." I whispered, "I need help."

"Jael? What's happened?"

She made me lay down on my stomach on her bed and helped me take my shirt off. As she inspected the bites with her sensitive fingers, she made disapproving clucking sounds with her mouth.

"I'll get something to disinfect these, and then I'll make up something to relax the muscles."

As she went into the kitchen, I called after her, "I'm in a hurry."

"Don't be. It'll take a minute."

"Then you can bring it to me at Becky's. I need to get back."

"You need to rest," she said.

"I can't." I burst into tears. Suddenly, the whole story came tumbling out of me. I rushed through it so quickly and through such thick blubbering I don't know how much she understood. When I was done, she stood quietly for a moment, holding a wooden bowl in her hands.

"You truly got attacked by a bear?"

I wiped a glob of snot on the back of my arm and nodded. Then added, "I sort of attacked it, actually."

Ama smiled. "Throwing your tota in the fire might be the most sensible thing you've ever done in your life. Now I'll put this on your back, and you sleep. I'll go down the mountain and see to your friend."

I began to cry again. "I can't afford to pay you..."

"Oh hush," she snapped. "Bearhie, child, I won't hear any more of that Klifrari foolishness in my cabin. Come down to Becky's when you wake up."

THE LOVE LETTERS OF CAPTAIN HARRISON CRADDOCK

My beloved, the light of my eyes and the joy of my heart,

Ever since I met you, you have been the thing that awoke me in the morning and gave me sleep at night. You are my sun, my moon, and my stars. Perhaps I made an idol of you.

But you are my Aphrodite.

My love has driven me places I never imagined I'd go. And, yes, I closed my eyes to some evil, and I changed my allegiances to protect your life, and, in the end, I put a knife to the lamb I raised in my own home.

But isn't that what you do for an idol? Spill innocent blood at its feet?

In these last moments, I do believe in a Creator and that I will not fare well before his throne of judgment. The blood of Abel cries out against me from the ground. But I believe that my motives were good to the end.

We will not ever be together, my love. I will never see your sweet face again or touch your white hands or wake up next to you to the glow of a new snowfall. And I curse myself that I couldn't protect you. All of this blood spilled for nothing.

You must run for your life. Find a safe place high in the mountains and hide there. Do not come down, and do not live among people again.

I'm dying now, and I'm dying with sorrow in my heart. Sorrow that we will never be together. Sorrow for everything I've lost. And anger. Anger with Paxton, who did this to me. Because he did. History may remember him as the hero, but I hope you won't. He thwarted me at every turn, and so I hold him responsible. For my death, for yours, and for his own. He pressed me to this. What was I to do? I couldn't let him live when he could so easily undo my deal with Aresis, could I? I got no joy from what I had to do. And, in the end, he and I did the same to each other. If I killed him, then he killed me.

My beloved, this is my last letter to you. Be safe. Seek shelter. Remember me always as the man who loved you most...loved you into the dark.

Yours through all the fire of eternity,

Crad

JAEL'S NARRATIVE

I slept dreamless and awoke in the dark. The fire was dead, and for a panicked minute, I didn't know where I was.

When I realized I was in Ama's cabin, I felt relief briefly, and then a heavy pelt of depression dropped over me. I wanted to go back down the mountain to Becky's, but I was afraid of what I might find there, and I wasn't sure I could handle it. My shoulders were better, and I could lift my arms enough to rub the sleep out of my eyes, so I found some rosemary bread and a honey tart Ama had left for me, and I chewed them slowly as I stoked the fire in the stove back to life. The bright taste of the rosemary and the sweetness of the honey compounded my guilt. I shouldn't be here, resting and eating good food while Luca was suffering alone with a stranger.

But every muscle, every nerve, felt stretched like wet wool.

I set the kettle to boil, and when the yau was ready, I squeezed a little honey into it and went around the back of the hut to the greenhouse. I savored the sweet, earthy tea as I wandered through the rows of herbs and flowers and vegetable plants. Now and then, I paused to pinch off a leaf of cilantro or lemon basil and rub it between my fingers so the smell stuck to my hands. Above me, the Northern Lights danced like soundless visible music, casting a blue-green glow through the glass roof. I stopped in front of a potted dogwood tree in bloom and looked at the lacy white four-petaled flowers.

I watched the lights for a moment.

"Is this because I killed the bear?" I shouted at the Creator I imagined must be just beyond the lights, conducting the dance. My voice echoed, and all the plants listened. "Then why Luca and not me?" I demanded. "What did he do wrong?"

I waited in silence for some kind of answer. I almost

expected a booming voice, the same that had answered ancient Job in his complaint, would come from the sky and scold me the way Birch used to.

But no answer came. The plants grew, and the dogwood bloomed. The Northern Lights kissed the mountaintops.

"It's not fair! I'm the one who killed the bear! Is all this because I killed the bear? I'm sorry! Can't you forgive me?"

I turned back to the dogwood tree and touched the flowers, and noticed the drop of blood red at the center of the blossom, and something like an answer came to me.

All those years of striving and longing, and the answer had been right in front of me, all around me. I saw now that everything – the dogwood flowers, the kindness in Luca's eyes, the song of a fiddle, a line of buffalo undulating across unbroken tundra – all the bright and beautiful things in the world were just signposts pointing to the Great Artist who reached out, not scolding but compassionate and full of love, and offered his blood without asking for payment.

The Klifrari didn't live that way.

And I was not, and never could have been, a Klifrari.

And I was glad of it.

I went back to the cabin, took my tattered coat, and started back down the mountain toward Becky's.

THE PERSONAL LOG OF OBSIDIAN, FATHER OF CREED, THE CROWN PRINCE OF GRAVARUS

Aresis did not die in the train crash because I am not that lucky. Aresis will probably never die. He is so stupid, and rash, and ridiculous, but he will outlive us all just to prove the absurdity of the universe.

I returned to the settlement, but as I walked through the streets to Ila's hut, I noticed something felt wrong. The other Gravarians stood around the village, staring into the middle distance like they were waiting for something. I turned, and I saw him.

Such a scraggy little individual with his missing eye and ear. Ever the underhog, even now. When we were children, I never understood how he could bully me so effectively, even though I was much larger than he. I should have taken my mother's advice and retaliated, but it hurt me to do it, and it felt unfair. It doesn't feel unfair now.

When I saw him, I realized what he meant to do. I realized what he was doing. He had the Remembering Box, and he was going to brainwash me like the others. So I closed my ears and ran to get Ila and Creed, but when I reached the house, they were nowhere to be seen, and all their scant belongings were gone. I can only hope they escaped.

Aresis stood in the doorway, and he frowned at me. When I turned to run, I faced a wall of hive-mind Gravarians. They closed in on me, with their eyes blank and their arms reaching, and I realized that I was about to be killed, captured, or torn to shreds. I took my cleaver, and I took the head off the nearest Gravarian. I expected the others to step back and let me pass, but they didn't notice. They didn't seem to care at all.

I cut my way through them and left behind a trail of carnage. It was my most valiant and horrible day.

Now I am free of Aresis and have made my way to a place called Becky's today.

I remember Jael speaking of it often, idealistically, like it was a dream place, but when I arrived here this morning, I found the front window broken and boarded up and the interior stained with old blood. Not a soul in sight. I searched the building and found a freezing cold basement walled with cabinets. Inside the cabinets were animal skin bags filled with human blood—also medical supplies, boxes of salt, needles made from filed bone, scalpels. There were plants trapped under glass domes and leaves distilling in glass jars. Racks, standing in rows, held furs, blankets, skeins of yarn, yards and yards of woolen material dyed various colors, and crates of leather. In human society, this was akin to finding a basement filled with gold.

I returned upstairs and found before the fire a mess of tangled tubing and animal skin bags on the floor and, cast off to the side in a heap, I found Luca's plaid shirt crusty with blood.

I can only assume the worst: That Aresis found the humans and killed them, or at least killed Luca. Probably, Jael has run off into the mountains somewhere. I know she can live there alone and undetected forever, and I will never find her.

This is my fault. I should have prevented this. I should have protected them from my brother.

I am angry to my core. I want vengeance. I want justice. I want to look Aresis in the eye and somehow make him understand what he has done – make him feel regret, or at the very least, I want him to second guess himself for the first time in his life. And I want him to look at me, and instead of that sneering look in his eyes, I want to see fear.

I will find that Melodiac, and I will take it to my mother, and I will be king, and when I am, then Aresis will be sorry for everything he has done.

JAEL'S NARRATIVE

The blood on my hands itched as I stripped the caribou meat from the carcass and laid the steak carefully on a strip of bark. The sun hung directly overhead, bleary behind a chintz gray cloud. I'd already been gone too long.

I rubbed my hands in the snow and covered the carcass with a tarp, hoping I could make it back before the wolves got into it. The bones would make good broth.

The view was nice here, looking out over the cliff at the endless mountain peaks striking into the sky. I took one of the caribou antlers and sat down next to the little mound of rocks I'd heaped that morning. I set the antler against my knees and, with one of Luca's knives, began to etch slowly and neatly into it: L-U-C-A

I paused before I started on the surname because I didn't know if Luca had a middle name. I didn't have one, but that didn't mean other people didn't. Then I wondered if I might have a middle name, and I just forgot it.

When I finished, I laid the antler at the head of the little grave and sat next to it for a long time with my eyes closed, smelling the mountain air and the pines, and resting. How long had it been since I rested?

Someone cleared their throat, and I opened my eyes. Jasper Judd stood before me, red sweater and all, his hands in the pockets of his frayed trousers.

"What do you want?" I asked.

"The Klifrari told me about the cave. They said if you left Becky's, you'd be there."

"Did you find the cave?" I asked, a little alarmed.

"No. Seems I found you first."

"What do you want?"

"Aresis hasn't left Earth," he said, sitting beside me in the snow and taking a cigar from his pocket. "Want one?"

I shook my head.

"Anyway, I don't think he means to leave anymore, and I think someone needs to get rid of him if any of us want to see another spring."

"How do you know that?"

"I know things."

He struck a match and lit up his cigar. "Sure, you don't want one?" He asked. "It's bitter grass. Klifrari grown. Clears your head."

"No thanks."

"Of course, Aresis has the Melodiac and the Remembering Box, but he's greedy and paranoid and wants the musician. I thought I could use your friend to get close enough to Aresis to kill him. I want the Melodiac."

I leaned to the side and pointed at the antler headstone I'd made. Judd's face fell.

"Oh, that's a pity."

"Why?" I snapped. "Because you can't use him to grow your cult?"

"Yes, actually," he blew smoke into the damp air and watched it dissipate. "You could still help me."

"Where were you," I asked bitterly, "when Aresis and his men had us pinned down weeks ago? Where were you then? Because we could have used your help."

"I was right about everything, wasn't I?" He said. It annoyed me that he changed the subject. "And I know that you and," he threw a glance at the antler, I suspect to remind himself of the name, "Luca were friends...perhaps a little more. Don't you want to avenge him?"

"No," I said, standing up and brushing the snow from my pants. "I want to stay here in the mountains where I belong."

"Even the mountains won't be safe for you if Aresis keeps the Melodiac."

I groaned. "Please, go away and leave me alone."

Judd looked me over for a moment and sucked thoughtfully on his cigar. Finally, he stood up and tugged on his sweater. "Come and find me if you change your mind. I'm staying at Becky's tonight."

"Becky's is mine, you know," I called after him as he walked away. "You owe me for the nights you stay there."

He laughed. "Then come down tonight, and we'll talk it over."

As I climbed up toward the cave, I didn't see any smoke or light. The fire couldn't have died already. I wasn't gone for...how long had I been gone?

When I walked into the dark entrance, the fire was dead. I turned to get more kindling and nearly collided with Luca as he came in with a bundle of kindling under his left arm.

"What are you doing?" I demanded.

"It got chilly," he said.

"I was on my way back."

I took the kindling from him, and he walked past me, yawning.

"You said if I don't get up and walk around, I'll get pneumonia," he said as he crawled under Old Yuma's pelt next to the fire and watched me sleepily as I stoked the dying orange coals.

"You shouldn't leave the cave when I'm not here. You could fall over and hit your head or something."

"I'm not going to fall over," he said as he reached surreptitiously inside his shirt and pulled out a little whittling knife and a piece of wood, "my legs are the only part of me that feels normal. Someone broke all my ribs."

"You were dead. I didn't think you'd mind, and I see you over there trying to whittle," I scolded. "No knives until the splint is off your arm."

"My splinted arm isn't doing anything; it's just holding the wood."

"But you're flailing that knife around with your left hand

now."

"I don't flail, and I'm ambidextrous."

"You are not ambidextrous."

"Wasn't five weeks ago, but I am now."

When he said five weeks, it spun me a little, and I couldn't decide if that felt too long or not long enough. The days and nights melted like candle wax into each other until I didn't know where they began and ended. Only in the past two weeks, when I knew when I lay down to sleep each night that Luca would live until morning, had I begun to feel clean lines between the days.

"I need to check your sutures," I said. I tousled his hair as I went past him toward the back of the cave where I kept the medical supplies. "Don't overwork your arm."

"You said I should move it a little to work out the stiffness."

I sighed. "I know, I know."

"You're very inconsistent," he called after me.

I'd hauled Luca and the supplies up from Becky's after I decided it wasn't safe for us there anymore, but I couldn't recall when. Perhaps a week after we arrived. Perhaps less. It had been a lonely, miserable five weeks. It was good to see Luca returning to himself, even though he worried me with his restlessness.

I returned with clean bandages and examined my stitching in his side and felt impressed with myself. It was good work, even under ideal circumstances. He lay still and uncomplaining as I ran my fingers over the tender tissue. His trust was a warm sweater.

Luca craned his neck to see the pink skin and the black knots. "Will I get a good scar?"

"A very good scar," I said, smiling at him. "Jasper Judd came and found me at your grave today."

"What does he want?"

I smoothed a bandage over his stitches. "Aresis is looking for you, but I told Judd you're dead."

"Did he buy it?"

I shrugged. "I think so."

"Shouldn't you be dead too?"

"I was planning to make myself a grave too, but Judd found me first."

"Does he want our help?"

"Maybe," I said as I set to cooking the caribou steaks over the fire. Luca got up. I opened my mouth to tell him to sit down, but he gave me a 'don't even think about it' look, and I decided to let him be.

He walked to the mouth of the cave and looked down the mountain.

"What happened to Sid?" He asked.

"He's probably out there following Aresis like the other Gravs."

"What are we going to do?"

I slid the caribou steaks onto a spit mounted over the fire. "I can take care of us," I said. "We can live up here for as long as we want. Forever, if we like."

Luca kept his back to me. "Shouldn't we do something?"

"Like what?"

He didn't reply, just kept looking down the mountain at a bank of cloud rolling in. Outside, it began to sleet.

"I need to go down and cut up the rest of the carcass," I said. "It might spoil, or the wolves will get to it. Can you see to these?"

Luca came back to the fire and sat down. The steaks dripped juice into the flames and sizzled.

It didn't take long to hike back down the mountain to the carcass. There was normally a vast view of miles of snowcapped pine and the mountain range running forever until it dissolved in slate blue mist, but because of the warming air and the sleet on the snow, a heavy fog lay over the valley below and rose almost to the cliff top. It looked like you could walk off the cliff's edge onto a pillowy floor of cloud.

Someone was standing over the carcass, looking at me as I picked my way over the slippery snow. As I came nearer, I saw it was Sid.

I wasn't happy to see him, and I felt guilty for that. But I knew if he was here, he had failed his mission with his mother, and we were more hopeless than before.

He smiled at me. “I knew you would be alive,” he said.

“I am.”

“And Luca?”

I hesitated. Somewhere, deep in my gut, something told me to lie.

“No.”

His face fell. “The old woman said...”

“Oh, you talked to Ama,” I swallowed. “It's been a few weeks, so...”

Sid looked struck, and my conscience throbbed.

I walked away from the caribou to a bare nose of rock standing out of the snow and sat down on it, gesturing for him to join me. He sat beside me awkwardly, with his hands on his knees. He still wore the red sweater I made for him. We sat in silence for a long time as I watched the clouds, and Sid watched me, and then, very gently, he reached out his arms.

“You smell sad. Would you feel better if I gave you an embrace?”

“No,” I replied.

He sighed. “Good.”

“Thank you, though.”

“You're welcome.” He laughed, sounding relieved. “I didn't want to, but if it makes you feel better...”

“That's ok.”

“Aresis is still on Earth. The shuttle was destroyed, and Mother hasn't sent a new one. She will take nothing but the Melodiac.”

My frayed nerves felt like a spiderweb trying to hold together under the weight of a tree.

“With the Melodiac and the Remembering Box, Aresis can control every Gravarian on Earth,” Sid continued. “He could kill every last human, start his own little Gravarus, and with all the solar power and Gravarus on its way to extinction, he could be king, and no one could stop him. He doesn't need to leave Earth now. And Ila and my son are gone. I cannot find them anywhere.

I do not think that Aresis has them, but I suspect Ila won't risk the child by coming out of hiding until Aresis is dead."

Fear billowed up in me like the clouds rising to the cliff's edge.

"He'll be looking for you and Luca."

"Well, Luca died, so he's wasting his time."

"That makes me very, very sad," Sid said quietly.

He did look deeply, profoundly sad...and tired. We were all so tired.

"What do you want to do?" I asked.

"I spoke to Jasper Judd, and he says he has a plan."

"No," I kicked at a lump of snow at my feet. "I can stay here for a long time. There are other caves deeper in the mountains. There are other mountains."

Sid shook his head. "He'll find you eventually."

"But he won't," my voice was a little choked. "I know how to hide. He won't ever find us."

Sid put his hand on my shoulder. "But don't you think you have a responsibility to..."

I shrugged his hand off, got up abruptly, and walked to the cliff's edge. I felt his eyes on me and his question following me like an annoying gnat. I felt hard inside, like I'd swallowed paste, and I didn't understand why. My teeth were set, and I began preparing a scathing argument in my mind. For some reason, I didn't want Aresis to die, and it frightened and puzzled me.

I looked back at Sid. He sat upright, his big hands playing with a loose thread on his pants. He looked so soft and un-Gravarian in his big red sweater. For the first time, I noticed that his eyes, and all Gravarian eyes, were not different from a human's. And he had a very human expression in them at that moment: he looked scared.

"Don't you want Aresis to pay for what he's done?" he asked. "For Powderkeg? For Luca?"

"Technically, it was Craddock and not Aresis that killed Luca. And that's not the type of thing Luca cares...cared about. Just come and join us...me on the mountain. We'll be safe.

Forever. We can hide."

Sid looked disappointed. "I'm going to talk to Judd and work something out. We'll be at Becky's Yau Hut."

I stripped down the rest of the caribou meat, swatting the guilt away the way you swat mosquitoes. When I was done, I returned to the cave.

The cave glowed orange. Luca slept by the fire, wrapped in Old Yuma's pelt. I sat down at his head and hugged my knees. He stirred a little, wincing like he was in pain, and turned restlessly from his side to his back to his other side. I took off my jacket, balled it up, and laid it over my leg, then eased his head onto it. Some of his dark hair had fallen over his forehead and covered his eyes, so I brushed it back gently with my fingers and wondered if I should cut his hair soon; it was getting shaggy. Soon, he settled back into a heavy sleep.

I sat for a long time, gazing at his face in the darting firelight and thinking. For some reason, I thought about my mother. I wondered if Aresis had burned her home – my old home. I wondered if I had brothers and sisters; If she'd loved them

How had she picked my name? Had she thought about it for nine months, waiting for me to arrive in the world, imagining me a certain way, and then when I came, was she disappointed? Was it the white patches on my face she disliked or was it the way I talked or my affinity for the outside? Did I leave the door open to the snow too many times? Did I frighten people away?

I looked down at Luca again and was suddenly seized by a terrible fear. We had been thrown together by danger, and we'd stuck to each other because we had to. Our survival depended on it. But if Sid killed Aresis and life went back to how it was before, I felt sure Luca's feelings would change. He would get sick of my face, or my rough habits, or the way I loved the mountains. He might stay with me out of gratitude even when his feelings went cold, but could he love me in the quiet as he had loved me in the noise? For I knew I could love him through song and weeping, storm and stillness, and all the vibrations of time and space.

My eyes welled, and I wiped my nose on my sleeve. Luca opened his eyes and blinked up at me.

"What's wrong?" He asked, rolling onto his back.

"Nothing," I whispered, "go back to sleep."

"Are you crying?"

"No. Go back to sleep."

"What's wrong?"

I hesitated, then said, "I just keep thinking...if Aresis ever goes away, what will happen to us?"

"What do you mean?"

"You said before that we had to part ways someday. You said you wanted to go back to Blockade Running."

"That was a long time ago," he said, sitting up stiffly. "A lot has changed since then. Besides, Aresis hasn't gone away, so we have to stick together."

"But let's say, theoretically, that someone killed Aresis, and everything went back to the way it was before. Would you go back?"

His expression cleared like he suddenly understood what I was trying to say. "You're asking me if I would leave you if I didn't have to stay."

"Well, maybe..."

"If I did, it would be a very, very silly thing to do."

"Why?"

"Well, where else will I find a girl who can break all my ribs?"

I rolled my eyes and turned away.

"I'm kidding, I'm kidding," he caught my shoulder and turned me back toward him. "I don't want to leave. I don't plan to leave. You see, I happen to like you a lot. And I don't just mean that I love you because you saved my life, or because we've been through all this scary stuff, or because I don't have any other friends. Take all of that away, and put us back in Powderkeg with no Aresis and no Sid, and nothing that happened happened, and I think, eventually, we would have ended up together."

"Why?"

"Because I'm so handsome."

"Luca..."

"Because I've never met anyone who cares about me the way you do, and I've never met anyone more interesting and more kind."

"But I'm not kind. I was raised Klifrari and..."

"That's it, Jae. That's what's so remarkable about you. You were raised by people without compassion, but you still have it. You learned that from Ama and her stories, and the Creator made that a part of you even when Birch and all your people tried to force it out."

I stared at him like he was describing someone else.

"I want us to stay together," Luca continued, "until your habit of climbing up freezing mountains or my habit of jumping from high places finally catches up to one of us."

I smiled. "Well, maybe I won't spend so much time climbing on freezing mountains anymore."

He laid his head back down on my coat.

"If I could have everything I want in the world," I said, "I'd open Becky's again, and you'd make the yau, and I'd make the gash cakes, and someday we'd have six little kids running around tracking snow all over the floors."

"Why can't I make the gash cakes?"

"I'll teach you to make gash cakes if you want."

"And all those six little kids will have silly nature names, aren't they?"

"Of course. We'll have a Cedar, and an Aspen, and a Winter..."

"Winter is a ridiculous name."

"I think it's whimsical."

He laughed. "It's not whimsical when it's been winter for four hundred years. How about this? How about you get to name three of them nature names, and I get to name three of them music names? That way, you get your Cedar and Aspen and Antler or whatever, and I get a Melody, a Lyric, and a Cadence."

"How about I name boys, and you name girls?"

"Done."

I ran my fingers through his hair for a while. His eyelids drooped like he might drop off to sleep again. Just when I thought he was asleep, he said, "What are Klifrari weddings like?"

"You're going to think they're stupid."

He opened his eyes. "I will not."

"You're going to laugh and mock me for days."

"I promise not to laugh."

"Alright then. They tie the man's right wrist to the woman's left wrist and send you off into the woods together. You must survive for seven days with your wrists bound together. When it's done, if you still want to be married, then they untie you and tattoo a rope on your wrists, and then everyone has a huge feast. They cut the arm with the tattoo off if you ever try to leave or betray your spouse."

Luca laughed.

"You promised!"

"I'm sorry, I'm sorry."

"I think it's very sensible!"

"But so violent!"

"It's romantic."

"Yes, amputations are very romantic," he chuckled.

"No, it is. You're bound together forever, and if you leave, you lose a piece of yourself. It's a beautiful symbol."

"I do like that part."

I wanted this quiet, simple night to last forever. I wanted to sit with him by the fire and talk about our future until we went gray, but he frowned and said timidly, "We need to help Sid and Judd get rid of Aresis."

"I'm afraid we do."

"We can't raise six kids in this kind of world, can we?"

I shook my head. "I don't think we can."

We heard footsteps at the cave entrance and turned to see Jasper Judd standing between us and the night, his arms folded over his round chest.

"You look very healthy for a dead man," he said to Luca.

"Apparently," Luca said to me, sitting up, "you're a bad liar."

"Well, you're a bad diaper," I replied.

"That joke makes me wish I really was dead."

"I thought it was clever."

"I'm going to get up and go crawl into my grave."

"Be quiet and listen to the man in the red sweater."

Judd hovered in the entrance, looking uncomfortable.

"Come and sit, Jasper," Luca beckoned to him. "Don't cave to your insecurities."

I let out a little shout. "That was worse! That was worse than mine! Judd, wasn't that one worse than mine?"

Jasper sat down on the other side of the fire. The watery heat waves rising from the flames distorted his face and made him appear phantasmal. Unreal.

"I want the Melodiac. And I want Aresis dead," he said without preamble.

"You've said as much," I replied.

"And I think you can help me."

"How?"

"I've heard that you have a gun. A large one."

Luca and I exchanged a look, and I was about to shake my head when Judd got up, walked to the back of the cave, rummaged around a moment, and returned with the rifle.

"This gun, to be specific," he said.

"Don't you have a stockpile of weapons in Eveness?"

Judd's eyes shifted, and he ran his fingernail through a vein in the gun's wooden stock. "I did, but my followers turned on me. I'm struggling to find many who are...faithful enough for me to trust."

"Meaning," Luca interjected, "that you have no followers right now."

"I have high standards."

"And high turnover."

"Getting back to the point," Judd said in a clipped voice, "I want to use your friend Obsidian to get close to Aresis."

"Where is Aresis now?" I asked.

"He's staying at the old train yard down outside the outpost. As you know, when the pass is closed, the trains lie dormant. He's keeping the Melodiac with him there."

Luca and I looked at each other, and I groaned.

THE PERSONAL LOG OF OBSIDIAN, FATHER OF CREED, CROWN PRINCE OF GRAVARUS

I have returned to the mountains to join Jael and Jasper Judd and formulate a plan. I am pleased that Jael wishes to help us, though I am also apprehensive.

When I reached the cave, I walked in and saw, of all people, Luca sitting by the fire with Jael.

I was so happy to see him. I shouted and startled everyone so badly that they jumped. Luca got up and came to greet me. He offered his hand, but I pulled him into a great embrace. He slapped me on the back, and I slapped his back and probably squeezed the breath right out of him.

My spirits are up considerably now. We have a plan that might work, and I'm certain I can get the Melodiac back and finally rid the Earth of Aresis.

We have made our plan.

Jael will bring me to Aresis, drawing him out into the open.

Judd will hide on a nearby train trestle with the rifle. Once Aresis is out in the open, Judd will shoot him.

Aresis' death will break the hive mind. I will burst free of my bonds and take care of Gregorikus.

We believe that the Melodiac and the Remembering Box are hidden in one of the steam engines. Luca will find them both.

I do think this plan is a little too simple. Mr. Looks-Silly-in-a-Red-Sweater came up with it, and I have no better ideas, so I can't argue with him. I tried, but he threatened to back out, and I can't do this without him. So, I'm committed. But no matter, it will work. I'll make it work.

Of course, Judd wants the Melodiac for himself, and I want it so I can regain my birthright and that of my son. Once we get it from Aresis, I may have to overpower Judd and take it by force. This will not be difficult, as he is a rather small man – even a little shorter than Jael. He will be angry, of course, which will be entertaining. I'm almost looking forward to watching the little man fume and spit as I run off, laughing. Jael and Luca will support me – I'm confident of that. Everything is turning out well despite all setbacks.

JAEL'S NARRATIVE

"Who keeps the Melodiac once we find it?" Luca whispered.

It was morning. Snow fell quietly outside the cave entrance, the fire crackled, the yau boiled, and we huddled together, watching intently as Judd and Sid stood together at the back of the cave. Judd was talking rapidly over Sid's shoulder as Sid bent over a map. Sid looked like he was trying with all his might to pretend Jasper Judd didn't exist.

"I can use it," Judd was saying, "for the good of humanity. Not like you."

This finally struck a chord with Sid, who straightened and stood over Judd with his arms crossed.

"And what did you imagine I planned to use it for?" Sid demanded. "I will become king and my son after me, and we will preserve mankind and our own planet."

"No," Judd snapped, "you'll hand it over to your mother, and she'll wipe out every living thing on Earth."

"Not if I can control her with the Remembering Box."

"That plan's already failed once. It's a fool who thinks it'll work a second time."

"Tell me, Judd, how you plan to help mankind with the Melodiac?"

Judd smiled sickly. "I'll hive mind all Gravs on Earth and make them walk single file off a cliff."

"You forget that I am a Gravarian too!" Sid shouted.

Despite his head barely reaching Sid's armpits, Judd squared up to him. "Obviously, you'll know better than to be standing, ears open, when I play the song."

Sid grabbed a handful of the front of Judd's sweater. "You think I will stand by and watch as you destroy..."

"Bearhie, you two, calm down!" I interrupted, standing.

"You're getting the cart ahead of the horse!"

Judd and Sid still stared at each other, but I could tell they were listening.

"I think, for the moment," I continued, "we need to focus on one problem at a time. Aresis has the Melodiac. All we need to do is get it away from him. Who gets it after that isn't something we need to worry about yet."

Sid let Judd go, and they stepped away from each other.

"That is sensible," Sid said. "We will have a civilized negotiation when all of this is over."

Judd tugged his sweater back into place. "That suits me."

Luca got up. "Jae, I'm just going to stretch my legs. Better come with."

I followed him outside into the snow. We walked a little way down the mountain and around a jut of rock until we were confident we were out of earshot of the cave.

"Neither of them can have that book," Luca said. "They're both right. Judd is crazy, and Sid is too naive to admit that it just needs to be destroyed."

"Destroyed?" I said in a loud whisper. "We can't destroy it."

"Why not? Name one good thing that's happened since we found it?"

"Lots of good things have happened. We met Sid and celebrated Christmas and saw buffalo."

"Yeah, and also I got stabbed."

"That was a bad thing that happened."

"From my perspective, it was a very bad thing that happened. I'd like to make sure that it doesn't happen again, and I think destroying the Melodiac will help with that."

I considered for a moment. "It is probably too powerful for any one person to have."

"It's definitely too powerful for any one person to have."

"So what do we do?" I asked. "Obsidian and Judd will panic if we tell them we plan to destroy it. Judd will probably kill us in our sleep."

"I don't think we can tell them. We'll have to destroy it

ourselves."

"Right," I rolled my eyes, "because I'm sure they won't notice when we throw it in the fire."

Luca drummed against his legs with his hands and made a ticking noise with his mouth as he thought.

"I could tell them that you're too weak to come," I said after a long minute. "Then you could sneak in and find the Melodiac before Judd kills Aresis. Then we have it, and we can control what happens to it."

Luca nodded slowly. "I like that. That plays to our strengths."

"I hate it, but it's the best I can think of."

When we returned to the cave, we were met by the sight of Sid holding Judd off the ground by his sweater as Judd kicked and swung his fists and shouted obscenities.

Luca ran forward to intervene, but Judd, in his mad flailing, caught him in the stomach with his foot. Luca doubled up and dropped to his knees, wincing.

Sid gasped and literally flung Judd off to the side and then crouched down next to Luca with panic on his face.

"Did the little man hurt you?" he asked.

I pushed Sid away and pulled up Luca's shirt to look at his wound. Judd had kicked him on the opposite side, and not very hard from the look of it. I doubted it would even bruise, but Luca kept sucking in his breath and looking like he was in pain. He caught my eyes for a minute, and I understood what he was doing.

"Look what you did!" I shouted, standing up and whirling to face Jasper Judd. "I swear, if I catch either of you fighting again, I'll shoot you. Is that clear?"

"How badly hurt is he?" Judd asked.

"Unless you can push the plan out at least a week, we'll have to do without him."

Judd grimaced. "Then we'll have to do without."

Judd left that night so he could climb onto the trestle under cover of darkness and set a timed charge of dynamite in the woods, which, he said, would draw the hive-mind Gravarians away and force Aresis to move into the open.

The rest of us had to wait until morning to set out.

For some reason, I was afraid that Judd, when he shot at Aresis, would miss and hit me. This thought ran around and around in my head until I finally dropped off to sleep. I dreamt I was standing in a muddy train yard with Sid, Luca, and Judd, and I had a gaping hole in my forehead that no one, including me, seemed very concerned about. Judd muttered excuses about wind conditions and the position of the sun. I felt annoyed with him, and my head itched for some reason, and I wondered if I would drop dead or just live with a hole in my head forever.

Luca shook me awake just before sunrise. Sid was already up, waiting for me in the mouth of the cave. My hands trembled as I tied on my snowshoes and pulled the straps of my rucksack onto my shoulders.

"I'll be right behind you," Luca whispered as he leaned in and kissed my forehead.

I hugged him tightly. "I hate this."

"It'll all be over soon."

I kissed him one last time. Deep inside me, in the same part of my stomach that guided me when I was lost on the mountain, I felt that this plan was going to go wrong. Something about it didn't click in my mind. Perhaps it was too simple. Perhaps I was just too cynical. I hoped for the latter.

As we hiked down the mountain, there was no wind, and a thick layer of cloud covered the sun. Sid walked in silence, picking his way clumsily over rocks and ice. He seemed uneasy, but I was too nervous to ask him why. And it was too late to turn back now.

The train yard was a muddy tangle of tracks, about a hundred yards across. In the center of the yard lay a lone green train car tipped onto its side with its steel roof toward us. On the far end of the yard, leaning against the rocky mountainside, stood a peeling green roundhouse. Three rusty steam engines dozed in its musty stalls like draft horses waiting for work. The lines splintered out from the roundhouse, then crisscrossed and intersected in the center of the yard before untangling into two lines. One line to our left ran into the forest. To our right, the second line crossed a trestle bridge straddling the river, which flowed through a deep ravine. The trestle lay even with the ground, but a network of iron beams stretched over it like a hood. I assumed that Judd was hiding somewhere in those beams, but I couldn't see him.

A few dozen blank-eyed Gravarians dragged wood from the forest to the roundhouse. More sat silently and looked straight ahead, waiting, I assume, for orders. As we stood under the shelter of the pine trees, Sid looked around at the Gravs and shuddered.

Aresis waited for us, alone, near the toppled train car. I took Sid's elbow, and we approached him, stopping seven or eight feet short.

"Judd was supposed to be here," Aresis said.

"I'm working with Judd now," I replied.

Aresis' eye rested on me, and a dark expression flickered across his face before he blinked it away. He was silent for a moment, looking directly at me – searching my expression. I met his gaze as steadily as I could, but there was no hiding the beads of sweat on my forehead or the way my heart pulsed in my neck. I knew that the plan had already failed. Aresis knew.

The ground rumbled, and Judd's explosion rocked the forest. Birds shot into the air in a swarm of screeching, trees groaned and tossed their branches, and a billow of black smoke rose into the sky. But the dead-eyed Gravs didn't move

Aresis didn't even blink. "I'll take my brother, then," he said as if nothing had happened.

I kept my feet planted. "I want the Melodiac."

Aresis shrugged but stepped backward until his back touched the roof of the train car behind him. It was tall enough to shield him completely from Judd's line of fire.

Aresis ran his hand over his bald head and said wearily, "Look, Klifrari girl – I can't remember your name – tell me where the sniper is hidden and save us the time."

My brain went white with panic. For a moment, I grappled around in my mind for something to say.

"Then let's just do this, ok?" I finally managed. "You give me the Melodiac, as we agreed, and we all walk away."

He shook his head. "I'm not going to give you the Melodiac. And that's not why you're here. You're here to kill me, and I don't want to die."

A little knot of crows flew overhead, laughing down at us.

"Oh," Aresis said, as an afterthought, "and we found your friend."

Gregorikus rounded the corner of the car, pushing Luca in front of him.

Sid creased his brow and looked at me, bewildered, but I avoided meeting his gaze.

"If your sniper wants something to shoot at," Aresis said, "he may need to shoot Obsidian."

Aresis smiled, held up a Remembering Box, and pushed play.

THE PERSONAL LOG OF SID

The music drilled into me. It hurt. I wanted to clamp my hands over my ears, but my hands were bound. My brain felt like a gear out of alignment, with the teeth grinding against one another. I fought against it, but my body obeyed commands I never issued.

Then someone cut the ropes around my wrists.

There was a gun in my hand.

I turned and pointed it toward the humans.

They pleaded with me, but I could not hear them. I didn't want to kill them or let them live. There was no anger or hate, only submission.

The blankness hurt like an empty stomach. I wanted it to end. I wanted to feel full again. My arms moved, but I felt like I'd left my brain behind. I was just a body now, moving through my master's commands without thought or objection.

I held up the gun, my finger touched the trigger, and I felt an irrepressible urge to do what I was told.

But there was something underneath. Something warm, a little sharp. It felt like a match suddenly sparking into flame. It nagged at me like a forgotten thought. An emotional impression. A memory of feeling.

I didn't understand it then, but it was the dregs of the joy I felt when I saw Luca alive.

And that feeling, like a fuse running toward gunpowder, made me think of Creed. And his face flashed into my mind. Then the blare of a train whistle. An evergreen tree covered in crocheted snowflakes. A flash of red yarn. Wool against my skin. A song about a thrill of hope. My hand moved to my pocket, and my fingers touched something small and smooth.

A little carved buffalo.

I turned the gun on Aresis.

JAEL'S NARRATIVE

When Sid fell under the control of the hive mind, and I realized we were about to die, I wasn't afraid. I was angry. Every miserable moment since I'd dragged Luca into Becky's five weeks ago came blundering into my mind. Cold fingers, aching muscles, hunger in my belly day after day – all for nothing.

Sid's finger brushed the trigger.

I wrapped my arms around Luca's waist and pulled him to the ground. We hit the mud, and I crawled on top of him, shielding him with my body, covering his head with my arms.

He realized what I was doing and tried to struggle free, but I pinned his good arm beneath him, and his splinted arm couldn't support his own weight.

"Skin you!" He shouted, "Get off!"

The gunshot deafened me.

I braced for the impact and pain, but I didn't feel anything. I glanced over my shoulder, but I didn't see Sid blank-eyed, mechanical, with a gun trained on us. Instead, I saw Aresis, his back pressed against the train car, holding a shard of what had once been the Remembering Box but now was shattered into a hundred tiny pieces. Sid stood in the sunlight looking composed and intelligent, a smoking pistol in his hand.

Luca wriggled free, got to his knees, and pulled me into his arms.

"Skin you," Luca's voice trembled, and a tear slipped down his cheek. "Skin you, Jae, you're insane."

A second gunshot cracked the air. My heart hit my ribs. Sid lurched back with a cry of surprise and fell heavily. Instinctively, we turned to Aresis, but he looked just as shocked as the rest of us.

Then I remembered Jasper Judd.

A third bullet whistled past my ear.

He was shooting at me.

My mind went blank. I couldn't move.

Sid, wiping blood from the side of his head, got to his feet, grabbed Luca and me by the backs of our coats, lifted us off our feet, and carried us back to cover. Once safe, he dropped us, *plop,* on our rear ends in the mud.

"W-what's happening?" I stammered.

"Judd is trying to kill me!" Sid shouted, indignant.

"Obsidian, contain yourself," Aresis sneered. "You reek of anger, and it's making my head swim."

"What do we do?" I asked, standing and flattening myself against the roof of the car.

Aresis smiled. All around us, the hive-mind Gravs began to close in. I realized with a shock that Aresis could command them silently, with his mind.

The gun Sid had left behind lay on the ground about six feet away. I stepped out to grab it, but a gunshot startled me, and a bullet pinged off a rail inches from my hand.

"JAE!" Luca gasped, grabbing the back of my coat and pulling me back.

The hive-mind Gravs stalked toward us, but Judd began to pick them off one at a time. They dropped or stumbled; a few fell and tried to drag bleeding limbs behind them before Judd cut them down.

Aresis frowned, and the Gravs turned away and moved back toward the forest, forming a blue wall between us and our best hope of escape.

"Whose side is Judd on?" I fumed.

Luca looked grim. "I think he means to kill all of us. That way, he gets the Melodiac and all the glory."

"Skin him!" I shouted, pounding my fist against the car. "But why kill the Gravs? Won't they kill us for him?"

"They'll kill you," Gregorikus said, "but they'll shield my master and me."

The sun broke through the clouds, casting the yard in

blinding light. We huddled together in a line: Gregorikus, Aresis, me, Luca, Sid — in the shadow of the train car and stared at the pistol glinting in the sun. I scowled up at Aresis, who looked calm like he could wait here all day. Standing next to him, our elbows inches from touching, sent chills up my spine.

"We'll have to kill him first," Aresis said.

"And how do you intend to do that?" Sid demanded.

All five of us turned our eyes back to the pistol lying in the mud the way starving men stare at a loaf of bread. I felt Luca brace beside me.

"Don't even think about it," I said, grabbing his arm and holding onto him so tightly he winced.

"Someone has to get it."

"Well, it won't be you."

"We have the Melodiac," he whispered. "I found it before they caught me."

"Good. Now stay put."

"On the count of three, I'm going to make a go for it."

"Luca, don't you dare."

"One..."

"Stop it!"

"Two..."

"Skin you, Luca!"

"Three..."

Gregorikus made a break for the gun a split second before Luca did. There was a crack, a burst of black blood, and Gregorikus fell dead on the tracks. Luca stopped short and jumped back to cover.

"Judd is a decent shot," Luca panted.

Aresis and Obsidian looked at each other, and then, in perfect synch, the wall of Gravs on the edge of the forest ran toward us.

Aresis pulled a knife and swept it at Obsidian, who was unarmed and unprepared. The blade cut Sid's arm, and he lost his feet and fell. Luca vaulted over Obsidian as he went down and went knife-to-knife with Aresis. Aresis brought up his knee, meaning to catch Luca in the ribs, but Luca was quick, and he leaped back. For a split second, Luca exposed his chest to Aresis, who thrust forward, his knife extended. Luca twisted his body, and the knife cut the front of his shirt. Aresis swept backhanded, but Luca ducked under his arm, and Aresis lost his balance for a second, stumbled forward, and, before he could recover himself, Obsidian got to his feet again and, ducking his head down, ran at his brother. He caught him around the middle, lifted him clean off his feet, and slammed him into the ground.

I backed against the train car as the Gravs who survived Judd's shots reached us. One of them grabbed Luca, two others got hold of Obsidian and tried to yank him away from Aresis, but with a furious cry, Sid threw them off. Another caught me around the shoulders, but I whipped my head back and hit him in the throat. He staggered back, wheezing.

I heard a yell behind me and, turning, saw two Gravs with their arms around Luca, pulling him away from the safety of the train car and into Judd's line of fire. Luca, his eyes wide with terror, reached out, and I grasped his splinted hand.

"Hold onto me!" I screamed. "Luca, don't let go!"

But Luca's grip was weak. I grabbed his arm with my hands, planted my feet, and pulled with all my weight. Luca screamed from the pain and dropped his knife. The Gravs dragged him away from me with a great heave, and I fell forward into the sunlight.

Bullets squelched in the mud inches from my head. I slipped and stumbled back into the shade.

Judd opened fire. The Gravs holding Luca dropped dead, leaving him standing exposed. Sid broke free of his attackers and dashed toward Luca.

"Look out!" I shrieked, but gunfire cut through the sound of my voice. Sid fell with a shout, and Luca turned back to help him, but, caught in the open, he slipped around in the mud, unable to move forward or back.

"Play dead!" I shrieked. "Luca, just play dead!"

Luca dropped onto the train tracks.

The Gravs stopped where they stood. I watched breathlessly as Sid and Luca lay motionless.

Were they faking? They lay so still, I couldn't tell. I wanted to burst from cover and run to Luca, shake him, make him look at me.

"Dear God, no," I breathed, "please, no."

The train yard fell under a heavy silence. The wind waited, the crows hushed their cries, even Aresis held his breath. Hot tears blurred my vision, then stung my chapped cheeks.

Then Luca opened his eyes. I put my hand over my mouth and smothered a sob.

Any second, Judd could decide on a whim to make sure they were dead and shoot either Sid or Luca. It would be easy. Like hunting sleeping grouse.

The helplessness, the hair-string instability of our position made me break into a cold sweat. I locked eyes with Luca and tried to say without words, 'what do I do?'

Another gunshot cracked the silence, Luca jolted, and my heart hit my collar bone, but the bullet struck a random Grav standing a few feet from the woods. Luca shut his eyes and let out a long, slow breath through his nose.

I began to panic. A few crazed ideas of running out into the open and dragging Luca back to cover raced through my mind, but Birch's voice broke through them.

Jael, he had said to me once when we found ourselves in a white-out on a strange mountain, *when you feel like panicking – don't!*

Then what do I do? I asked.

Birch's voice, scoffing, came to me, *Bearhie, stupid child, keep moving.*

I kept my back to the cold steel behind me and tried to gather my courage. Aresis stood maybe four inches from me in the same position as we waited.

Then the Gravs began to move toward Luca and Sid.

"What are you doing?" I asked.

Aresis let out a quick huff, almost a laugh, and said, "I know they're not really dead. Let's make sure Judd knows as well."

"No, please, please," I pleaded, "Don't do this! Skin you! Stop!"

Aresis smiled and watched as his followers moved toward the two prone bodies in the mud. Judd picked the Gravs off one at a time, but they kept coming.

Then an idea struck me, and I couldn't believe I hadn't thought of it before.

I swung my rucksack off my shoulder. Judd's constant firing sent shocks up my nerves like electric pulses. I dug around, pulled out my little flute, put it to my lips, and began to play the Buffalo Song.

"NO!" Aresis screamed. I turned my back to him and fell on my knees, hunching forward over the flute as I played. He pounced on me, and we both fell away from the train car.

The song worked. The Gravs moving across the muddy yard stopped suddenly, straightened like they'd all had the same shocking idea, and cast bewildered looks at each other, then at their dead companions scattered around them. Judd shot one of them, and the others turned and ran for the woods. Aresis crawled quickly back to safety, swearing and nearly crying with fury. I followed him and crouched as far from him as the train car would allow. Aresis glowered at me with murder in his eyes.

Luca had managed to stay still, but sweat rolled down his face.

I had to do something. Time was running out like an avalanche down a mountain. I caught Luca's eyes and nodded at the gun still lying where Sid dropped it and held up three fingers. I meant to make a break for it, and when I did, I'd draw Judd's fire, and Luca and Sid could run back to cover.

Luca shut his eyes and tightened his lips. I could tell he wanted to shake his head and tell me not to do it, but he couldn't move.

I counted down.

Three...

Two...

One...

The instant the car's shadow was off my neck and the warm sun touched me, I felt naked and exposed. Aresis lunged at the gun at the same moment.

I reached it first, but I dropped to the ground and slid past it to throw off Judd's aim. I reached back and snatched the gun from under Aresis' fingers. Gunshots split the air around us, but I couldn't think about that. Aresis grabbed my arm. I rolled onto my back and squeezed the trigger.

Aresis lurched. There was a spray of black blood, and he fell, shot through the temples.

I pried off his dead hand, which still clutched my arm, and sprinted madly for the forest. Judd fired after me. I felt one of the bullets punch a hole in my coat sleeve. The others fell at my heels.

When I reached the woods, I ducked behind a white pine and took one of my laces from my boot. I shoved the gun into my belt, then used the shoelace to shimmy up the tree. Once I reached the bottom branches, I began to climb.

Below me, back in the train yard, I saw Luca and Sid safely under cover again and Luca watching me tensely as I moved upward.

When I'd climbed high enough to be equal with the top of the trestle, I finally spotted Judd laying flat on one of the beams, looking through his scope, trying to find me. He had an ammunition belt around his body and still wore his ridiculous red sweater. I laid my left arm along a sturdy branch and rested my right wrist on my left forearm. I aimed carefully through the trees. It was a long shot—over a hundred yards. I didn't know if this gun could even shoot that far. What would happen if I missed?

I checked the chamber. I had three shots.

I felt lightheaded. I lay my forehead on my arm for a moment and took long, deep breaths.

Steady hands are good for more than just stitching.

I could do this. After everything I'd been through, this

would be easy.

I lined up my sites again, took a deep breath, exhaled slowly, shut one eye, and squeezed the trigger.

The bullet struck the iron two feet above Judd's head. I saw him startle, then look frantically around. I fired a second time, and the bullet scraped the side of his bald head.

In a panic, he began to climb quickly down the side of the trestle. I shot at him again, and he let go of the beams and fell backward into the river below.

THE PERSONAL LOG OF SID

Well, that was an ordeal. We did all live, which is, I suppose, more than I could have hoped for. When everything began to slide rapidly downhill, I was sure that at least one of us would be killed before everything was over, but Jael and Luca proved more clearheaded and sturdy than I imagined, and we got through it, if not entirely unscathed, mostly unharmed.

We met Jael at the bottom of the tree, and she and Luca fell into each other's arms, and there was a great deal of human emotion I'd rather not describe.

Then, to my surprise, they wrapped their arms around me, and we all three embraced, which was very nice. We were happily embracing and enjoying the relief of victory when there was a great concussion in the air and then an explosion that nearly sent us all deaf, and the bridge exploded in a great spray of fire and black smoke.

We were all so surprised we dropped to our knees and covered our heads with our arms. I suppose Judd survived his ducking and meant for us to know it.

When we had quite gotten over our startle, I asked Luca to please hand over the Melodiac, but, to my great surprise and annoyance, he didn't.

"I'm sorry, Sid," he said, "but Jael and I agreed it needs to be destroyed."

"Luca," I said, restraining my sudden urge to knock him down and wrestle the Melodiac from his hands, "that is very silly. I need it to gain my birthright and that of my son."

"It's not safe. No one should have it," Luca said, like an idiot.

He looked to Jael for confirmation, and she frowned. "He's right. I don't think anyone should have it."

I hate it when humans get ideas in their heads.

"I need that Melodiac," I said through my teeth. "I need it for my future, for my son's future, for the future of my planet and yours." I held out my hand. "Give it to me, or I'll take it by force."

Luca backed away from me, shaking his head, and then, to my surprise and annoyance, he turned and ran.

He would have outrun me easily if he had been at his best before the wound. He nearly got away, but I was angry, which lent me speed.

I caught up to him, grabbed him by the shoulders, and dragged him to the ground. He fought against me, but I climbed on top of him and began to tear at his jacket, trying to get the Melodiac from him.

Jael caught up to us and shouted at me, but I was too angry to heed her. Annoyed, I swung at her with the back of my hand and knocked her away from me and onto the ground.

Luca struggled to get out from under me, but I pinned him down and tore the Melodiac roughly from him. Then I noticed blood on my knuckles. The color of it brought me back to my senses, and I jumped away from him with a wash of horror.

Luca lay in the snow, panting but not bleeding. I turned and saw Jael kneeling behind me, holding her face, blood running through her fingers.

I got to my feet, gazing at them as if through someone else's eyes. I didn't hear what they were saying, but I saw Luca pulling Jael's hands away from the bloody mess of her nose as he tried to stem the blood with his own sleeve.

The sickening smell of their anger and fear filled my nostrils, made my stomach churn. I turned away from them, and I ran.

When I stopped running, I stood in the glaring sunlight in the middle of the gore-soaked train yard. To my right sprawled my brother's body, with a hole blown through his head. To my left lay my cousin shot through the heart. And all around me, flanking me in like a siege of the dead, lay a dozen bodies of my people, slowly freezing. A powerful and dredging emotion made my insides flip, rise to my throat, and I fell to my knees and vomited. For the first time since I came to Earth, the first time I could remember in my life, I wept. I bent over, my hands planted in the mud, and I wailed and sobbed like a human. My tears mingled with trickles of black blood dribbling from the bodies of the lost.

Still weeping, I got up, took up the Melodiac, ran madly to the burning wreck of the trestle bridge, and, without hesitation, hurled the book into the fire. It landed on a piece of shattered wood standing in the open air like a broken rib and steamed quietly for a moment before it caught fire and went up in flames. I watched it blaze out and then burn slowly down. I cannot explain it, but watching the Melodiac burn brought years of bound-up emotion tumbling down on me, like someone cutting loose a bundle of logs. In a moment, the death of my father, the neglect of my mother, the hatred of my brother, the lost years with my wife and son spilled out of me almost as if the very smoke of the Melodiac enchanted my emotions. When it was done, and the book was no more than a pile of ash blowing away in the wind, I felt lighter inside.

Jael and Luca joined me by the bridge. Jael's nose looked a little swollen but no longer bled. She put her hand on my shoulder, which was higher than her head, and said,

"Would you feel better if we embraced?"

"No," I replied.

"Good," she said, smiling. "I didn't want to, but if it made you feel better..."

"Thank you."

"What do we do now?" Luca asked.

I was contemplating an answer when we heard footsteps crunching behind us and turned to face a group of a dozen Gravarians, all staring at us with great gravity.

"Are you Obsidian, the son of the queen?" one asked.

I replied that I was.

"We want to speak with you," he said.

JAEL'S NARRATIVE

The fire crackled nervously as we waited for Sid. Luca unfastened the splint on his arm and flexed his fingers slowly, whistling to himself. I held snow against my swollen nose and pressed my shoulder against Luca for warmth. My eyelids were heavy, and I kept nodding off.

Finally, as the sun dipped behind the mountain, Sid returned with a grave expression. He sat across from us and wrung his hands for a long time before he said anything.

"Well?" I demanded impatiently. "What happened?"

Sid looked up at me, and I thought he looked frightened. "Some of the Gravarians want me to be their king."

"Yes, after your mother dies..."

"No," he said, "here. Now. They want me to be their king here, on Earth."

I gaped at him. "But...they're criminals."

"Some of them are, but some of them are enemies of my mother sent here on some unjust conviction. These Gravarians have lived here in poverty and chaos for too long. They want to make Earth a new home, and they want me to lead them. Also," he looked into the fire thoughtfully, "Gravarus is dying. My mother needs Earth to keep it alive, and someone must oppose her."

"Your mother could start a war over this," Luca said. "She might destroy Earth anyway."

Sid nodded thoughtfully. "I know."

"What are you going to do?" I asked.

His voice was hardly more than a whisper. "I don't know."

We sat in silence for a long time.

"I have to find Ila and Creed before I do anything else," Sid finally said. "That must be my first priority. And I need to think. If I unite the Gravarians on Earth and provoke my mother, there's no telling what she could do."

"What should we do?" Luca asked. "Do you want us to come with you and help you look for Ila and Creed?"

Sid shook his head. "It's too dangerous. Go back to the mountains and wait for me. I'll come find you when I know they're safe."

When we walked in the door, we found Becky's clean and swept, with a kettle boiling over the fire and the smell of cardamom in the air.

Ama bent over the kitchen stove, stirring a pot of potato soup and humming to herself.

"Ah," she said when she heard us enter the kitchen, "I knew you'd be back soon. Luca, I scrubbed the stain out of your shirt and mended it. It's drying by the fire. Jael, come help with the gash cakes; the lunch rush will be here soon."

"Ama," I said, "you know I kicked all the Klifrari out."

"There's more people in the world than the Klifrari, Jael," she scolded. "And they can smell my gash cakes all the way down the mountain. I told everyone that came to my hut that Becky's was opening up to the public and business has been quite good. Now, the cow needs milking, and there's butter to churn, and we need to get these gash cakes in the oven." She handed me a bowl of dough. "Don't be conservative with the cinnamon."

Ama walked heavily out of the kitchen, leaving me stunned in the middle of the room.

Luca laughed. "You heard her, Jae. Don't be conservative with the cinnamon."

Luca grabbed a pale from the counter.

"Well, Jae, you promised to teach me how to make gash cakes."

I handed him an apron. "I suppose I did."

The kettle sang, the fire crackled in rhythm, and I finally stood in Becky's, and I belonged.

The setting sun poured orange light through the kitchen

window.

I SEE A CITY IN THE DISTANCE

Spring may come, ice may soften, snow may melt, but winter always returns. For Jael, Luca, and Obsidian, the adventure has only begun.

ABOUT THE AUTHOR

A. R. Maxwell

A. R. Maxwell has a passion for writing and reading across multiple genres. When she isn't indulging in her literary pursuits, she loves to travel, hike, sing, try new foods, and watch good movies. She believes that story is the ultimate form of human expression because it reflects the image of God in us. Her stories are filled with adventure, hope, humor, and the human struggle to overcome. She lived in Maine for four years and now lives in the beautiful mountains of Western Maryland with her husband and children. Follow her on Instagram, TikTok, and Facebook.

BOOKS BY THIS AUTHOR

Random Man: A Superhero Novel

Randy Regal, a clumsy teenager in his first year at The Academy of Super Police, can't control his seventeen unruly superpowers. When a disastrous accident gets him kicked out of The Academy, he reluctantly turns to The Western Academy for Super Police - a rundown school buried in a secret canyon town with only 5 students, a handful of reluctant teachers, and a super villain who seems to want Randy dead. Can Randy stay alive, impress his crush, and pass superhero ethics all in one explosive school year? He's not sure he can.